THE DROWNING RIVER

THE DROWNING RIVER

KIM BYRNE

FIVE STAR
A part of Gale, Cengage Learning

Detroit • New York • San Francisco • New Haven, Conn • Waterville, Maine • London

GALE
CENGAGE Learning™

LIBRARY OF CONGRESS CATALOGING-IN-PUBLICATION DATA

Byrne, Kim.
    The drowning river / by Kim Byrne. — 1st ed.
    p. cm.
    ISBN-13: 978-1-59414-769-2 (hardcover: alk. paper)
    ISBN-10: 1-59414-769-8 (hardcover : alk. paper)
    1. Women college students—Fiction. 2. Drowning victims—
Fiction. 3. Cape Cod (Mass.)—Fiction. I. Title.
    PS3602.Y763D76 2009
    813'.6—dc22   2009005239

First Edition. First Printing: June 2009.
Published in 2009 in conjunction with Tekno Books and Ed Gorman.

Printed in the United States of America
1 2 3 4 5 6 7 13 12 11 10 09

For Mike

ACKNOWLEDGMENTS

I'm grateful to John Helfers and everyone at Tekno Books and Five Star Publishing. You've all been wonderful to work with. Big thanks to my family for their love and support: Mike, Ryan, Dan, Barbara, Ann, and Tony. Props to Heather for reading my first drafts.

PROLOGUE

Tonight was the night of her death. The morbid thought surfaced from nowhere and scratched at the dark corners of her mind as the freezing February wind nipped at her skin. The road to the bridge was empty. The few houses they passed were dark and quiet with sleep.

Hannah McPhee dismissed the notion of her own mortality as quickly as it came as the thoughts of a drunken, paranoid idiot. She silently cursed herself for overindulging at the bar. So much for being a changed woman. But how was she supposed to know tonight would end up being so important? So much had happened in the last few weeks. Her life had changed so drastically, so quickly. Her thoughts were muddled with the haze of alcohol, but she hurried on, making a cursory attempt at small talk with the person beside her.

East Street ended with an empty parking lot—no one visiting the beach in the middle of a February night. The three-quarter moon played hide and seek with the clouds, casting intermittent light ahead of them. She heard the rush of the Drowning River below as they stepped onto the pedestrian bridge. The moon peeked out, and she used the light to gaze down the length of the bridge, to the hills of sand that rose from the banks of the river. The beach was on the other side, and she was briefly amazed at how the sand dunes muffled the sounds of the sea pounding the rocks.

As a cloud drifted across the moon, the dunes seemed to roll and slide along the horizon. Much like her life. Sliding down, then building up, only to erode once again. Things were going to change for her now, though. Tonight was a turning point, a night she would remember forever.

Halfway across the bridge, a two-foot space gaped open where part of the splintered wooden guardrail must have rotted off or given way. She inched herself to the edge and peered down. The drop had to be at least twenty feet. The past few weeks had been so cold that even the river had a thin layer of ice. She glanced at the blackness below and flirted with the idea of jumping. But it was just a fleeting thought. She would never do that, especially not now. She'd been in rough spots before and always clawed her way out of the holes.

Her companion must have sensed this fighter quality in her. And that's why the coward pushed her from behind.

At first, she thought it was her own dizzy thoughts. *Did I actually do it? Did I actually jump?* No. She still felt the spots on her back where hands had shoved her a moment ago.

The river's icy crust rushed at her in seconds that felt like minutes, during which her life didn't flash by, but instead the future she would miss out on did. She should have felt fear but instead felt immeasurable sadness. Until the moment when she saw the reflection of her face—pale green eyes, short blond hair—in the ice. Then, she hit. And it was over.

CHAPTER 1

Seven Months Later

Dolan's Pub smelled like Murphy's Oil Soap and beer. With dark paneling on the walls, Gothic arches, and a long, mahogany bar, it tried hard to look like an authentic Irish pub. But a quick look around at its pool table and jukebox confirmed it was merely an American college haunt. The air hung above the crowd of bodies, thick and hot. Elise Moloney used a bar napkin to dab the sweat off her neck. Large, block-lettered print on the napkin read: DO NOT OPEN THIS. It was probably a marketing gimmick, but she caved and opened it to find a list of appetizers the bar served. She balled up the napkin, now moist from her sweat, and searched the bar for a familiar face.

A convenient two-minute walk from the Wickman College campus, Dolan's was crowded with new and returning students on this, the eve of the first day of the academic year. Girls screeched and hugged friends they hadn't seen since May. Guys patted backs and punched arms in their ritual of manly greeting. Elise doubted they were all graduate students like herself. Half the bar looked like under-twenty-one undergrads, but the owner was probably too busy counting his profits to notice.

She pulled her long, blond hair up from her damp neck as Kat Herrera returned to the table with two frozen margaritas held up in victory. They had abandoned their quest for a waitress in the crowded bar ten minutes ago, and Kat had gone to the bar herself.

Elise took a sip of the green concoction and sighed with relief. "I'm so happy you ordered them frozen. I didn't even think to mention that."

Kat shrugged. "I'm not just a pretty face and a good time. I'm also intuitive."

"And modest," Elise added with a wink.

Kat wore tight jeans and a low-cut red blouse that clung to her curves. She was the physical polar opposite of Elise. Elise was fair, with pale skin that never tanned, light green eyes, and her signature straight blond hair. Kat was exotic, with wavy, lustrous black hair, skin bronzed by the summer sun, and dark chocolate eyes. Elise was petite, with a slim, boyish figure. Kat was tall and curvy, with unimaginably perfect breasts that made Elise want to hate her.

Kat scanned the room like a predator. "So many men, so little Kat to go around."

She smiled at Elise in a way that was quickly becoming familiar. They had only known each other six hours, long enough to pick bedrooms and start unpacking in their apartment, but Elise already knew this smile. It was a devious one that said, "Come on, guess, am I joking or am I serious?" In this case she didn't know.

Kat stirred her drink and eyed her. "You're single, right? No boyfriends?"

Elise lowered her eyes like she always did when she lied and said, "Yeah, none right now," though she wasn't quite sure if it was a lie or not. She didn't want to probe her feelings about Nick at the moment. Tonight was about new beginnings.

"Good. Women tend to be more fun when they're unattached," Kat said and flashed the smile again. Her top left eyetooth was crooked. Elise liked that. It made her human. Sure, she had the body of a supermodel, but she had a crooked left eyetooth.

"So, what's your deal?" Kat asked.

"My deal?"

"You know, life story in under five minutes."

Elise nodded and sucked another sip from her straw. "I grew up in Hingham, Massachusetts, about an hour from here. An uncommonly pleasant childhood—no dysfunction, parents still together and actually in love. I went to Providence College for my Bachelor's in English. Now I'm here getting my graduate degree."

"Still English?"

"Yep."

"What do you want to be when you grow up? A writer?"

"I'd love to be a novelist. I don't know how practical that is. Maybe teach. I'm not sure yet." Elise took a long drag from the straw and her mouth puckered. It had been a while since she had a margarita. She was more of a beer girl herself. "Your turn."

Kat leaned back in her chair and slid her fingers through her hair. "I'm the youngest of four—three older brothers. One is a mechanic, one is a lawyer, and one is a cop, so I'm set for any trouble I run into in life. I grew up outside of Miami. I went to Florida State and now I'm here."

Elise pondered the melting slush in her drink and pretended not to notice the two men at the bar staring at them. "What was your major at Florida State?"

Kat laughed and threw her head back. Her hair cascaded like a Pantene commercial. Drool collected in a pool under the guys' mouths at the bar. "Which year? Freshman year, I was undecided. It didn't matter much then because you just take required core courses. Sophomore year, I chose accounting. It seemed practical. My brothers were always shoving practical down my throat. Then, junior year I switched to history. Completely unpractical, but passionate and interesting. History and art have always been my favorite subjects, but I figured if I chose art my brothers would simultaneously hemorrhage. So history it was. I had two years' worth of senior year to make up for time wasted in accounting. Now I'm here."

"And what do you want to do when you grow up?"

She smiled wickedly and glanced at the men at the bar. "Marry rich and never work a day in my life."

Elise couldn't help but laugh. "Your poor brothers."

"Poor brothers? What about me? Any boy that even looked twice at me in high school got shoved into a locker." She pulled the straw out of her glass and sucked leftover margarita from the tip, letting the straw linger on her lips.

"You're making up for it now, though, you straw tease. Do you really want those guys to come over? They look a little cheesy."

"Not your type?"

"No, I prefer oil in a car, not on hair. Gold chains don't do it for me, either."

Kat laughed. "I get the picture. You like the shy, preppy types."

"I'm not sure what my 'type' is, but I do know that they don't fit the mold."

"They'll buy us drinks."

Elise made an effort out of sighing and stretching. "These margaritas are so strong; one is plenty for me. If I have more, you'll need to carry me home. Plus, I'm tired. I'd like to get back to the apartment and get a good night's sleep. First day of classes tomorrow."

"Mind if we join you?" The skeevy men had already ambled their way to the table. They were a walking, talking *Saturday Night Live* skit.

Kat stood. She was two inches taller than one of the men, as if her looks weren't intimidating enough. "You were too slow, boys. My new best friend here is too tired now. Better luck next time."

The cool night air rushed at Elise's face as she pushed the heavy oak door open. Much to the dismay of all males in Dolan's, she led Kat onto the sidewalk for their quick walk home to Wickman's graduate student housing. She wrapped her arms around her chest as she walked.

"You know what they say about that?" Kat asked.

"What who say about what?"

"Wrapping your arms around yourself like that. It means you're holding something in. Hiding something."

"I thought you were history and not psychology."

"So you are hiding something?"

"No, I'm just cold. Sometimes things are just the way they are, nothing deeper."

Kat made an exaggerated yawn.

"Oh, I'm boring you?" Elise walked faster. It was cool for Labor Day weekend. Though the ocean was a mile away, she could smell the salt water in the breeze. Dolan's Pub was in the center of Oceanside, Massachusetts, a small town whose population of 8,000 swelled to 13,000 from September through May with the addition of students at the private liberal arts college.

"Just tell me there's something exciting there for me to find out about you. A skeleton in the closet for me to trip over while borrowing a sweater, perhaps? You seem too . . ."

"Boring," Elise repeated.

"No, I don't like boring people, but I like you. That means there's something there."

"I'm telling you there isn't." Elise raised her arms above her head. "I've got nothing."

"Maybe you just don't know what it is, but it's there. I can sense it in you." Kat sniffed the air like an animal.

"What exactly can you sense?"

"A mystery," Kat said with an eyebrow raised.

A loud crash behind them stopped their footsteps. Elise glanced around for the source. East Street was a picturesque main street with small stores side by side lining the sidewalk. Village Pizza was open, but that was a few buildings back. The other stores all had closed doors and windows, and this noise was definitely outside.

"Sounds like it came from there." Kat pointed to a darkened alley nestled between two short brick buildings. "Let's check it out."

"No way," Elise said, shaking her head.

Kat clucked like a chicken and turned toward the alley.

Elise sighed and lagged behind.

They crept up to the red brick building and peered around the corner down the alley. It felt surreal, like Elise was trapped in a *Scooby Doo* episode. Of course, she'd be Velma the nerd and Kat would be Daphne the beauty queen.

The alley was dark, but a streetlight on the sidewalk illuminated enough to make out the bumps and shadows. A large dumpster leaned against the wall overflowing with greasy pizza boxes. A shuffling noise startled Elise, and she jumped back. Kat, on the other hand, pushed forward into the alley.

A moment later, Kat cackled. "What do we have here? Need some help, girl?"

"Screw you. I'm fine," came a slurred female voice.

"Just a drunk girl, Elise. You can come out now!"

Elise rolled her eyes and rounded the corner into the alley. An obviously wasted woman lay on the ground amidst a bunch of trash. Her unnaturally red hair resembled a bird's nest, and her right high heel had the remains of a garbage bag attached to it.

"I just tripped and fell. I'm okay." She refused Kat's hand and tried to push herself up using her arms, but slipped and reluctantly grabbed Kat's arm.

Elise moved closer and asked, "Do you want us to walk you home?"

The woman looked up into Elise's face and froze, her mouth gaping open, her eyes widening, until she sucked in a sharp breath and shrieked like a horror scream queen. Elise covered her ears with her hands as the echo amplified off the walls. The woman scrambled up Kat's arm and ran the other way down the alley, intermittently screaming and pointing at Elise until she was out of view.

Moments later, in the stunned silence left behind, Elise realized she couldn't breathe and fell to the ground.

He scrubbed the whole apartment out of boredom. The floors shined, the counters sparkled, and still he paced, unable to get his mind off her. He tried watching TV but that only pissed him off. All those reality shows with dumbasses making fools of themselves.

He gazed out the apartment window and watched the anonymous bodies mill back and forth under the light of the streetlight. Her picture burned against his chest from the pocket of his button-down shirt. He slipped it out and stared at it, tracing her features with his thumb. Blond hair like flowing silk. The soft angles of her face. Her full lips.

He collapsed into a chair and leaned his head back, her name tumbling out like a sigh. "Elise."

He closed his eyes and wondered how this would end. Would she have to die, too?

CHAPTER 2

"Are you sure you're okay?"

"For Christ's sake, Kat, I'm fine." Elise leaned back against the faux-brick interior hallway of the Wickman College Graduate Classroom Building. Students hurried back and forth, schedules in hand, peering at room numbers, searching for their first class.

"No need to get the claws out."

"I'm sorry," Elise said. "I'm still freaked out by last night."

"Because of your asthma attack?"

"No, that had an explanation."

The woman's screams had frightened Elise enough to trigger an attack. The first sign was always tightness in her chest, but she had ignored that as anxiety. Then came the pain with each wheeze, like breathing in ice. She was fine moments later, once she retrieved her inhaler from her bag, but still shaken by the strange reaction the woman had to her.

"Then what's bothering you? Not that dumb girl."

"Come on. She took one look at my face and screamed like I was the devil."

"Maybe it's the horns sticking out of your head."

"I'm not kidding around."

Kat pulled a pencil out of her backpack and tucked it behind her ear. "You should be. Lighten up. She was wasted. She could have been doped up, too. Who knows? She probably hallucinated a big hairy monster standing behind you."

"I guess you're right."

Kat slung her backpack over her shoulder. "Learn that statement well. I'm always right. But now I'm going to be late for class. See you back at the apartment, my girl."

Elise watched her walk away—as did almost all the males in the vicinity—and decided that she should head into her classroom as well. Her first class in graduate school: Studies in Romanticism. Oh, the irony. She had run from real romance with Nick, and now entered a class where she would study the work of masters.

She found a seat in the middle—not the eager-beaver front row, yet not the slacker last row—and leaned back in the seat, taking a deep breath. Classrooms have their own special smell, a blend of wooden desks, old books, and chalk. Elise had always found comfort in classrooms, and the smell calmed her first-day jitters.

The professor was nice enough, a bit of a hippie, but that meant he could be talked into having class outside every now and then, and that was a plus. He passed out the syllabus and did the obligatory "this is what I expect from you this semester" speech. Then he got right into it and began his first lecture on *Wuthering Heights,* which they were all supposed to have read before the first class. Elise had read it in the seventh grade.

She drifted off fifteen minutes into the lecture and scanned her classmates. She had expected graduate school to be more diverse than her four years of undergrad. Maybe some older students, more international classmates, perhaps. But a look around the classroom quickly told her that Wickman wasn't that kind of school. Each of the twenty-four desks was filled with the same sights she had seen while at Providence—the preppies, the casual jocks, the bespectacled intellectuals, the beauties. All the same people, just four years older.

She jotted a few notes as the professor winded down his

lecture, then looked up and spied a fellow classmate staring at her. He turned away when caught and didn't look back. It wouldn't be the first time she caught a cute guy checking her out, but something in his expression reminded her of the woman last night.

After class ended, she wandered back down the hallway toward the exit until she felt a hand on her shoulder.

"I thought . . ."

She turned to face the guy from class staring at her again, open-mouthed.

"You thought what?" she asked.

"Um . . ." He looked utterly confused.

She reached out and pushed his chin up, closing his mouth. "Wouldn't want you to catch any flies in there."

That seemed to snap him out of it. "I'm sorry," he said, his cheeks flushing.

He was tall, at least six-three, and thin, on the gangly side. She sensed that he was probably clumsy, but in a cute way. He had a smattering of freckles across the bridge of his nose and his sandy-blond hair was short in back but long in front, nearly touching his gray-blue eyes. He looked like a California surfer.

"I'm Parker Reilly," he said and offered his hand.

She took it, sensing a light tremble in his fingers. Was he really that nervous to talk to her? "I'm Elise Moloney."

He nodded and seemed to absorb the information. "Would you like to go to the Café with me and grab some lunch?"

She had no reason to say yes, but no reason to say no, so she went.

The Café was full of bustling undergrads who seemed so young. Even though the freshmen were only four years younger than Elise; it seemed a lifetime ago when she was that age.

Parker returned to the table with two sandwiches and two sodas on a checkerboard tray.

"Thanks for lunch. You didn't have to buy," she said.

"But now you owe me one. I'm guaranteed a second lunch with you," he replied with a tentative smile.

Elise bit into her turkey sandwich and chewed through an awkward moment of silence while she noticed Parker staring at her. To end the uncomfortable moment, she asked, "Do you live in graduate housing or off campus?"

"Graduate housing. Bourne Hall, fourth floor."

"Really? I'm Bourne, third floor. Three-oh-two. Where did you go to undergrad?"

"Here. Most Wickman undergrads who go on to grad school go somewhere else—for a change, like the city maybe. But I always liked it here in Oceanside, and I've never been a big proponent of change, so here I stay. I think there are only about one hundred of us from last year's class in the graduate school now. The other thousand or so grad students are from other colleges. Like you."

"That's good, then. You can give me tips—about professors, things to do, places to go."

"Definitely," he said, and took his turn to ask a question. But instead of one, he asked twenty. "Where did you go to undergrad? How old are you? Where are you from? Do you have any brothers or sisters? Why did you pick Wickman? What was your undergraduate major?"

The list went on and on, and Elise was exhausted until she put her hand up to his face. "Stop. I need a moment to catch my breath. What's with the interrogation?"

He blushed again, as he had outside the classroom, and looked away from her. She waited, but he would not look back.

"Why did you really ask me to have lunch with you?"

He locked eyes with her but made no motion to answer.

"Why did you stop me after class? You said, 'I thought,' but you never finished the sentence. What were you going to say?"

His lips moved slowly. "I was going to say, 'I thought you were dead.' "

CHAPTER 3

That certainly wasn't what Elise expected to hear. Great way to start out at a new college. She gets a hormone-crazed, supermodel roommate and the first guy she meets is psycho.

"I'm glad to report that I'm not dead. Thanks for lunch. See you around." Elise stood and Parker grabbed her arm.

"Wait. It's not what you think. I'm not some crazy guy. Let me explain."

"I have another class I have to get to."

"Let me walk you there and I'll explain along the way. And if you still think I'm nuts, I'll never go near you again."

Still wary of him but interested in what the story was, she nodded and began walking.

"A girl died last year, in February. She was a senior, same age as you and me. She looked exactly like you."

Elise felt better now that they were back outside and only minutes from her class. "They say everyone has a twin," she said.

"No, it's not that she looked kind of like you or almost like you. She looked exactly like you. Except her hair was shorter and she dressed different, more provocatively."

She glanced down at her jeans and baggy sweater and felt like a bag lady. A bag lady with ninety-dollar running shoes, but still a bag lady. "How did she die?"

"She drowned in the river. She was drunk and fell off the bridge. It was only a line item in the newspapers, but it was big news here on campus."

"What was her name?"

"Hannah McPhee."

The name meant nothing to her, but immediately Elise felt something stir, deep inside. She quickly dismissed it.

Parker continued. "I wasn't in her group of friends. I actually don't know much about her at all."

She stopped at the door to the Graduate Classroom Building. "Thanks again for lunch. I guess I'll see you around, in class and in Bourne Hall."

"That's it? I tell you that you are a carbon copy of a student who died last year and you don't want to know any more? You're not curious?"

A couple of passing students slowed. "Keep your voice down," she whispered. "It's no big deal. I look like a girl who died. It's creepy, but that's the end of it. Plus, you said you didn't know any more about her."

He obliged with a lower tone of voice. "That doesn't mean I couldn't find out. Her old roommate is a grad student here, too. I know who she is. We could look her up in the directory to find out where she lives and go see her."

"Why, though? To dredge up bad memories for her? I'm sure she misses Hannah, and to see someone that looks exactly like her would be hurtful."

"She's bound to run into you eventually. It's a small campus." He paused. "But I understand if you think the whole thing is creepy. If you change your mind, I'm right upstairs. Four-oh-four."

Bourne Hall was the last in a line of three, five-story brick buildings purchased by Wickman College for their graduate housing. They were named Brewster, Barnstable, and Bourne after towns on the Cape, while they waited for donors to contribute enough for the halls to be renamed after them. They were old, drafty, and furnished poorly, but the only affordable choice for a graduate student on a budget. Elise and Kat's apartment had scratched hardwood floors and paint that originally was most likely a pale yellow but was now a darker mustard. But Elise couldn't complain because at least she and Kat had their own bedrooms. Considering that today was the first day of class and two men had already called for Kat tonight, she had the feeling she'd appreciate that separate bedroom quickly.

Elise sat curled up in a corner of the couch, furiously highlighting passages in a textbook. Kat reclined in an overstuffed chair with one leg draped over the arm.

"So let me make sure I have this straight," Kat said. "Cute surfer boy stops you after class, takes you to lunch, tells you that you are a dead ringer—excuse the pun—for a girl who drowned last year. A girl your age who looked exactly like you, except sluttier. Quite the elaborate pick-up line. No wonder he's an English major. Very creative."

"I think the story's true. It would explain why that drunk woman freaked out at the sight of me. She literally thought she was seeing a ghost."

"If the story is true, then why don't you want to find out more about this chick?"

"Because it's creepy."

Kat exaggerated a yawn. "A hot guy who is obviously interested in you enough to buy you lunch offers to take you on a mystery-solving adventure and you decline. You disappoint me, roomie."

"I'm not going to show up at this girl's apartment and start asking questions about her dead best friend. Don't you think that's rude? Plus, I'm sure it's one of those things where I look almost like her. Everyone has someone out there that looks almost like them."

A knock on the door interrupted the conversation.

"Go get that," Elise said. "It's probably one of your suitors."

Kat snorted and pulled herself up and to the door.

A male voice asked, "Is Elise here?"

"Ah," Kat purred. "You must be cute surfer boy. Come in."

Parker entered and turned toward Elise. "Cute surfer boy?" he said with a lopsided grin.

"Ignore her," Elise said. "What's up?"

He held out a book in front of him. "This is my yearbook. There's a whole page dedicated to Hannah's memory. Please, just look at her picture. If you still don't want to know anything more about her, then that's fine, but I won't accept no for an answer until you look at her."

Elise sighed and shifted uncomfortably. "Listen, Parker, I don't know why you care so much, but I—"

"Give me that." Kat grabbed the book. "I'll settle this once and for all. What page, surfer boy?"

"Twenty-four."

"Twenty-four, twenty-four, twenty-four," she flipped through, searching for the page and then, silence. She stared for a long moment, then handed the book to Elise and said one word. "Look."

Elise allowed her eyes to drift down to the page of photos dedicated to Hannah McPhee, and for a few moments her lungs forgot to take in air and her heart forgot to beat. She was looking at herself.

The Christmas Tree Shop looked more like a shop on Main Street in Disney's Magic Kingdom than a discount store on the Cape. An ornate dome topped the building and multicolored lights adorned the perimeter. A look inside the stained-glass windows showed the store packed as always. Tourists flocked for bargain-priced souvenirs, and locals rummaged through the aisles for home decorations. Despite its name, it was one of those stores that sold everything—from Cape Cod mugs to artwork and lamps.

"What the hell is this?" Kat held up a stone carving. "A crazed lion or something?"

Elise looked up from the cookbook she had taken off a shelf. "That's a gargoyle."

"What's it for?"

"Decoration. You've never seen a gargoyle on someone's steps before?"

Kat shook her head. "You creepy New Englanders. Why did I leave Miami again?"

Elise tossed the cookbook into their already full shopping cart. "Actually, you never did say what brought you all the way to Massachusetts."

"Yes, I did. Three brothers. A girl needs a buffer zone."

"A fifteen hundred mile buffer zone?"

"You do what you gotta do." Kat reached back and tightened her ponytail. Even with her hair up and in a casual outfit of gray sweatpants and a tight black t-shirt, she was still a knockout.

Elise glanced around. "I think we've hit every aisle. We got the pots and pans we need, plus another hundred dollars worth of stuff we don't need. Time to go."

The checkout line was so long, she expected a velvet rope at the end. Elise tapped her foot and bit her thumbnail for a few moments until Kat said, "Want to talk about what we're not talking about?"

"What's that?"

"Your big date tonight. Most likely the reason you're terrorizing that poor thumbnail of yours."

Elise clasped her hands in front of her. "There, no more biting. And it's not a date."

They inched forward as another customer left the line.

"Are you having second thoughts about agreeing to see this chick?"

"I'm just nervous."

"You're looking at this the wrong way," Kat said. "Think of it as a fun adventure. You and a very cute guy are going off together to solve a mystery. How cool is that? Very cool. Instead, you're dreading it. It's not that big of a deal."

"Come on, Kat, you saw the picture. It *is* a big deal. This could be a life-changing event."

"Yeah, I saw the picture, but still . . . what is it that they say? Everyone has a twin they don't know about?"

Elise took a deep breath and looked Kat in the eye. "Yes, that's what they say. But not everyone is adopted. I am."

When Elise graduated second in her class at Providence College, she had two options—go to work or attend graduate school. She had covered all the bases by applying for both jobs and graduate programs. She had an offer on the table for an entry-level position at a Providence newspaper. She had acceptances from all three graduate programs she applied to. And she had another, more serious offer she was considering from her boyfriend, Nick.

Her parents were supportive when she decided she wanted to travel abroad during the summer and start graduate school in the fall. They told her she had the rest of her life to work and were proud of her academic accomplishments.

Wickman College wasn't the most competitive school. It was actually her safety school choice, as if she needed one. Wickman was considered elite, but not for its rigorous academic standards. It cost ten grand more per year than the average private school, mainly because of its location—an oceanside college where the children of the rich can study amidst breathtaking views.

Elise had preferred to attend Harvard University's Graduate School of Arts and Sciences and was accepted into their graduate program. But then Wickman came through with a full merit scholarship. Elise knew that her parents would insist she go to Harvard, but they were already saddled with enough debt from her four years at Providence. They made too much money for financial aid, but not enough to pay for school, so they took a second mortgage on their home to pay for her education.

Not wanting to end up in debt herself and not wanting her parents to take on more left her with one choice, she lied. She told her parents that Harvard had rejected her, but hey, great news, I got a free ride to Wickman.

And here she was. About half of Wickman's graduate students lived on campus in graduate housing. It was convenient, a quick walk to class. Plus, it was cheaper for those students for whom money was something tangible. Then there were those students whose parents thought on-campus graduate housing was beneath them. They were usually set up with a nice seaside apartment for themselves or they split a townhouse with other students.

Faith Petrucci was one of these students. Elise and Parker pulled into the parking lot of Beachview Condominiums, an upscale condo complex with a private beach. Parker slid his cherry red Jeep between two BMWs and killed the engine.

"So, she's expecting us, right?" Elise asked.

"Yeah, I told her it's someone who has some questions about Hannah. I was pretty vague. I want her to see for herself."

Elise smoothed her green blouse and khaki Dockers as they walked to the door. "And she agreed to the meeting, just like that?"

Parker rang the doorbell. "She knows who I am. We're not friends, but she knows me, so it's not like a complete stranger is coming. I suppose curiosity got the best of her, too."

The door opened, and Elise instinctively turned so that her back was to the door. She didn't want to scare Faith, but knew showing her face was inevitable.

"Parker, nice to see you," a sweet, high voice said.

"Thanks for agreeing to talk with us. This is Elise Moloney," he said with a hand on Elise's shoulder. He gently forced her to turn around and immediately Faith gasped.

"What is this? What's going on?" Faith's olive skin paled, and she put one hand up on the doorjamb.

Elise took a deep breath and said, "I was hoping you could help me figure that out."

Elise and Parker told Faith their story as she poured them drinks with trembling hands. They sat on ornately carved, yet highly uncomfortable, wooden chairs in the living room with a view of the sea advancing and receding outside the bay window. The apartment was nicely furnished, with trendy décor from Pottery Barn and Crate & Barrel.

"So, after seeing the yearbook picture, I finally agreed that we look too much alike for it to be coincidence, so I told Parker it was okay to contact you."

Faith threw herself back in the chair. She had shoulder-length brown hair with loose curls that framed her small face. Her large, hazel eyes dominated the rest of her tiny features, child-like nose, thin lips. Faith was cute in every sense of the word. She looked like a teenager rather than a twenty-something.

"I'm sorry if I'm staring," she said. "I just can't get over it. It's like I'm looking at Hannah. Of course, your hair is much longer and you carry yourself differently, but those are just minor things."

"Do you have any pictures of her that I could see? I've only seen the yearbook ones."

Faith leaned forward, plucked one of the many framed photos

off the glass coffee table, and handed it to Elise. "She's in this one."

The picture was taken on a beach, but it must have been in cool weather because the trio wore sweatshirts and jeans. Faith on the left, Hannah on the right, and a guy in between. Hannah had her head thrown back and mouth open in laughter.

"Who's the guy?" Elise asked.

"That was her boyfriend, Gavin Shaw."

"He was on the football team, right?" Parker asked.

Faith nodded. "Hannah went to all his home games. I went along, too, most times."

Elise stared at the photo in silence for a couple of minutes, taking in every line and curve of Hannah's face.

"So, what do you think the explanation is?" Faith asked.

"We must be twins. It's the only explanation I can see."

Faith shook her head. "That's not possible. You can't be Hannah's sister. She was an only child. Maybe you're a cousin she didn't know about or something."

Elise placed the frame back on the table. "It is possible. I'm adopted. Hannah and I were most likely separated at birth and adopted by two different families."

Faith's eyes darted from Elise to Parker and back. "I'm sorry, Elise. But Hannah wasn't adopted."

"Maybe her parents never told her she was adopted," Parker said.

"It's the truth. I was her roommate for four years. I met her mother several times. The resemblance is undeniable. That's her biological mother. Her father's not in the picture, never was, but she has a stepfather. There's no doubt that Beth is her mother, though, especially when you see her eyes. The same exact green eyes."

"My eyes, too," Elise whispered, reeling from Faith's announcement.

"Yes, that's true," Faith conceded. She shook her head. "None of this makes any sense."

Parker leaned forward. "I know how to figure this out. Elise, when is your birthday?"

"Valentine's Day. February fourteenth."

Faith covered her mouth with her hand and said in a muffled voice, "That was Hannah's, too."

CHAPTER 4

Only an hour's drive from Oceanside, Hingham was a picturesque New England town. Settled soon after the Mayflower hit the rock, now historic homes mingled with new McMansions. Eleanor Roosevelt once proclaimed that Hingham had the most beautiful Main Street in America, and Elise agreed. Hundred-year-old antique homes waved American flags. The elementary schools had shiny, new playground equipment. The lawns were meticulously cared for. The driveways held minivans and abandoned bicycles or Cozy Coupe toddler cars.

Elise grew up happily in Hingham, oblivious for many years that this wasn't how nice every town was, how happy every child's life. Her parents bought an old colonial years before Elise entered their lives. They fixed it up inside, painted the outside pale yellow, and added a farmer's porch complete with swing.

Marie and Ed Moloney were blessed from the start, as they told Elise every time she wanted to hear the story of how they became a family. They met at a dance at Ed's college (Marie and a hundred other girls were shipped in from their nearby all-girls school). They fell in love, got married, bought the house of their dreams, and spent two years working hard, making it perfect for the family that would inevitably come.

Money was never a problem. Ed managed the plastics plant in the next town over. Marie taught high school English. They spent their extra time with friends, volunteering at church functions, working on their home, and trying for a family. But month after month, year after year, the baby that was already so loved and wanted never came.

They prayed. They saw doctors. They asked advice of others. Nothing worked. Marie spent some time in a depression, during which she would sit on the porch swing and stare into the empty yard for hours.

Even though their priest could not give them any practical advice on the matter, they turned to him to help restore Marie's faith and spirit, as her depression was only making the waiting worse. When Marie asked tearfully what she had done wrong because God had not blessed her with a child, the priest opened their eyes to the blessing they had not considered—adoption. They were excited about the idea, and the priest found a Christian adoption agency in Rhode Island that was eager to meet with them. Within a matter of weeks, Elise was in their arms and Ed and Marie finally felt complete.

Elise could not remember a time when she did not know that she was adopted. She always felt very special because of it. Most children were born—she was chosen. Marie always said that God had intervened. That Elise was meant for them, and God found a way to lead them to her.

Elise rounded the bend of Bluebird Road and pointed. "The yellow one. That's mine."

Kat looked up from her textbook in the passenger seat. "Nice house. Very *Better Homes and Gardens.*"

By the time Elise opened the door of her black Honda Civic, her father was already halfway down the driveway with his arms open. He wore thick eyeglasses, jeans, and a flannel shirt. His hair was white, but still thick, something he was proud of as a sixty-three-year-old.

"My little girl, come here." He embraced her strongly. "Mom was so happy when you called and said you were coming. We didn't expect a visit for at least three more weeks. What, they don't have laundromats at Wickman?" He laughed and glanced at Kat.

"You caught me. I did bring laundry, but I also wanted you to meet my roommate, Kat Herrera, and show her around my hometown. Plus, do I ever need a reason to visit?"

"Of course not," he said and kissed her forehead. He shook Kat's hand. "Nice to meet you. Interesting name."

"My mother named me Candy. Being that I didn't want to be a stripper when I grew up, I got it legally changed when I turned eighteen."

"Smart move," Ed said and winked. "Let's head to the house. Mom's whipping up some lemonade. We can sit on the porch. It's a beautiful day."

As they walked up the driveway, Kat whispered in Elise's ear. "I don't know why you didn't just ask them over the phone."

"I need to see their faces, look into their eyes. Now shut up. You're getting free laundry done."

A half-hour later, the lemonade glasses were empty, and Elise's parents were officially in love with Kat. The bright midday sun had dimmed as clouds gathered for a gray afternoon. After a short silence, Kat announced that she was going to the basement to check on the laundry. She tossed Elise a meaningful look on her way inside the house.

Elise watched as her father gently took Marie's hand in his. Physically, they had changed so much since she was a child. Ed's hair was white and his posture slightly stooped. Marie had gained some weight, and her long straight hair was now cut above her shoulder and permed into tight curls. But after all the changes the decades had brought upon them, they were still madly in love.

Elise wiped her clammy hands on her jeans. "Mom, Dad, I did have an important reason to visit you today. I need to ask you some questions."

"About what, dear?" Marie's fingers absently traced the smooth face of the gold watch on her wrist. Elise bought it for her birthday several years ago. It wasn't that expensive, but Marie treated it like the Hope Diamond. Elise looked up from her mother's wrist to her father's honest, loving face. Could it be possible that they had lied to her? Kept a secret like this her entire life?

She said the words quickly, as if the answers would come as swiftly as the questions. "Am I a twin?"

Confusion settled over her parents' faces. Her father was the first to break the silence. "Of course not. Why would you even ask such an odd question?"

Elise pulled a photograph out of her pocketbook. Faith had allowed her to take the picture of Hannah, Faith, and Gavin with her.

"Take a look at this," she said, handing the photo to her mother.

Ed leaned over, looked at the picture with Marie, and shrugged. "Who are these people with you?"

"That's not me."

"Of course it is," Ed said, getting frustrated. "Elise, are you playing a game with us? Some sort of practical joke? We're not going to be on one of those MTV pranking shows, are we?"

Marie lifted her eyes from the picture for the first time and immediately quieted Ed with a soft hand on his arm. "She's right. It's not her. Elise's hair has never been this short. Who is this girl, honey?"

"Her name was Hannah McPhee. She died last year at Wickman. In addition to our identical looks, we share the same birthday. We're obviously twins. And I'm here today to find out if you knew." She became unexpectedly emotional, her voice climbing higher. "Did you know there were two of us, but you chose only one? You could have afforded both of us, right? I mean, I don't understand."

Marie rose from the wicker chair and joined her daughter on the porch swing. She embraced her as tears welled in Elise's eyes. "It's okay," Marie said, patting her back. "It's okay. This sudden knowledge has to be confusing. Let it out."

Elise pulled back and wiped her tears. "I'm fine, really. I just want answers."

Ed spoke quietly. "This is news to us. The agency only told us about you. If you really were a twin, we would have eagerly taken both of you. We never would have separated sisters. We didn't know. They didn't tell us." He paused and added, his voice shaking, "You believe me, don't you?"

"Of course, Dad. I believe you. I just had to know. There are other explanations, of course, but I just had to know if you knew."

"I wish we had known," Marie said, looking wistfully at the picture. "We would have done anything to keep you together, if this is true."

"What are you going to do now?" Ed asked.

Elise looked across the front yard, once full of memories, now full of what-ifs. "I'm going to find out what really happened."

If Parker's roommate, Robbie Deluca, ever needed some extra cash, he could easily earn it as a Buddy Holly impersonator. Though a modern-day version, he looked just like him, right down to the thick black glasses. He was a conspiracy nut— anything from Area 51 to LBJ killed JFK. While most students drank beer, Robbie ordered whiskey on the rocks. He loved to drink, and when drunk loved to theorize about government conspiracies and cover-ups. Tonight, Elise was glad that the topic of conversation was light.

"All I know," Robbie said, slamming his glass on the table, "is that we were gypped. The time to go to college was the eighties. Drugs were okay. Casual sex was okay. Hell, even the music was better. Can you imagine how great it must have been to go to college during the time of The Clash? Imagine sitting in your dorm room blasting 'How Soon is Now?' from The Smiths? Priceless, man. Now, we got shit."

"Someone should tell Kat that casual sex isn't okay anymore," Elise said with a smile.

"Blow me," Kat muttered, and kicked her under the table.

They were seated in a dark booth in the corner of Dolan's Pub. Confronting her parents the day before had exhausted Elise, and the normality of spending a night drinking a couple of beers with friends was comforting. She stared at Robbie as he spoke of the grand conspiracy to make college less fun than it used to be and wondered why the hell he went by Robbie anyway. He could go by Robert, Rob, Bob. Hell, even Bobby was better than Robbie. She didn't think anyone over the age of five went by Robbie.

"What do you think?" Parker asked her.

"Oh, sorry, I wasn't listening. Think of what?"

Parker flashed her a look of sympathy. "Are you thinking about Hannah?"

It was actually the first moment in the last twenty-four hours since she left her parents' house that she wasn't thinking about Hannah. She drained her beer and placed it near the end of the table for the waitress. Parker, Kat, and Robbie all stared at her expectantly.

"It's just so overwhelming. I went through my whole life thinking one thing, and then I find this out and everything is different now. I feel an emptiness. What could have been."

Kat tossed her arm over Elise's shoulder. "Any luck with the adoption agency?"

She shook her head. "They're not in the Yellow Pages. I Googled them and got nothing."

"Parker's Dad could get you any info you needed," Robbie said.

"Yeah, definitely," Parker said. "He's a D.C. lobbyist, and he can get information on anyone or anything. One of the perks."

"A lobbyist? Eww!"

"He's not Satan, Kat. Not all lobbyists are corrupt, working for big tobacco or insurance companies. He works for a group that makes an algae-based product that cleans up oil spills and other environmental disasters. Not very exciting, but he believes in it." He turned to Elise. "He'll find out what's up with the adoption agency. Just give me the name and any other information you have, like their last known address, and he'll work on it. He has a lot of contacts with access to a lot of databases."

"Thanks. I just want answers. This whole thing is so crazy. I was just going along through life and then bam, I have a sister and oh, by the way, she died last year in an accident."

"Accident?" Robbie snorted. "That was no accident."

"Excuse me?"

Parker placed a hand on Robbie's shoulder. "Now's not the time, pal. She doesn't need to hear this particular conspiracy theory of yours right now."

"It's not a conspiracy theory. It's common sense. It's nearly impossible to just fall off that bridge. And, before you say it, she did not commit suicide. You didn't know her, Parker. I did. She would never have committed suicide."

"You knew her?" Elise leaned forward over the table. "Tell me. Tell me everything."

"He didn't know her that well," Parker said. "He likes to think he did, but he didn't. They just slept together a handful of times, before Gavin."

"So you were like her boyfriend or something? You must have

known her well."

Parker's voice was barely a whisper, "That's just the thing, Elise. He wasn't her boyfriend."

Elise's eyes drifted back and forth between Parker and Robbie. "I don't understand."

Robbie said, "Your sister, assuming she was your sister, she . . . um . . . how do I say this?"

"Slept around?" Kat said. "Big deal."

Robbie shrugged. "Yeah, it's no big deal. I just, you know, don't want to say anything bad about her."

Elise leaned back and stared up at the light above their booth. It had begun to flicker. "So, she wasn't innocent and pure. I want to know everything anyway. The good and the bad. Robbie, tell me what you think happened, how she died."

Robbie glanced at Parker for permission, and he nodded. Elise wondered when and why Parker had slipped into the role of her protector and information gatekeeper.

Robbie looked around the bar, which was nearly empty—it was still early. Then he whispered, "The idea that it was an accident is just plain stupid. Wickman students go over that bridge to get to the beach and the dunes all the time. Hannah herself probably walked over it hundreds of times. How can you just fall off of it?"

"She was drunk," Parker said, "and part of the railing was missing."

Robbie rolled his eyes. "Parker, how many times have you walked over that bridge absolutely wasted? Have you ever fallen off? No. No one has. She didn't fall by accident. And it was no suicide, either. Hannah loved life. She lived it to the fullest. Sure, after she started dating Gavin she was tamer, but she seemed very happy with him. I can't think of any reason why she would ever commit suicide. None. Some people have the capacity in them to do that and some people don't. Hannah didn't."

"So you think someone pushed her?" Kat asked.

"Yeah, it's the logical conclusion. She was drunk, walking with someone over the bridge, maybe to go to the beach together. I don't know. Lots of students hang out at the beach at night sometimes."

"Not in February," Parker said.

"Okay, I'll grant you that it's rare for a couple of students to want to hang out on the beach in the middle of the night in February, but I'm sure it happens. Especially if the people want privacy."

Elise rested her chin in her hands. "How would the person have known she would drown?"

"They call it the Drowning River for a reason. It doesn't look threatening, but that river will suck you under in seconds. It has a strong current and rip tides. Plus, the temperature of the water in February alone could kill a person."

"So you think she was drunk, walking over the bridge with someone for some reason, and they pushed her. On purpose."

"Yes, I do. But don't ask me who. That's the part I've never been able to figure out." Robbie took his glasses off and looked hard at Elise. "But maybe you can."

CHAPTER 5

The sunset bled across the skyline and disappeared behind the rising sand dunes on Oceanside Beach. Elise remembered hearing once that a red sunset meant a hot day for tomorrow, but she didn't know if it was true or an old wives' tale. Either way, it was a warm evening for September. She felt comfortable in denim shorts and a gray Old Navy t-shirt.

The afternoon's high tide was receding, leaving trails of seaweed and shells in the sheen of wet mud left behind. Seagulls cried as they circled and swooped through the air. Elise sat cross-legged and observed a little girl search for seashells, then delightedly bring her prize to her mother, who praised each one as the most beautiful shell she'd ever seen.

Elise picked up a fistful of sand and watched the tiny pebbles sift between her fingers. The wind picked up and she closed her eyes to protect them from the flying dust. A moment later she opened them, and a person stood facing her.

"Sorry I'm late. My professor wanted to talk to me after class."

"No problem." Elise rose and brushed sand off her bottom. "Want to walk?"

Faith fell in line beside Elise. She wore a long, pink sundress and walked barefoot while holding a pair of strappy sandals in her hand. Before Elise had a chance to speak, Faith began.

"A couple months before Hannah started dating Gavin, she got busted for possession—a little bit of weed. It was her first offense, so they gave her parole and community service. She did her service with disadvantaged kids at this after-school place. Tutoring, stuff like that. She went about five hours a week. I teased her about it, and she acted like it was such a chore, but I had the feeling after a few weeks that she didn't mind it at all. That she looked forward to it."

Faith's curls bounced as she walked. Elise wondered why she had just started talking like this and where the story was going, but she kept silent, encouraging her to continue.

"After Hannah died, I stopped by the center so I could tell them that Hannah would not be in to do her community service anymore."

Faith stopped walking, and Elise knew the point was about to be made.

"They told me that her community service requirement had been fulfilled in the first six weeks. She stayed on for months after that, not because she had to, but because she wanted to. She loved those kids. Every single one of them came to her funeral."

Her voice softened, and she looked away at a distant point out in the ocean. "All these little boys and girls, dressed up, sad, not really understanding what happened."

She was silent for a moment, then resumed walking, signaling that the story was over.

"Why did you tell me that?" Elise asked.

"Because I know you asked me here to find out more about who Hannah was, and I know you've probably already heard some things. Yeah, she wasn't the most innocent person. She didn't always make the right decisions. But I wanted you to know what kind of a person she was on the inside, and that was one small example of how big her heart was."

A jogger went by, his running shoes kicking up sand in their wake.

"So, about the things I've heard," Elise started.

"Whatever you've heard is probably true. Hard drinking, soft drugs, casual sex. What can I say? She loved life. She lived it fast. I never judged her, you know. She didn't have the dream of suburbia childhood."

Like me, Elise thought.

"She grew up in the city, poor, with a single mother who wasn't always there for her. Men came in and out of her life until her mother finally married a guy Hannah didn't like. She's a success story, really. She had to deal with things every day that the rest of us only saw on after-school specials. But she made it to college, and she would have done great things with her life."

"How did she pay for college? Loans?"

"She had a rich grandmother who paid for the whole thing. She wasn't in Hannah's life, but the money gave Hannah an opportunity she wouldn't have had otherwise."

Faith stole a glance at Elise and smiled. "Sometimes when I look at you, I forget. It's like she's back." They walked in silence for a moment. "She was the greatest friend I ever could have wanted or deserved. So she was a little wild. I never faulted her for it."

"What about this Gavin guy?"

A sigh slipped from Faith's mouth. "No one ever really affected Hannah. Hannah affected you. That is, until Gavin Shaw." She giggled in a way that made her seem very young. "No one saw that coming. Gavin was a straight arrow, goody-two-shoes, football quarterback, homecoming king. He and Hannah couldn't have been more different."

"How did they get together?"

"They were in the same history class and the professor lumped them together to do a group project. Pure chance. Spending that time together did it. They both fell madly in love.

I didn't think Hannah was capable of that kind of love with a guy. I never thought she would trust someone enough to love him that much."

"And Gavin?"

"He loved her back just as intensely. He was never into hooking up or one-night stands, but he jumped from relationship to relationship. I don't think he was ever single for more than a week. He was in love with being in love. Does that make sense?"

Elise nodded.

"He always treated his girlfriends well at the beginning. He would drown them with his love—compliments, gifts, passion. No girl could refuse him, really. Not even Hannah."

"Why just at the beginning?"

"He has a habit of losing interest after a few months and moving on to another, just as intense relationship. I don't think any girl has dumped him. He always does the damage."

A ship in the distance blew its horn. Elise gazed out at the ocean, but couldn't find it. The glare of the setting sun turned the water an impenetrable dark.

"Hannah changed after they became a couple?"

"Drastically. She was still fun, don't get me wrong. She still went to parties and drank a little, but never got wild anymore. No more drugs, never cheated on Gavin, never took risks."

They reached the base of the bridge that not only made the Drowning River passable, but also connected Oceanside Beach to the parking lot and East Street, the main road into town and campus. Elise didn't want to stop, so she tried to keep Faith talking as she stepped onto the first wooden plank of the bridge. "And this was Gavin's influence?"

"He liked to save women. And I give him credit. He did save Hannah. She really turned her life around. She went from a straight-C student to As. For the first time, she started talking about a life after college. She was researching careers, optimistic about the future."

Faith's composure shattered, and she dropped her face into her hands.

Elise had expected a few tears tonight—that would be natural in a woman reminiscing about her deceased best friend—but this sudden change shocked her. Faith grabbed her tight as hard sobs wracked her small frame. Surprised, Elise hugged back, not knowing what to say. After a long minute, Faith pulled back but kept her hands on Elise's arms. She looked deep into Elise's eyes and said, "I'm sorry."

"It's okay," Elise muttered, feeling uncomfortable. On the surface, it would seem that Faith's apology was for her outburst of grief, but she had an unnerving suspicion that the urgency in Faith's eyes and words weren't for Elise at all, but to someone else through Elise.

They began walking again, and Elise broke the awkward stillness with a question. "Where is Gavin now?"

Faith brushed away her tears with the palms of her hands. "Here in town. He's a cop. He was a criminal justice major here at Wickman. His dad is the chief of police, so he easily got a job on the force. I don't think Gavin ever had a choice in the matter."

Faith stopped and placed a hand on Elise's shoulder. She gazed down at the water below and whispered, "This is where it happened."

"Where she fell?"

Faith nodded and grazed her fingers along the wooden railing of the pedestrian bridge. "The railing was out right here. They don't know why. Maybe one of the townie teenagers broke it. But anyway, the railing was out and . . . she was drunk . . . and I don't know. She fell. There was a thin layer of ice on the water below. The police said that the force of breaking through the ice knocked her unconscious and then she drowned."

Goosebumps rose on Elise's arms and she involuntarily shuddered. It was a long way down to the cold water below. She leaned against the railing and peered down. She imagined herself falling in slow motion, head over feet and head again, unable to stop, unable to think, unable to scream, unable to do anything but stare at the reflection of her face in the river as the water rushed up and engulfed her.

Faith pulled her back. "Please don't lean on the railing. You never know. These rickety old bridges."

Elise hadn't noticed, but Faith had been crying again. Fresh tears shimmered on her cheeks. Faith turned and walked away. Wanting more information, Elise followed.

"Was Hannah sad about anything that last week?"

Faith glanced at her with an understanding of the unspoken question beneath. "She and Gavin had broken up so she had reason to be sad, but I never really felt like she was honest with her emotions. She always put on a tough facade no matter what."

"Why did they break up?"

"I don't know. I wasn't around much that week."

Elise paused, waiting for her to add more, but she didn't. "What about her mother and step-father? Anything going on with them at that time?"

"Her mother was trash, if you ask me. I met her a few times and never liked her. Hannah and her mother never got along that well to begin with, but about a week before she died something big happened. Hannah and her mother got into a huge argument. She didn't want to talk about it, though, so I never found out what it was about. She really kept to herself those last days."

The bridge ended, and they stood on the banks of the river. Only three cars were left in the parking lot. The ocean was no longer visible in the distance, hidden by tall sand dunes. The sun had set, and the sky was gray. A mist slithered in from the salt marshes.

Faith fidgeted, twirling a curl around her finger. "I should get going. Do you want a ride back to campus?"

"No, I'm going to walk. But can I ask one last question?"

Faith struggled to stand on one leg while putting her feet in her sandals. "Sure, shoot."

"Do you think Hannah was sad enough those last few days to commit suicide?"

Elise knew the answer immediately from the look in Faith's eyes. No. No way. Hannah McPhee loved life and even when she was knocked down, she always came up swinging. She would never have done that.

"Maybe."

"What?" Elise asked, bewildered.

"It was February thirteenth. The day before her birthday, before Valentine's Day without Gavin. It's a definite possibility that she committed suicide."

With that, Faith disappeared through the sea mist back to her car, leaving Elise alone with her thoughts. Hannah didn't commit suicide. She couldn't explain how she knew; she just did. And Faith did, too. Then why would she want Elise to think that suicide was a possibility?

Elise knelt on the riverbank and wondered if Faith's previous outburst was caused by grief or guilt. She leaned forward, peering into the water. A face in the river stared back. A face with eyes as green as the sea, hair as pale as the sand—Elise's face. Hannah's face.

She felt as if Hannah was reaching out to her from the murky depths. Telling her to keep searching for the answers. It was no accident, the reflection said. It was no suicide.

Help me.

Save yourself.

Before it's too late.

CHAPTER 6

Elise hung up the phone and groaned with dread. She got the information she wanted, but now she had to do something with it and that thought knotted up her stomach. The afternoon sunlight poured through the apartment's large front window, and Elise leaned back with her eyes closed and enjoyed the warmth of it on her face. It had been a long week of classes. She had a paper due next week that she hadn't even started yet. She was behind on her reading, behind on her sleep, and the stress was beginning to build up.

The door slammed, and Kat entered like a tornado, tossing her backpack in the corner while belly flopping onto the couch.

"I'm so tired," Kat said. "This is day three without diet soda. I've been clinging to consciousness all day."

Knowing her moment of peace was over, Elise took the bait. "Why did you give it up?"

"Robbie said there's a conspiracy of silence surrounding that fake sugar stuff. He said it causes all sorts of diseases with longtime use, but the FDA is allowing the soda companies to use it because they're in cahoots with the company that makes it. It will be the tobacco of the next generation."

"Then why not drink regular?"

"Too sweet."

"Aren't you wearing the same clothes you wore yesterday? Did you even come home last night?"

Kat raked her fingers through her hair. "He was this gorgeous art history major, had a nice pad with a beach view." She closed her eyes and moaned. "Anyway, what were you meditating about when I barged in?"

"I just called Faith and got the address of Hannah's mother."

"Your mother, too. Biological anyway."

Elise didn't need a reminder. She had to see her, and she wanted answers. But at the same time, a certain level of ignorance can be bliss, and part of her wished she didn't have to meet her, didn't have to find out the truth.

She tilted back again into the path of the sun and closed her eyes. "It's the strangest thing. I feel like I should cry. My sister is dead. I should cry. But I feel nothing."

"You can't mourn someone you never knew existed." Kat picked at a lint ball on the cushion. "You're probably still in shock. Give yourself a break." She pulled herself off the couch. "I'm making a grilled-cheese sandwich, want one?"

Elise shook her head no, but followed Kat into the kitchen. "I saw where it happened. The place where she died."

Kat whipped around, frying pan in hand. "What? When?"

"A few days ago. I met Faith there. I wanted to see it for myself." Elise sat at the kitchen table and rested her chin in her hands. "Hannah didn't commit suicide. I know it. We're twins. We have the same genes."

"Hannah did a lot of things you wouldn't do."

"That's true, but this I just know. Instinctively. I can't explain it, but I just know that she didn't kill herself. She wouldn't have done it, ever."

Kat expertly placed the cheese on the toasting slices of bread. "I had lunch with Parker and Robbie yesterday at the Café. Parker had done this research on twins at the library. He found some interesting stuff."

"I don't understand why he cares. Why does he want to help me so much?"

Kat glared at her over her shoulder. "Girl, that's obvious. The real mystery is you, not him."

"What's that supposed to mean?"

"Parker is perfect for you. He's smart, kind, funny, and cute. I'd go after him if he'd even glance my way, but his attention is all on you. The real question is why you're not interested in him."

Elise stared at a cloud-shaped stain on the linoleum floor. "I never said I wasn't interested in him. He is everything you say he is. I just don't want a relationship right now. I want to be friends with him until I figure some stuff out."

"What are you scared of?"

"I'm not scared."

Kat stared at her until Elise relented and turned away. "Someone hurt you bad, huh?"

"No, that's not it. I was in a serious relationship last year. His name is Nick Carrano. We were engaged. But I got cold feet in May and ended it without really understanding why I was doing it. And I didn't give him an adequate explanation either. I acted like a coward."

Kat brought her plate to the table. "You're regretting it now? Miss him?"

"I regret the way I did it, yes. And I'm undecided about him. All I know for sure is that between my confusion about that relationship and now everything with Hannah, this is no time to start a relationship."

Kat shrugged and took a bite of her sandwich.

"So, what did Parker come up with in his research on twins?"

Kat took a moment to finish chewing. "Identical twins share a hundred percent of their DNA. And he read some study about identical twins separated at birth and raised apart. The study showed strange similarities between the twins as adults—some smoke the same brand of cigarettes, drive the same model car, have similar hand gestures, voices, phobias. It was pretty interesting."

"What does that have to do with Hannah's death?"

"Parker believes that the best clues to solving the mystery lie in you. Sure, you and Hannah are two separate people who made different choices, but you have the same DNA. One hundred percent. You probably think alike in ways you don't even know. So if your gut tells you she didn't commit suicide, Parker would agree that you're right."

"And you? You think I'm wrong?"

"I just want to make sure you're not getting into this too deeply. Becoming too obsessed."

Elise opened her mouth to speak, but Kat silenced her with her hand. "I know that you have to find out what happened to Hannah, that you need answers. I would, too, if I were you. But just do me a favor. Don't lose yourself in the process of finding Hannah."

Faith cursed as her sneaker sank in mud. She pushed on through the marsh, periodically looking over her shoulder to make sure she was alone. The shed was only a hundred feet away now, cloaked in the darkness of night.

He said it would be unlocked and it was. She closed the door behind her and took a moment to catch her breath. The smell of the sea was strong tonight. She peeked out the small window and saw only black. Even the moon was hiding.

The shed contained signs with the beach rules, life vests, buoys, and other town beach fixtures. Her sneakers scuffed loudly as they dragged sand across the concrete floor. She looked for somewhere to sit, but there was nothing. The floor was dirty, so she stood, even though the small shed seemed like it was closing in on her.

Where was he?

She glanced at her watch. He was five minutes late. Was he playing head games? Was he outside right now, watching her?

A rustling came from behind the shed, the side with no window. She held her breath and listened. Silence.

Then a crackling, closer this time. Coming toward the front of the shed, the door.

Should she open it? Is it him?

She peeked out the window, but it was too dark to see anything. She pressed her forehead against the glass, straining to look to the left to see if anyone was at the door.

A flash of white burst in front of her eyes and banged on the window. She screamed and fell backward.

"Damn it!"

She opened the door, ran outside, and there it was. A large white bird had been scavenging around the shed and flown up and flapped against the window. She shooed it away and her heartbeat slowed with relief.

"What are you doing? I told you to wait in the shed."

The booming voice made her jump, but she was no longer scared. There he was, a dark form walking toward her.

"One of those stupid endangered marsh birds just scared the shit out of me," she said.

With long strides he reached her quickly, took her by the elbow and led her inside the shed. Her skin burned where he touched her. She was now thankful for the small size of the shed as it forced them to stand close together. Heat radiated from him. She had never seen him in uniform before, and she took the sight in and savored it.

"Is she for real?" Gavin asked.

Faith nodded. "The looks are undeniable. She must be Hannah's twin. She hasn't gotten any official word yet, but she called me today asking for Hannah's mother's address, so I'm sure answers will come soon."

"How could that be? How could Hannah have a twin?"

"I don't know. Elise obviously doesn't know. She didn't even know Hannah existed."

He wouldn't look her in the eye. He just kept asking questions while staring into the space over her left shoulder. She moved a step to the left, but he looked the other way and asked another question. "Did Hannah know?"

"She never said anything about it, but that doesn't mean she didn't know." She gently laid her hand on his arm. "She didn't tell us everything, you know."

He pulled his arm away.

"Everyone has secrets, Gavin. Even Hannah did," she said with the slightest hint of venom in her voice.

He turned to leave and she stepped in front and blocked him. "Why did we have to meet all the way out here? Why all the secrecy?"

"Isn't that obvious? No one ever found out, and I don't want anyone finding out now."

"Don't be so sure they won't. Elise is doing a lot of digging around. She thinks Hannah was murdered."

He rubbed his chin. "Don't worry about that. Just keep your mouth shut."

With that he left her alone in the dark shed with nothing but the memory of his touch on her elbow.

CHAPTER 7

Dorchester, Boston's largest neighborhood, often appeared in the news for gun violence and gang trouble. Triple-decker homes with no space between them lined the streets. A young girl, probably three years old, sat in a tiny front yard playing with a ball behind a chain-link fence. Parker and Kat both begged to go with her today, but Elise declined. This was something she had to do alone.

The street was dry, but the clouds were dark and full with imminent rain. Elise sat parked in her car across the street from house number 118, a gray triple-decker, obviously over one hundred years old and in desperate need of paint. She stared at the windows looking for something, anything. Shadows, movement, a glimpse of the mother who gave her away.

Curiosity, anger, and anxiety battled at her nerves as she reached into her purse for her asthma inhaler. She took two puffs and sank back into the upholstered seat.

How could a mother separate twin sisters?

She gathered her courage and left the shelter of the car, beeping the alarm on her way to the black door that stared at her like the open mouth of a cavern. The weight of her index finger on the doorbell brought a rustling from inside, and the thought that in a moment she would shock and possibly even scare her biological mother washed a pleasing calm over her apprehension.

The door jerked open, and a woman stood before her. She

was very thin, and wore out-of-date acid-washed jeans and a blue, oversized Champion sweatshirt. A cigarette dangled from her left hand, and her right hand tugged at her tangled mess of gray and blond hair. Her vivid green eyes implored Elise to say something and immediately in those eyes Elise recognized herself.

The woman's face held no surprise, no emotion. She stepped back and looked Elise up and down, finally letting her eyes rest upon her face. Then she leaned against the doorframe, tapped her cigarette on the porch railing, and said, "Hello there."

Elise watched the ashes fall to the ground in slow motion as the knowledge sank in. Faith had called the house and warned her. Fury rose to the surface. She felt cheated. She wanted to scare this woman. Shock her. Shame her. She'd earned that much; this woman owed it to her. But all that was taken away by one phone call.

The woman looked both ways, presumably for nosy neighbors, then motioned with her hand for Elise to enter.

"I'm Beth Wells," she said in a raspy voice. "I'm your mother. What's your name? Elsie? Eloise?"

"Elise." She followed Beth Wells blindly up a narrow staircase, sweat making her hands slip on the rail.

"Weird. I don't like it. I named you Holly. I wish they would have kept that."

Her name at birth was Holly McPhee. That new and seemingly innocent information rocked her. It was like she was two people. Elise, the person who existed with the life that she had, and Holly the person she might have been. She would have grown up with her sister—Holly and Hannah—but also with this mother, with this life she didn't want.

Beth opened a door on the second floor that led them into the living room. "I own the second and third floor apartments."

The air smelled of room deodorizer, probably one of those

sprays called Spring Morning or Flower Meadow. Two faded couches sat behind a large wooden coffee table. As she approached the nearest couch to sit down, Elise saw junk—newspapers, paper plates—stuffed underneath. Beth had done a quick clean-up job after the phone call. The idea that Beth may have wanted to impress her felt strange, but then again, wasn't that why Elise wore the sundress with the tiny green flowers that brought out the color of her eyes?

"Can I get you some coffee or something?"

"No, thanks." She just wanted to get some answers and leave. She didn't want this woman to be a part of her life. She already had a mother. She just wanted to know why. No coffee, no small talk, no sharing stories. "Faith told you I was coming."

Beth nodded nervously and coughed into her hand. "Yeah, she told me everything. I figured I'd have to face you someday. I mean, that's what most adopted kids do when they grow up. They try to search out their birth moms and blame them for anything bad that happened in their lives. I figured someday you'd knock on that door, but never imagined it would be today when the phone rang early this morning."

"I'm not here to blame you for anything." Elise felt like ice. Each word carefully chosen, each sentence as small as possible so as to expend as little effort as possible on this woman.

Beth stubbed her cigarette out in an ashtray shaped like two dice. She rubbed her hands back and forth on her jeans and avoided Elise's eyes. "What do you want then?"

"I think you know what I want."

Something strange resonated in Beth's face. Panic? A flash of rage?

Elise crossed her legs, amazed at how casual her voice sounded. "I want to know why you put me up for adoption and separated me from Hannah. I would think that's the obvious question."

Beth relaxed, and the expression of alarm left her face. "Oh, of course you want to know that. Only natural. Your dad was Jesse McPhee. I couldn't tell you where he is now. He was never in the picture. Took off with his band to tour California or something. I never heard from him again. I'm married now. Roger Wells is his name. He adopted Hannah when we got married, but she didn't change her last name. Hannah was in high school then. Anyway, I was nineteen when I got pregnant with you two."

Elise mentally added and figured that made Beth forty-two years old. She looked much older.

"I wanted to keep you both. I did. But that was impossible. I was dirt poor, living in a one-room apartment above the pizza place on Newport Road. Financially, it would have been impossible to care for both of you. So I did what I thought was best. I put you up for adoption."

"You thought it was best to separate twin sisters?"

She rolled her eyes. "Obviously, that's not ideal, but neither was getting knocked up at that time in my life. I made the adoption agency promise me you'd go to a nice, rich family. One with a big house in a nice town. And you did, didn't you?"

"Money isn't everything."

Beth smiled. "You sound just like her. Naive."

Elise ignored the insult. "Do you know where my father lives now?"

"No."

"Did he ever come back to Massachusetts?"

Beth traced her finger along a scratch on the table, back and forth, like she'd rather be anywhere else in the world. "No idea."

Elise sighed. She was getting nowhere. The only information she had gained so far was that she viscerally disliked her biological mother and never wanted to see her again. One last question.

"Did Hannah know about me?"

Beth's finger stopped moving, but she kept her eyes down, staring at the scratch. "No." She pulled another cigarette out of the pack lying on the table and lit it.

"You should quit," Elise said.

"Been smoking since I was thirteen. Can't ever stop."

Elise thought of her asthma. "Not even while pregnant with twins?"

Beth raised her eyebrows and blew a puff of smoke from the corner of her mouth. "I cut back a little bit. The doctor said to stop smoking would be bad. The sudden withdrawal would be too hard on the fetuses."

"I suppose the sudden withdrawal was easier on the newborns, then."

Beth lowered her eyes, caught in her lie.

Not the only lie she's told today, Elise thought.

Beth rested her head on the couch pillow and closed her eyes. She was glad that Elise had offered to see herself out because she didn't want to watch her walk away, watch the car drive off until it disappeared around the corner, and she was gone again. Beth found that if she didn't think too much about the bad things she had done in her life, then she didn't think she was a bad person.

"Pretty girl."

Beth lazily opened her eyes and watched her husband lumber into the room. Roger Wells had let himself go in the past few years. He was always a big man, which was why she was initially attracted to him. He reminded her of those football players in high school who were too busy chasing the cheerleaders to look at a girl like her. But after a few years of marriage, he started to look less like a football player and more like a coach. His dirty jeans hung low under his gut and his pecs had turned into floppy breasts. Beth didn't mind too much. What did she expect? He was forty after all, and she wasn't a prize herself.

"Were you listening the whole time?" she asked.

"Yeah. It's amazing. She even sounds like Hannah."

Beth sighed. She didn't want to talk about Elise or Hannah. She just wanted to sleep and dream.

Roger hoisted himself into his recliner and spread the sports pages across his lap. "So, she doesn't know?"

"No idea."

"Good. You think she'll be back?"

Beth closed her eyes. "No. She got what she wanted— answers, someone to hate. She's gone. We're fine."

CHAPTER 8

All the desks at the Oceanside Police Station were the same standard metal variety, but Officer Federico's stuck out like a drunk aunt at a wedding. It was immaculate. No pile of files with papers sticking out at every angle. No clutter of coffee mugs and pens. No newspaper, no picture frames, nothing but a telephone and the reflection of Elise's face in the shiny metal.

Either Officer Federico was a compulsive organizer with more time on his hands than the other officers or—

"Elise Moloney?"

—she was a rookie.

Elise rose and shook hands with the tall, broad-shouldered young woman. "Thank you for meeting with me, Officer Federico."

Her black hair was tied back in a ponytail so tight it made her eyebrows arch, and her voice was as masculine as her frame. "You can call me Lisa. Please have a seat. Sorry to keep you waiting. I was just getting the file."

"No problem. I'm glad I could get an appointment to speak with you. You investigated this case?"

Lisa retrieved a pen from her desk drawer and laid the file down in the perfect center of the desk. "No. What gave you that idea?"

"When I called, I requested an appointment to meet with the main officer on the case."

Lisa frowned. "Well, you got me instead. What can I do for you?"

Elise glanced around the open room. All the other desks were empty except one, where an officer sat whispering softly into his phone. Another officer was out front drinking a cup of coffee with the dispatcher.

"I wanted to ask a few questions about the case."

"Are you a family member of the victim?"

Elise sighed. "Have you even opened the file, Officer Federico?"

"Again, call me Lisa. And no, I have not read the file. I am new to the department and wasn't here when the accident occurred. I was briefed about the case and handed this file, but haven't had a chance to study it myself."

"Please open it."

Lisa opened the file, and Elise spied Hannah's yearbook picture paper-clipped to the first page. Lisa stared at it, then glanced at Elise and quickly looked back down at the papers.

Her cheeks reddened. "Twins, eh?"

Elise nodded.

"Why have you waited seven months to ask questions? Do you have new information?"

Elise rested her elbows on the desk and gave Lisa a Cliff Note's version of how she found out about Hannah. She left out a lot, including the fact that she thought Hannah was murdered, but figured if Lisa was the slightest bit intuitive, she would figure out that there was a reason Elise was here.

"When was Hannah's death ruled an accident?"

Lisa lifted a page and ran her finger down the paper. "February twentieth."

"A week after she died. Isn't that quick?"

"We had no evidence to the contrary."

"But still, it seems like it was written off as an accident

without deeply investigating it."

"Her blood alcohol level was double the legal limit. Drunk people fall all the time. They fall walking a straight line. Do you know how easy it would be to fall from that bridge when you're tired and numb with booze?"

"If it were that easy, Wickman students would be falling off of it every day. How many other drunken students cross that bridge every night in the good weather? Plenty. And how many others have fallen off?"

Lisa ignored the question. "There was no evidence of a struggle."

"No marks on her body at all?"

"Of course there were marks, but they were all consistent with being knocked around the river and the rocks along the banks."

"So there could have been marks from an assailant, but they were brushed off as typical riverbed damage." Elise's voice cracked, and the other officer in the room quietly hung up his phone and leaned forward, not hiding his interest in the conversation.

"There were no easily identifiable struggle signs, Miss Moloney."

"Do you know how easy it is to push someone into the river when they're drunk and not expecting it? You don't even need to leave a bruise to do it! Were people even questioned?"

The two officers in the dispatch area stared openly at her. She was about to cause a scene, could see it coming in slow motion like a reckless driver in the rearview mirror, but was unable to stop herself.

"Please stay calm."

Elise plowed on, her voice rising. "Was her boyfriend questioned? Or was he covered for because he's the son of the chief?"

Officer Lisa Federico had a line, and obviously Elise had just crossed it. She placed a hand on Elise's shoulder and squeezed, speaking through clenched teeth.

"You look here. This isn't like the movies. We're not all part of a crooked brotherhood. I take my job very seriously and so do all the other officers in this town. You can bet your skinny little ass that if the chief's son gave his girlfriend the nudge into the river, we wouldn't have looked the other way. But there is no evidence that Gavin, or anyone else for that matter, murdered your sister."

Elise's shoulder was starting to throb. "How do you know? Did anyone question him?"

"Yes, we did. He had an alibi."

"What was his alibi?" Elise tempered her voice, and Lisa returned the favor by removing her giant hand.

"He was in Hannah's dorm room with her roommate, waiting for her to come home."

"Where was Hannah?"

"She was spotted by several witnesses at Dolan's Pub— drinking, flirting, dancing, talking to a lot of people. No one remembers her leaving, but obviously she did."

"And Gavin and Faith were waiting for her back at the dorm the entire time?"

"Yes."

Elise tapped on the desk. Lisa seemed genuine, but something wasn't right. "I thought you said you didn't read the file."

"I didn't, but I was briefed on the important facts."

Elise leaned back in the chair and rubbed her forehead, frustration eating away at her like acid on metal.

"Listen, Miss Moloney, I know that this is all new to you. You didn't even know her and you'll never get the chance to, and that has to be tough on you. But there's nothing to this case. It was an accident. Period. Instead of looking into the case, you should look into why you desperately want there to be more to it. Why you want your sister to be this tragic heroine rather than what she really was?"

"What was that?"

"A drunk girl who fell."

Elise stood and the chair screeched. She had everyone's attention now and she didn't care.

"I've got something for you to consider, Officer. Maybe instead of just blindly following orders and automatically believing what you're told, you should try thinking for yourself. Think about why they put you, a young female rookie who knows nothing about the case, out here to talk to me. Think about why the person who briefed you—Gavin or the chief—had enough time to cherry-pick certain facts about the case to give to you, but didn't have time to meet with me. Think about how quickly the case was dismissed. Think about how differently this case would have been handled if it had been a rich townie girl it happened to and the chief's son wasn't involved. Think about why they obviously told you to discourage me from looking into the case further. Think about that."

CHAPTER 9

Elise loved the smell of the ocean, especially on days when rain was near. The air smelled sweeter, stronger, and even though rain clouds hadn't rolled in yet, she could sense that they were near by the scent in the air. A textbook lay open on the blanket beneath her, but she hadn't read a word for several minutes. The river's currents rushed and swirled, and she found herself leaning forward for glimpses every now and then, expecting to see her own reflection. But each time the face that looked back was not her own—it was Hannah's.

Parker closed his book beside her. "It's kind of chilly. Do you want to head back?"

She ignored the question and stared off at the sand dunes in the distance, past the river, on the other side of the bridge. They didn't seem real. They looked like a landscape painting or a photograph to be framed and hung on a wall.

"I can't believe it will be October in two days," she said. "This first month of school is like a blur to me."

After meeting her mother last weekend and going to the police station Monday, she still hadn't felt any closer to the truth. So she put the truth aside for the rest of the week to hit the books. She finished her paper on time and caught up with her reading. But as the academic pressure diminished, the urge for answers returned.

"It doesn't seem like you're getting any reading done," Parker insisted. "Maybe we should head back."

"I'm not in the mood to do homework. But I do want to stay here a little longer."

After a pause, he asked softly, "Do you feel close to her here?"

She nodded, and pulled her lavender sweater tighter against her body. Satisfied, he returned to his textbook and highlighted a passage.

On the opposite bank, a father and son fished for bass. The boy was about five or six, and by the gentle way the father instructed him on his cast, Elise wondered if this was their first time fishing. She wondered what Parker had been like as a boy. Probably cute, inquisitive, asking why a thousand times a day.

She leaned back on her elbows and took in the sight of Parker beside her, sharing a blanket on the riverbank. He wore loose-fitting jeans and an ivory sweater. His hair was blond like hers, but darker with honey tones, whereas hers was as pale as champagne. His hair stuck out in all angles, disheveled from his habit of running his hands through it when he reached a passage that challenged him.

He was handsome, she couldn't deny that. She also couldn't deny that she did have feelings for him that grew every day. A month ago, she didn't know this man and now she couldn't imagine being at Wickman without him. He and Kat had become her best friends and confidantes. But her life was so complicated right now. She didn't want to muddy it further by starting a relationship with Parker. She needed him as a friend. She needed his help. If they started something and it didn't work out, she'd lose him completely.

Even so, she found herself gazing at the smooth skin of his cheek, at the line of his jaw that led to his full lips.

He looked up and caught her stare.

She felt the red flame of embarrassment burn up her neck. She stammered, "Um, I was wondering. Where does this river go?"

A small smile of satisfaction lit up his face. He closed his book and turned to face her. "It's interesting, the river is actually a combination of fresh and salt water. Fresh water comes from the groundwater and a few streams and mixes with the salt water from the sea. The river feeds the salt marshes and ends up pouring into the Atlantic about a mile down through the marsh."

"Why do a lot of the wooden planks of the bridge have names carved into them?"

"The bridge dates back to the late 1800s, but the original bridge was destroyed by Hurricane Bob in 1991. The community rebuilt it by selling planks. If you made a donation to help rebuild the bridge, your name would forever be etched into one of the planks. Or at least until the next hurricane."

The bridge over the river led people to a labyrinth of paths through sand dunes. A right turn would lead to the salt marshes, a left turn to the town beach. She wondered where Hannah was headed the night she was on the bridge. Was she headed to the beach with someone? In February? It didn't make much sense. She pushed the thought away.

"Can you walk through the salt marshes?"

"They're not deep, but it's not recommended. They stretch out pretty far. Some of the area is protected land, for the birds."

"What birds?"

"Mostly ospreys. They were an endangered species for a while, but have rebounded. Robbie says that a crazy bird-man lives in one of the old shacks way out there in the marsh, and he takes care of the osprey nests. I don't know if that's true or just town legend, though."

"Oh, good. I was beginning to think there wasn't anything you didn't know." She paused. "Can I ask you something that might possibly offend you?"

He leaned back on his elbows. "How can I say no to that?"

"I've heard you in class ask Professor Marston questions so challenging that he couldn't answer them. I've read two of your papers and found them . . . well, there's no other word for it . . . brilliant. And nearly every day I listen to you rattle off facts about things that no one else knows."

He blushed slightly and looked down at the ground. "So, what's your question?"

"No offense, but why the hell did you pick Wickman? It's pretty here, but it's not the most competitive school. You could have gone Ivy League."

"Easy. My mom works here."

"I thought you were from D.C."

"My dad is in D.C. My parents are divorced. My mom lives in Hyannis and works at Wickman as a secretary. As one of the perks, all employees and their children get free tuition. Wickman is one of the few colleges that will cover dependents for both undergrad and graduate, so I took it."

She leaned back as well and it drew them closer. "Is that the only reason? The money?"

"No, to be honest the main reason was something else. At heart, I'm nothing but a mama's boy. Dad moved to D.C. after the divorce when I was thirteen, and Mom came to rely on me for a lot. Yard work, house repairs, friendship. I didn't want to go too far away. Her parents are in Florida, my sister is in California, the rest of the family is scattered around the south. I'm the only one up here. I like knowing that if she needs me, the dorm is ten minutes from the house."

He rolled his eyes and added, "I know, being a mama's boy isn't a very attractive quality."

"Actually, it is. That's one of the sweetest things I've ever heard."

He leaned toward her and she closed her eyes. Desire battled with anxiety. She needed a relationship right now like she needed a brain tumor, but she wanted nothing more in the world than to feel the light touch of his lips on hers.

It never came.

She opened her eyes as he retreated with a paper in his hand.

He handed it to her. "This came out of your notebook and was trying to escape in the wind."

"Oh," she said, flustered, shoving it in her notebook. "Thanks."

"Kat says that you were engaged."

Her heart beat again as she realized that maybe that was why he didn't try to kiss her. She tried to restrain her smile.

"His name is Nick Carrano. We met last year in Providence. I was a senior. He had graduated the year before from Brown. It was intense, and we moved fast. We met in November. He met my parents over Christmas break. He asked me to marry him a couple months later. We were engaged for a few months and were supposed to elope to Jamaica after graduation in May, but I got cold feet and broke it off days before."

He nodded as he gazed down at the river. She assumed he would ask more questions, but disinterest covered his face and silence settled between them, so she changed the subject.

"Why was it named the Drowning River?"

He shook off whatever thoughts had occupied him and returned his attention to her. "It's actually not. I forget its real name." He rubbed his chin as he thought. "A man's name, one of the Pilgrims, I think. But it's been known in town as the Drowning River for as long as anyone can remember."

"As a warning because of the currents?"

"I suppose that serves as a dual purpose, but its reputation created the name."

"Reputation of people accidentally drowning in it?"

"Not accidentally. People have used this river for a hundred years as a way to easily and quickly end their lives. It was a common method after the stock market crash and during the Depression. After that, a decade could pass by with no incidents. But one year in the late eighties, four Wickman students drowned themselves in the river, one after the other over a period of two weeks. They didn't know each other, and they all had their own separate reasons."

"That's so sad."

He nodded. "Since then no one bothers to call it by its proper name. It will always be the Drowning River."

She closed her eyes and listened to the rush of the water, the final sounds her sister heard before her death. She opened them to find Parker staring at her.

"Do you think my sister drowned herself on purpose in this river like the others?"

Even though she already guessed how he would answer, the intensity in his voice surprised her. "No," he said. "Absolutely not."

He stood and gathered his books, shoving them into his backpack and swinging it over his shoulder in one fluid movement. "I'm heading back," he said and left with no offer for her to walk with him.

She sat in a cloud of confusion, wondering if she'd said or done something wrong. After a few minutes, she collected her things and headed home. Thankfully it was only a five-minute walk to the apartment, because she could barely wait to collapse onto her bed and rest.

She reached Bourne Hall and trudged up the stairs. Kat was splayed across the couch watching *Jeopardy!* Her face lit up when Elise came in.

"The strangest thing just happened," she said.

"What?"

"I was watching TV and I heard this whoosh noise and I looked behind me, and someone had shoved an envelope under the door. I jumped up and ran into the hallway, but the person must have been quick because I couldn't find him."

"What was in it?"

"I don't know. I didn't open it."

Elise tossed herself into the armchair beside the couch and wished Kat would get to the meat of the story. Her bed was calling. "Why not?"

Kat produced a plain white envelope from the floor and handed it to Elise. "Because your name is on it."

Her first name was handwritten in block letters on the front of the envelope. She slid her finger through the back and opened it. A thin piece of folded paper fell out with one word written in the same block writing.

"Is it a secret admirer?" Kat asked, rubbing her hands together in delight.

"No."

"What does it say?"

" 'Stop.' "

"Stop? Stop what?"

Elise sat motionless, staring at the letters, letting the knowledge that she had just received a mild threat settle into her mind.

Kat looked at the one-worded note and said, "Whoever wrote this would have explained it further if they thought you wouldn't know what it meant."

Elise nodded slowly.

"So, what does it mean?"

"It means stop asking questions and stop looking into Hannah's death."

CHAPTER 10

The bedroom door clicked shut behind Parker, and he quietly knelt down beside his desk chair. He slid his hand underneath it, looking for the object he knew was there and felt a painful prick. He withdrew his hand to inspect it and found one finger bleeding.

He sucked on his finger and used the other hand to gently feel under the chair again, this time avoiding the exposed nail or staple that had hurt him. The tips of his fingers grazed the object, and he ripped the tape off and it fell to the ground. He picked up the silver key and inspected his finger. The bleeding had already stopped. Key in hand, he crawled over to his bed and peered underneath. A square shape sat in the darkness. He reached the full length of his arm under the bed and brought it out.

The key slid easily into the metal strongbox. Parker rifled through papers—birth certificate, Social Security card—until he found what he wanted. He relocked the box, kicked it back under the bed, taped the key back to the chair, and sat at his desk.

He hadn't looked at the photograph in quite some time, but every part of it was familiar. He brushed his thumb over her face with regret. He flipped it over and read the inscription again. He closed his eyes, willing tears not to form, willing his tightened throat to loosen.

The door burst open, and Parker threw the picture into the

desk drawer and slammed it shut.

Robbie looked at him curiously. "Your face is all red. You all right?"

Parker couldn't look him in the eye. "Yeah, what do you want?"

Robbie laughed. "Were you jerking off? You have to lock the door when you do that."

"I wasn't jerking off, asshole. I always do that in the bathroom and make sure I use your towel."

"Very nice." Robbie sat on the edge of the desk.

"What's up?"

"I was getting the mail and the guys downstairs in one-oh-three told me they're having a huge party tomorrow night. Wanna go? You could ask your new little best friend to come, and maybe she'll bring her hot roommate for me."

Parker tipped back in his chair, confident now that Robbie hadn't seen the photo. "Yeah, sure. I'll go downstairs and invite them, but that's no guarantee that Kat will even look twice at your ugly mug."

"Hey, me and Kat have had several conversations. She digs me. She just doesn't know it yet." Robbie slid his glasses down his nose and added, "You've really got the hots for Elise, huh?"

Parker rolled his eyes. "Shut it."

"She likes you too, man, don't get defensive. Why haven't you two gotten together?"

Parker sighed. He wished he could tell Robbie everything, tell him his true motives for befriending Elise. "We're not dating because she's got issues to clear up from a previous relationship. Why is it that all the girls I'm interested in have issues?"

Robbie laughed and patted him on the back. "I hope it works out this time. I haven't seen you fall this hard since . . . her."

That's one subject Parker wanted no part of right now. "Yeah, I know. All right, I'll go invite the girls and you run along and get some plastic surgery that will make Kat swoon."

Friday mornings were the best time to grocery shop. Sure, there were a few retirees and a couple of moms milling about, but no crowds or lines like evening or weekend shopping. Elise was struggling to choose a salad dressing from the thousand or so offerings when Kat caught up.

"I love this. There was only one other person in line at the deli counter and by the way, he was smokin' hot," Kat said, emptying her arms into the shopping cart. "We should start grocery shopping every Friday morning. The place is empty."

"Seriously, what's the difference between Zesty Italian and Old Time Italian? Do they both need to exist?"

"You have to go for the Zesty."

Elise tossed it into the cart. "Okay, but if it sucks, I can blame you. So, did you invite the hot guy to the party tonight?"

"No, I tried every shameless trick in the book to get his attention, but he was really focused on choosing a deli roll. Anyhow, Math Boy is going to be at the party."

"Math Boy?"

"Yeah, you remember. The math major I met in the library two weeks ago? Oh, there is nothing better than a good-looking dork because, since he's a dork, he has no idea that he's good looking and that makes him even more attractive."

Elise giggled as she steered the cart to the next aisle. "What time did Parker say this party starts?"

"Eight, so we'll stroll in at nine. Want to go for warm-up drinks at Dolan's beforehand?"

Elise tossed a bag of chips into the cart. "No, I need to do some research at the library after class today. I'll probably be home just in time to get ready for the party."

A loud crash came from the end of the aisle, and Elise jerked her head up.

"Holy mother of crap," Kat said. "It's the hot guy from the deli."

He stood at the end of the aisle with a smashed jar at his feet. He was undeniably gorgeous. Tall, broad-shouldered with faded jeans and a black cable-knit sweater that matched his hair, he looked like he'd slipped out of the J. Crew catalog and into the chip aisle. His lips were slightly parted and his dark eyes were set, unblinking on Elise.

Kat elbowed her in the ribs. "I couldn't even get his attention, and you made him drop his pickles."

Elise couldn't take her eyes off of him. He looked slightly familiar, but she couldn't quite place him. She was instantly attracted to him, but at the same time she felt a knot of fear in her stomach. She wanted to approach him, but at the same time wanted to run all the way home.

The decision was made for her as he turned on his heel and walked off, abandoning his cart of groceries.

Friday night at dinnertime, Wickman Library was as quiet as a morgue. Without any distractions, Elise had motored through her research. She stood and stretched. Only one more quote to find and then she could head home. Maybe she could join Kat for warm-up drinks after all. A small smile spread on her face as she thought about seeing Parker at the party tonight. Despite his odd behavior at the river, she was looking forward to spending time with him.

She silently repeated the book's call number, 211.13, as she searched for the right aisle. She found the book she needed and began leafing through it when she got the distinct feeling that someone was standing behind her.

She spun around, but she was alone in the aisle. Still, the feeling that someone was near, watching her, grew stronger. Her body tensed as she listened.

There. A snap, like the sound of someone's ankle or knee cracking as he tiptoed down the aisle. It came from her left side. She gazed at the row of books and wondered if there was truly someone on the other side, standing there, waiting.

She ran her hands through her hair. This was crazy. Even if there was someone there, he was probably looking for a book. This was the library.

Nevertheless, her instinct told her that she was being watched. She moved closer to the books and held her breath, listening. A drop of sweat tickled a path down her back as she realized that even as she held her breath, she still heard a constant inhale and exhale inches away. She grabbed a thick book from the row in front of her.

An eye stared back at her.

She gasped and fell backward, knocking books off the shelf behind her. She scrambled up and looked into the hole again, but the eye and its owner were gone. Filled with sudden courage, she ran down the aisle. Whoever it was had a head start because of her spill, but she pushed herself to the limit, running and looking down every aisle she passed.

She finally reached an open study area and skidded to a stop. She felt foolish, standing there out of breath, searching the room for who? An eye? She didn't even know if it was a man or woman.

Her neck tingling, she felt watched again. She turned around and saw a familiar woman sitting cross-legged in an armchair, surrounded by books and notes. Caught staring, the woman immediately lowered her eyes, and that was when Elise remembered her. The drunk woman from the alley. Though her hair was combed and smooth this time, Elise would recognize that bad dye job anywhere. Her reaction to Elise had never settled right. Now seemed like a good time to get some answers.

Elise marched over and sat in the empty chair beside her.

"Remember me?"

She didn't look up. "Yes."

"You're not going to scream this time?"

She motioned to her notes. "I'm kind of busy here."

Elise ignored her dismissal. "Care to explain yourself?"

She sighed. "I don't drink often, so I have a low tolerance."

"I don't care why you were so wasted. I'm more interested in the screaming and hysteria part."

"I thought you were a nightmare. When I woke up the next day, I was sure I had hallucinated the whole thing in my drunken stupor. But, then I heard the rumors. And sure enough, here you are."

"You don't seem too happy to see me."

"What? You want to be friends or something? Sorry, I don't have time for any new friends right now. Plus, you seem busy enough with Parker Reilly."

Elise raised an eyebrow. "You seem to have enough time to know who I hang out with."

"No one can help but notice. You two are always together." She rolled her eyes. "He leaves a trail of drool in his wake."

"We're just friends."

"Yeah, you believe that, but does he?"

"We're getting off the subject."

She slammed her book shut and another student shushed them. She whispered, "And what subject is that?"

"Oh, the little fact that when you first caught sight of me, you screamed as if I were the headless horseman."

"Are you slow or something? You are the twin of a dead girl. No one knew this dead girl had a twin. I was wasted. I thought I was seeing a ghost. Anyone would have screamed."

"Actually, you were the only one."

"Whatever. Leave me alone."

"What's your name?" Elise asked.

"Anita Hardwun."

"Creative. How about your real name?"

"Suck it. How's that one?"

Elise stood and looked around. She marched over to another grad student she recognized and asked him, "Do you know who she is? What's her name?"

His eyes followed her pointing finger. "That's Abby Frost."

Elise smiled. "Thank you."

She straightened and walked past Abby on her way out, making sure she had her attention before she called, "See you around, Abby," over her shoulder.

Chapter 11

Music pulsed through the crowded apartment. As soon as she entered, Kat turned heads with her short skirt and thigh-high black leather boots. Elise felt eyes on her as well, and immediately regretted caving to the pressure of wearing something from Kat's closet. Kat had basically forced her to wear one of her shirts—a deep blue, low-cut blouse—along with her own slim-fitting black pants. She did look sexy, but it wasn't her style and she felt uncomfortable out of her sweater and jean uniform.

"There they are," Kat said, pointing.

Elise scanned the faces in the living room and saw Parker and Robbie waving them over to a corner near the window. They made their way through the thick crowd, and Elise had a change of heart regarding her outfit when she saw the reaction on Parker's face.

When Kat told her the day before that Parker had come to the apartment to tell them both about a party, she felt immense relief. The way Parker had left her at the riverbank had filled her with unease. She needed him. His friendship meant so much to her. And now as he smiled and casually tossed his arm over her shoulder, her heart felt light.

"Where's the keg?" Kat asked.

"In the kitchen," Robbie said, his eyes drifting south from her face.

"Ugh. I don't want to go back through the crowd again. I

already had one strange person grab my ass on the way here."

"I'll go with you," Robbie offered.

"Oh, a bodyguard!" Kat grabbed him by the collar and disappeared into the mass of bodies.

Alone with Parker, Elise couldn't find words that didn't sound stupid or forced. She gazed up at him, reminded of how tall he was now that they were side by side. He sipped his beer and smiled. As a girl squeezed past them, she used the opportunity to move closer to him. She felt so comfortable with him, so safe. She instinctively felt that no matter what happened, he would die trying to protect her.

She glanced over her shoulder and her skin crawled. "Ugh, not her."

Parker followed her eyes. "Who, Abby?"

"Yes, Abby Frost. I've had a couple run-ins with her. You know her?"

"Yeah," Parker said in an intriguing tone.

"What's her story?"

"Ever heard of Senator Frost?"

Elise thought for a moment, then remembered. "The Republican senator from Texas who had a DUI and the illegal fundraising scandal?"

"That's the one. Abby is his only child."

"No way. I never thought twice about her last name when I heard it. Did she go to Wickman for undergrad, too?"

"Yeah, she graduated at the top of our class. She tries hard, works hard, but has issues with alcohol. It runs in her family. She does her best to suppress it, but sometimes the genes get the best of her."

"So, the night I saw her wasted in an alley wasn't the only time."

Parker raised his eyebrows, but didn't ask. "Abby and I . . . uh, we dated last year. When we broke up, she went on a two-week drunken bender. Made a fool of herself in public, too."

"That explains one part of her hostility. The part toward you."

"What part remains unexplained?"

"The part toward me."

She was hoping he'd suggest that perhaps Abby was jealous, thinking that they were becoming a couple, but he only shrugged.

"I'm going to go get a beer," she muttered, and made her way to the keg, filled with a sudden need to numb herself with the rest of the partiers. It bothered her that Parker hadn't made a move. Even though she felt she wasn't ready for a relationship, she still wanted him to want her.

She waited in the line until it was her turn for the burly guy holding the tap to fill her plastic cup with cheap barley and hops. She finally reached the front, and her outstretched hand was pushed aside by another.

"Thanks, Randy," Abby said, glaring at her. "Oh, I'm sorry, Elise. Did I cut you in line? I just assumed that your puppy-dog Parker would get you a beer." She swayed a bit where she stood. "When I was Parker's girl, he would never have made me wait in line for cheap beer. Maybe he's lost his sense of chivalry along with his taste in women."

A thousand ideas surged through Elise's mind, ranging from pouring Abby's beer over her obviously dyed red hair to punching her right in her pinched-up nose. She finally settled on a smile and a hushed voice.

She leaned in close and said, "That's okay, Abby. I realize you're probably in a hurry to pour more booze into those veins. Can't go for long without it, can you? I wonder how much the D.C. gossip pages would pay me for information about how Senator Frost's daughter is wasting her father's money getting shit-housed every night at college and falling down drunk in alleys like a common hobo."

Abby's face paled and she opened her mouth, but nothing came out. Elise immediately felt remorse. She'd let her anger get the best of her and thrown a low blow.

"Abby, pick your jaw up off the floor. I'm kidding. I would never do that."

Color returned to Abby's face and she slurred, "You're just like your tramp of a sister," and stormed off.

Elise turned back to the keg and gave Randy a look that said, "Don't even ask." She drained her first beer on the spot and got another. The party was just beginning, and already she'd been in an argument. Could it get any worse?

She needed a friendly face. She searched the apartment for Kat and finally found her in a corner of one of the crowded bedrooms, in deep conversation with Math Boy. Robbie stood at the other end of the room, pretending to listen to some guy play a guitar while he stared longingly at Kat. She didn't want to be a shoulder for unrequited love to cry on, so she set out to find Parker instead.

She found him, back turned to her, in conversation with a pretty brunette who was petite in every way except for the voluptuous breasts that peeked out from her v-neck sweater. It was obvious to Elise as the girl threw her head back in laughter and rested her hand on Parker's arm that whoever she was, she was completely enamored with him.

Elise's hackles rose. She wanted to kick herself because her utmost desire was to scream, "He's mine, bitch!" and claw the girl's doe-eyes out. He most certainly was not hers and she had no right to feel any sense of ownership over him. A glutton for punishment or competition, she sidled up to the cozy pair and was rewarded by a toss of perfume-scented hair in her face.

"Oh, sorry," the brunette said, and pulled her long hair to one side.

"Hey, this is Brittany. She lives in our building. We met this morning in the mailroom. Brittany, this is my friend Elise. She lives on the third floor."

Elise bristled at the emphasis he put on the word *friend,* but still managed to extend her hand.

Brittany shook it, said, "Nice to meet you," and immediately turned back to Parker as if Elise didn't exist.

"I can't believe you grew up here!" she bubbled. Elise detected a slight Southern belle accent. "It must have been fantastic to grow up on the Cape. I haven't really gotten to know the area well, yet"—another hair toss—"maybe you could show me around sometime?"

Elise swallowed the bile that lurched its way up her throat and walked off without excusing herself, chugging her beer as fast as she could. Despite its bitter aftertaste, it was cold and refreshing. She polished it off and filled up for the third time.

She wasn't one to binge drink. A humiliating and life-threatening stomach pumping incident on prom night turned her off of that. But she did enjoy getting a two-beer buzz every now and then. She couldn't remember the last time she had been really drunk, and that old familiar feeling was rearing its ugly head now.

Time ticked by as she talked to people whose names she forgot as soon as she heard them. She laughed and smiled at the appropriate moments in conversation, but barely listened. The music changed—from alternative to hip-hop—and now the living room was full of sweaty, grinding bodies. Elise held up a wall in the kitchen, close to the keg, and willed the room to stop spinning.

She couldn't remember how many beers she'd had. All she wanted was to be safe in her bed. Away from strangers' imploring eyes, away from Brittany and Parker, away from the temptation to drink any more than she already had.

In a feat of courage, she left her wall and searched the apartment for Kat. Parker stood with Robbie in the living room, and she was delighted to find that he and Brittany weren't one of the living room's dirty dancing couples. She breezed by them and checked both of the bedrooms, but there was no sign of Kat or Math Boy.

"Shit," she muttered.

"You okay?" Robbie put a hand on her shoulder.

"I'm fine. Just looking for Kat."

"You're really drunk. You should go home."

"Yeah, thanks for the tip."

She pushed past him, back into the living room. Brittany the hair-tossing vixen was back with Parker and using the loud music as an excuse to shove her gigantic breasts up against him as she whispered in his ear.

Alcohol makes people do crazy things. Elise had heard that statement a lot in her lifetime. She was about to prove it true herself.

She sidled up to Parker and nudged the girl away with an elbow. "Excuse me, Ashley."

"Brittany."

"Yeah, whatever, I need to talk to Parker."

Aghast, Brittany stepped back. Elise reached up, pulled Parker's face down, and pressed her lips against his. His lips were hard at first, with the shock, but then softened and opened, and then his hands pulled her back and away from him and it was over.

He grabbed her by the arm and led her into the empty bathroom. "What was that?"

"It's called a kiss, dipshit," she said, feeding her urge to insult him after rejecting her. She added, softly, "I thought you'd want me to."

"You only kissed me because you're plastered."

The venom with which he said the last word struck Elise like a fist. He was disgusted with her. He'd already gone through having a drunk for a girlfriend and now she had done this. She felt like a fool.

He closed the bathroom door on his way out, not looking back at her as she slipped down the wall to the floor, hugging her knees. Why did she get so drunk and act like an idiot? She may have lost his friendship now.

After a few minutes, someone banged on the door and threatened to piss on the living room rug if she didn't open it, so she complied. As nausea swept over her, all she wanted was to get back to her apartment. Thankfully, it was only two floors up. She dragged herself up the stairs slowly, feeling dizzy any time she looked down. After what seemed like a marathon, she reached her third-floor apartment and froze.

The door was open.

Just an inch, but open. Kat wouldn't have left it like that. She was always lecturing Elise about locking the door behind her after she came in, especially at night. And they didn't leave it like that when they went to the party because, drunk as she was, Elise specifically remembered locking and closing the door behind her when they left.

She stood transfixed for a few moments, until she heard a slam from inside the apartment. That snapped her to attention and she pushed the door fully open.

"Kat? You home?"

Silence.

She stepped through the threshold. The lights were on, and she couldn't remember if they had left them like that. Despite her rising panic, she regulated her breathing and focused on the simplest explanation. Kat and Math Boy came here and in the midst of their passion, they left the door ajar. They were getting it on in Kat's bedroom and didn't hear Elise's voice. And Elise was going to barge in there and beat them senseless with a pillow for scaring her.

Except that Kat's bedroom door was open, and Elise's was closed.

Her breath caught as she realized that someone was definitely in the apartment. The slamming sound had been her bedroom door closing. It was open when she left, and there was no reason for Kat to be in there. It had to be someone else. The room spun and she shook her head, damning herself again for drinking so much.

"Kat?" she called out, louder this time, and faced silence once again.

She turned left into the kitchen and grabbed a carving knife from the drawer, statistics about weapons more likely to be used on the homeowner than the criminal be damned. She crept toward her bedroom door, noticing the darkness in the bottom crack.

She placed her hand on the brass doorknob and tried to turn it soundlessly. Then she pushed the door open. Darkness rushed at her. Her blind eyes darted from shadow to shadow, taking too long to adjust to the blackness.

Her trembling hand reached along the wall, searching for the light switch. Too low. Too high. Where was it? The moment her fingers touched the plastic, she flipped it and the sudden brightness blinded her worse than the black.

Wielding the knife in front of her, she advanced into the bedroom, spinning around as her eyes took in the familiar surroundings. No one visible in the room. No one behind the door. She roughly opened the closet door and it slammed against the wall. With one last place to check, she dropped to her knees and looked under her bed.

A swoosh from the living room stole her attention. She bounded back up to her feet and raced into the living room.

Her feet froze as she saw a single, black-gloved hand close the door to her apartment.

She willed herself to run, open the door, sprint down the hallway, and find out who it was. But her feet did not move. Despite her brave intentions, she also wanted to cower in the corner of the room and pray the person wouldn't come back.

A third possibility revealed itself when a wave of drunken nausea hit her stomach with the force of a punch. She quickly reached the toilet and vomited. The bathroom spun and tilted like a sinister funhouse. She slid down to the cold tile floor, her last thought resounding in her head.

"Don't pass out."

CHAPTER 12

The campus police officer was middle-aged and tired-looking, with bags under his eyes that matched his brown uniform. An unidentified bit of food—probably part of his breakfast—clung to his mustache, and it jiggled when he spoke, making Elise want to vomit again. But then, in her current state, merely breathing occasionally forced bile into her throat.

"Is anything missing?" he asked, his miniature notebook open, pen poised. He hadn't written a word yet.

"No," she said, rubbing her temples to ease the pain caused by the echo of her own voice.

"Is anything broken?"

"No."

"And you're not hurt."

"No." Unless you count the gnome that crawled into her brain last night via her ear and began pounding on her cerebral nerve centers with his tiny, evil-gnome needles.

"And you were pretty drunk. I mean, drunk enough to pass out on the floor."

She stopped massaging her head for a moment to toss him a look that could start a forest fire. "Thanks for reminding me. Yes, I was drunk."

"Don't take this the wrong way, lady, but are you sure someone was even here?"

She groaned. "I was drunk, not high. I didn't hallucinate the whole thing. Yes, someone was here."

He snapped his notebook closed with finality. "There's nothing we can do right now. Keep your doors locked at all times—"

"I told you, they *were* locked!"

"—and if you have any further trouble, give us a call."

He slammed the door on his way out and the noise reverberated in her head like a jackhammer against metal. She slid down in the armchair, avoiding the morning light peeking through the blinds of the living room.

"This is what you need," Kat said, returning from the kitchen. "The Herrera hangover concoction, guaranteed to reduce your hangover in thirty minutes or your money back."

Elise accepted the mug, but placed it untouched on the coffee table after one glance. It was a murky green color with an unbeaten egg floating on top.

"That's about as helpful as he was," she said.

"You can't blame him. He had nothing to go on. There was no theft, and you weren't hurt."

"So what, you think I'm making it up, too?"

"Of course not."

Kat looked hurt, and Elise regretted lashing out at her. She tossed a thin, pale arm over her eyes, blocking all light. "Whoever it was had been in my room and when he heard me coming, he ran out, closing the door behind him, and hid in the bathroom until I went into the bedroom to investigate, then he slipped out."

"Or she, right?"

"Yeah, I only saw a gloved hand. It could have been anyone. But what if I went to the bathroom first? What would he have done to me?"

Kat put her feet up on the coffee table and twirled a long, dark strand of hair around her finger. "Whoever it was didn't want to hurt you."

"How did you come to that conclusion?"

"Closing the bedroom door was a way to distract you so he could get out. If he wanted to hurt you, he would have waited for you in the bedroom instead of hiding in the bathroom."

"I guess that makes sense." A thought occurred to her. "Where were you, anyway?"

A slow smile spread over Kat's face. "I slept over at Math Boy's place. I came home early this morning. I was hoping to find you with Parker, but instead I found you sleeping with the toilet."

Memories Elise had placed in a drawer marked *humiliating,* hoping never to surface again, pushed through the fog of the hangover, making her groan.

"What?" Kat asked.

"I don't want to discuss Parker. Actually, I don't want to even see him or talk to him ever again."

"Why? Tell me!" Kat leaned forward, eyes lit up with girlish gossip delight.

"I got drunk and made a fool of myself."

"Who hasn't done that? What did you do, rip your top off and dance on the kitchen table?"

Elise lifted her arm to glance at Kat. "Um, no."

Kat grinned. "Yeah, I've never done that either. Wink, wink."

"I kissed him," she said, covering her face again.

"And that's a problem because . . ."

"Because he pushed me away." It hurt to say it out loud.

"Huh? That makes no sense. Did you puke before or after you kissed him?"

Elise sat up, not in the mood for conversation anymore.

"Oh, come on, I was just joking." Kat put her hand on her shoulder, encouraging her to stay. "A little hangover joking, come on."

"Forget it. I can't even talk right now, I'm so tired. I'm going back to bed. I'll talk to you later."

The more Elise thought about the kiss, the more it bothered her, and talking wouldn't help. She crawled onto her bed, without the strength even to get under the covers. She closed her eyes and drifted off with questions swirling in the mist of early sleep. Did she miscalculate Parker? Did he not have feelings for her? If not, then why was he spending so much time with her? What did he want?

Sylvester and Tweety were cool, but he much preferred Road Runner and Wile E. Coyote on a lazy morning after a late night. Fortunately, they were on next. Parker lay on his side on the couch, still wearing his flannel pajama pants and white t-shirt. He'd shower later when he could open his eyes more than halfway. Several minutes and close calls for Road Runner later, he still hadn't laughed. His eyes were on the flickering screen, but his mind was elsewhere. On Elise Moloney.

The party was a good time, long overdue for him. He needed to relax, have a couple beers, listen to music, hang with friends, and not think for a few hours. He had been able to do that until she kissed him. He was shocked, both by her sudden boldness and by the way it made him feel. Thinking about it now made the feelings return.

He pulled himself off the couch and schlepped into the bathroom. The faucet squeaked as he turned it and splashed cold water over his face. He scrutinized himself in the mirror. He looked a few years older than twenty-two, but he didn't mind. He felt several years older than his classmates anyway, probably due to the self-inflicted baggage he carried on his shoulders. He raked his hands through his honey blond hair, dried the remains of the water on his face with a hand towel, and headed back to the couch.

But he still wasn't able to think about anything else.

He pushed on his forehead with the palms of his hands. He

had to be careful. Elise reminded him of a porcelain doll, so fair, so fragile. He worried that if he made one wrong move, she would break. He had to work carefully. He had to always remember his purpose.

The door opened and Robbie swooped in amidst the smell of fresh coffee and donuts.

"They were all out of honey-dipped, so I got you a couple of jellies instead," he said, laying the bags down like prized treasure on the coffee table. He nudged Parker aside and made room for himself on the couch.

Parker took a sip from the large Styrofoam cup, and the hot coffee burned sweetly down his throat.

Robbie bit a chunk of donut off, then mumbled between chews, "Did you hear about Elise's intruder?"

Parker was about to nod along, mindlessly agreeing with meaningless breakfast chatter, when the words sank in. "What?"

"I just ran into Kat in the stairwell. Apparently someone broke into their place last night and scared the puke out of your girl."

Parker ignored the "your girl" comment to pull the rest of the story out of Robbie faster. "Is she all right?"

"She's quite hung over, and rightfully so. A girl with a small frame like that isn't supposed to drink so much—"

"Robbie! Is she all right from the intruder? Did he touch her?"

"No, she's fine. She caught a glimpse of him on his way out. He could have even been a her, Kat said. The person didn't steal anything. The campus rent-a-cop thinks she imagined the whole thing, but Kat believes her."

Parker sat in stunned silence, donut in hand, suspended midway to his mouth. Who was it? Was she in danger? Did the intruder have to do with Hannah? He wanted so badly to see her, to prove to himself that she was fine.

"What happened between you two last night, anyway? Kat said Elise kissed you and you pushed her away like she was a hundred-pound sewer rat."

"I'm just not into PDA. That's all."

"That's bullshit. You and Abby used to have your tongues down each other's throats at parties all the time last year."

"Well, I'm older now, and besides, it's different with Elise. I want to move slowly."

Robbie stared at him for a moment, then smiled and plunked the last bite of donut into his mouth, chewing and nodding.

"What?"

"There's someone else. It makes perfect sense now. I was wondering what the hell was wrong with you. I mean, you haven't made a move on Elise, yet at the same time you're always hanging around with her, keeping her on a short leash. You've got someone else you want more and if things don't work out with her, you want Elise in your back pocket. Am I right? Who is she?"

"No, that's not true. There's no one else."

Robbie frowned. "So you just want Elise?"

"I don't know what I want," Parker said, his voice louder than he would have liked.

"If you're not sure about her, then why are you with her all the time? Why are you trying to help her investigate Hannah's death? I mean, if it's to get in her pants, I can understand. But if you're not interested in Elise in that way, then why the hell do you care so much about Hannah?" Robbie's voice cracked. "You didn't even know her. If anyone should care, it should be me. I knew her. I liked her a lot. Hell, I might have even loved her if she gave me the chance."

Parker tossed his uneaten donut in the bag. He had lost his appetite. "You and your obsessive crushes are as common as sand on the beach. You're in love with a different girl each

Sunday of the month."

Robbie's face burned crimson and his hands curled. For a short moment, Parker thought he would take a swing at him. Instead, Robbie rose and wordlessly walked into his bedroom, slamming the door behind him.

CHAPTER 13

During the day, rounding the corner of Chapel Road and East Street gave a view of the ocean, a vast expanse of blue reaching as far as sight travels. But it was after dark, and as Elise jogged around the corner and turned down East Street, the only hint that the ocean lay at the end of the road was the scent of salt in the air. She preferred to run in the afternoon, but her hangover had lingered through dinner, so she didn't make it out until the sun had set and the night sky deepened to a navy blue. Her fanny pack thumped against her hips with the weight of her keys, mace, and inhaler.

Asthma is the Greek word for panting. Elise learned that at a young age. She remembered waking in the night as a child, gasping, wheezing, groping at the dark with her little hands, searching for air. She explained it to the bespectacled doctor with the white coat as drowning above water. He made her breathe into a machine, told her to push the little ping-pong ball up the tube with her big, strong lungs. She tried and tried, but the ball never went far. She felt as though she had failed a test and began to cry. Her mother took her in her arms and comforted her, assuring her that now that they knew what was wrong, she would never again wake in the night drowning in her bed.

Ever since then, an inhaler had always been near, her lifeline to the air. She didn't let her condition control her, though. *She* controlled *it*. Most of her friends probably didn't even realize she was asthmatic.

Her breathing was regular now, in and out to the music of the *whoosh-whoosh* of her nylon jogging pants. She reached the end of East Street and the empty beach parking lot with the lights from storefronts, homes, and streetlights behind her. In front of her, the river rushed in near darkness, aside from a sliver of moon and the black blanket of sky pierced by a billion twinkling flecks of light.

She slowed to a walk as she approached the riverbank. Her lungs burned slightly from the cool October air. She searched the sky until she found Orion, her favorite fall constellation. She easily found his belt, then mentally traced the lines up to his shield, outstretched to defend the mighty hunter from Taurus the bull.

She never had any interest in astronomy until the night Nick showed her the constellations during a romantic rooftop dinner. He had thought of everything: music from a portable CD player, a candlelit table for two, her favorite foods, a little dancing. Then they made love in a swathe of blankets beneath the night sky with Orion and his fellow legends watching from above.

She sighed with longing. Everything was so jumbled in her head. Did she miss Nick or just the romance? He was so sweet, so thoughtful. He treated her like a maiden out of a fairy tale. But when she woke up beside him some mornings, she couldn't imagine doing that every day for the rest of her life. Maybe it wasn't him; maybe it was her. Maybe she was a commitment-phobe. She hadn't dated anyone since Nick, despite a couple of offers. Maybe she was just destined for a life spent alone.

Her self-indulgent introspection was interrupted by a strange, guttural human sound she associated with primal fear. She turned around, but no one was behind her. The rhythm of the water disguised the direction of the source, and she squinted in the darkness until movement caught her eye. Someone was standing on the bridge.

The shadow of a person darted across the bridge away from her, and she immediately made the decision to follow. She sprinted across the moist dirt of the bank to the base of the bridge. The pounding of her running shoes against the wood planks echoed above the sounds of rushing water. By the time she was halfway across the bridge, the person had vanished into the mist on the other side, but she pushed on. When the bridge ended, she looked for tracks in the sand, clues as to whether she should go left toward the beach or right toward the marsh. She saw nothing.

She went straight and clambered up a steep dune, the brittle sand grass slicing and stabbing at her hands as she pulled herself to the top. From this height, she could see the beach, the darkness of the ocean, the full length of the bridge, the endless expanse of salt marshes stretching to meet the horizon. And a person, almost certainly a man, tall and skinny with long limbs running toward a small shed in the direction of the marsh. Something was on his shoulder, something out of place, but she couldn't recognize it.

She tried to run down the dune, but slipped and rolled most of the way. At the bottom, she stood, dusting herself off as she ran. He had a large head start, but if he hid in the shed, she'd catch him. The sand turned into muck and her sneakers sank with each step. Mud splattered on her shoes and socks as she closed the distance.

She slowed to a walk as she approached the shed and weighed her options. She could ask him to come out, but that would let him know she was here. There was a good chance he hadn't looked out the small window and she could surprise him if she silently slunk up and burst through the door.

She sided with a surprise entrance, and crept toward the door, her shoes making small sucking sounds as they were pried from the mud with each step. She reached her hand out until she felt the cool knob. Then turned.

It was locked.

"Get out here!" she yelled, angry now. "I want to talk to you."

She stepped back and waited. Not a sound.

Maybe he wasn't even in there. Maybe he'd found it locked, too, and continued to run. He'd be long gone now.

She tried to look in the window, but saw only darkness from this distance. She took a deep breath and pressed her forehead against the glass, squinting at the dark shapes. It looked like town property, signs, beach equipment. A larger item huddled in the corner furthest from the window. She stared at it, waiting for movement.

"What are you doing here?" a loud voice boomed behind her.

She spun around and the beam of a flashlight blinded her.

"Get that light out of my face," she said, with her hand raised to protect her eyes.

The bright light turned to the side, and as her eyes adjusted a man slowly came into view. A young, handsome, familiar-looking police officer.

"What are you doing here?" he repeated.

"I was following someone." Then, realizing that sounded bad, she added, "He was watching me. I had been jogging, and I stopped down by the river and he was watching me from the bridge. When he saw that I noticed him, he took off."

"Where is he?"

"I don't know. He might be in there." She motioned to the shed. "It's locked."

He rifled through a large key ring, until he came to a small silver key, which he slipped easily into the shed's lock. The door swung open and he shined the flashlight up and down. Elise peered over his shoulder as the beam reached the dark corner where she thought the man was hiding. It was just a pile of rope and a life preserver.

"No one here," he said.

"He's long gone, then."

"Did you get a look at him?"

"Not really. He was tall and thin, and he wore a dark knit hat, but that's all I saw."

"Age? Race?"

"I don't know," she said, frustrated. "What are you doing here, anyway?"

"This area gets checked during every shift, to make sure no teenagers are having beach bonfires, stuff like that. It's town property." He relocked the shed and attached the key ring to his belt. "Why did you follow him?"

Because her presence had terrified him, and she wanted to know why. Because she needed to know if he was following her. Because she wanted to know who he was, if he was the person threatening her. She looked into the cop's face and again familiarity tugged at her. "I wanted to ask him some questions," she said.

"All about asking questions, aren't you?"

"What?"

"I know who you are, Elise. The first time I saw you, I made a fool of myself because I wasn't prepared for"—he gazed at the ground—"how much you look like her."

Then it hit her. The guy from the grocery store. "You dropped your pickles," she said, lamely.

"You're not making fantastic first impressions, either. I heard you made quite the little scene at the station."

It occurred to her that he was more than just a random guy. He obviously had known Hannah. He was a cop. And he had looked familiar in the grocery store, too. Then the pieces pulled together. Faith's picture.

"You're Gavin Shaw, aren't you?"

"Yeah. I was your sister's boyfriend. You *are* her sister, right? It's true?"

"Yes, my biological mother confirmed it."

He paused, letting the information settle in. "I'm sorry for your loss, then. I've had several months to grieve, but it's all new to you. It must be overwhelming."

She nodded. He was very handsome, much more so in person than in the photograph. His broad shoulders and muscular upper body stretched the fabric of the uniform taut against his skin. His black hair was cut short and his eyes were impossibly dark, almost black, and she had to look away from him in the awkward silence.

"Let me walk you back to your car."

"I jogged here."

"I'll drive you home, then."

"No, I'll jog back."

"After possibly being followed tonight? I don't think so."

She didn't like him telling her what to do, yet at the same time felt flattered with his desire to protect her.

"If you jog home, I'm just going to follow you anyway. You'll look kind of strange running down the street with a patrol car following you at five miles an hour."

She smiled. "Okay, I'll take a ride."

His car was warm, but she felt uncomfortable. It was her first trip in a police car, albeit in the front. And her deceased sister's boyfriend sat next to her. Her apartment was only a couple of miles away, so the ride was thankfully short. She had made a mental list of a thousand things she wanted to ask Gavin Shaw when she met him, and now she could barely put into words which building she lived in.

The car slowed to a stop, and he put the gear in park and turned to face her. Her heart beat faster.

"I'm glad I ran into you tonight, despite the strange circumstances. Ever since I heard about you, I've wanted to see you in person and talk."

"I've been curious about you as well," she admitted.

"Will you have dinner with me some night this week? I'm sure you have questions about Hannah, what she was like, stuff like that. I'd be happy to share some memories of her with you."

She stared down at her fingers, which had begun to gently shake. Gavin was one of the people she wanted to talk to about Hannah, but now that she had met him, she felt uneasy about it.

"Please," he said. "I'll take you to the nicest townie restaurant in Oceanside. My treat."

"Okay," she said, her throat dry. "Pick me up Thursday night at seven."

She shut the car door and spun around, motion in one of the windows of Bourne Hall catching her eye. A shade snapped down. She counted across and up and quickly figured out whose apartment it was.

CHAPTER 14

The call came early in the morning. Her back had gone out again. Parker emailed the professor from his nine o'clock and told him he'd miss class, then drove straight to his mother's house and gently eased her into the car. The chiropractor worked his magic, and now Parker watched his mother stare out the window as he made the twenty-five-minute drive from Plymouth back to her house in Hyannis. Her short bob of brown hair was streaked with silver, and fine lines circled her lips and mouth.

"I'm sorry you had to miss class," she said, her somber gaze focused on the passing trees. "I didn't know who else to call."

"You know I don't mind, Mom. I'm glad you called me. I'd rather miss class than have you in pain all day or have you stuck in a car with one of your nutty neighbors."

Her cheeks lifted as she smiled.

He knew she felt conflicted about his decision to stay on the Cape. Guilt and relief had flashed equally in her eyes the day he told her he wasn't going away to medical school. Instead of using his psychology degree, he was going to stay at Wickman for graduate school. Get a masters in something for free. Maybe English; he always liked that subject. Experience had proven that he wasn't cut out for psychology.

As he maneuvered his car through the rotary and onto the Sagamore Bridge, he was reminded that it wasn't just loyalty to his mother that rooted him. He truly loved living here. He didn't mind the tourists like so many Cape natives did. Not only for the money they brought into the local economy, but also because he loved the Cape and enjoyed seeing that love reflected: in the eyes of a child holding a seashell to his ear, a couple holding hands on the breakwater, an old man walking past the dunes and seeing the ocean for the first time in his long life. These were sights most Cape Codders took for granted, but not Parker.

He craned his neck to look down at the Cape Cod Canal passing below the bridge. The U.S. Army Corps of Engineers built both the Sagamore and Bourne bridges from 1933 to 1935. Boston traffic used the Sagamore while Providence, Connecticut, and New York traffic used the Bourne. Oceanside sat on the Upper Cape just over the bridge, unspoiled, as tourists mostly passed it over on their way to the Mid-Cape towns of Yarmouth, Hyannis, and Dennis. The eastern shores of the Cape faced the cold, rough Atlantic. The other side was the more calm and warm Cape Cod Bay.

Parker passed the exit for Oceanside now, Route 6 nearly empty. In summer, he'd be stuck in the traffic that continued to Exit 7, with a long line to take a left at Higgins Crowell Road to Route 28, a Mecca of motels, restaurants, and family amusements.

He glanced at his mother and felt relief at her closed eyes. Despite how much he enjoyed time spent with her, he didn't want to maintain small talk right now. His mind was elsewhere. Seeing Elise get out of Gavin's patrol car last night was a shock. Sure, she'd see him eventually, but Parker had hoped he'd be with her when she did. Gavin had power over women. He could talk a lamb into the slaughterhouse with a smile on its wooly face.

Parker had to talk to Elise after class this afternoon. He wouldn't lecture her on Gavin today, though. His father had received the information they wanted and, though he was bound to share it, he wasn't looking forward to the conversation.

She wasn't going to like what he found out.

Marie Moloney whipped off her blouse and sank into the cherry-wood kitchen chair, fanning herself with a newspaper. If Ed walked in now, he'd have a good laugh at the sight of her in her dress pants and bra. Damned hot flashes were so unpredictable. Never knew where or when one would hit. She always thought her monthly period was a curse, but now that it hadn't visited in eight months, she realized the joke was on her. The real trouble was the curse of the fifty-five-year-old woman: menopause.

She sighed and tried to focus on something other than the fire burning up her neck and the beads of sweat forming between her large breasts. She wanted to get through menopause naturally, without taking any artificial hormones her drug pusher, ahem, doctor kept telling her to take. She wanted to stay away from all those fad herbs, too. Those were probably even more dangerous, being unregulated and all. Who knew what they would do to her. Turn her into a nympho like Sally next door when she started stealing her husband's Viagra.

No, she'd do this naturally, like a real woman. She closed her eyes and thought of the one thing that always made her feel better: her beautiful, smart, charming daughter. Marie was still so shocked that Elise was a twin. After she'd left that day with the picture, Marie had locked herself in the bedroom and cried and cried, not even letting poor Ed in. She felt as if she'd just found out that she herself had a daughter she didn't know about. A daughter she never knew she had. But that was foolish. Some other woman had that baby and reared her. And now she was gone.

She swallowed hard and tried her best to suppress the self-righteous feelings of how different Hannah's life would have been if Marie and Ed had reared her, too. Maybe she'd still be alive. Marie would have two beautiful daughters.

What kind of a woman separated sisters like that? Twins, nonetheless. Marie would love to drive to Dorchester and give that woman a piece of her mind. Yet, ironically, she was grateful. If the woman had kept them both, Marie would not have Elise.

The shrill ring of the kitchen wall phone startled her, and she jumped up to answer it.

"Is Elise there?" a weak male voice asked.

"No, she's not," Marie answered, offering no other information.

"Can you tell me where she is?"

"Who is this?"

A pause. "It's Nick." His voiced cracked on his name.

She sighed. "I told you she left for Europe in May after graduation."

"You can't give me any other information? Please? I just want to talk to her. I just want to know why."

"No, that's all she wanted me to tell you." She did feel bad for the boy. Despite her inherent belief that her daughter was perfect, she did think it was cowardly of Elise to break up with the poor boy via letter and not hash it out in person like most folk. But, right or wrong, she would always take her daughter's side.

A small, sniffling sound came through the wire, and she realized he was softly crying.

"Is she . . . is she seeing someone else?"

"No, there's no one else. But, son, you really need to move on. You're a nice young man. Handsome. I really liked you. But you're both still very young and obviously, for some reason, it just didn't work out. Good luck, Nick."

She gently placed the phone back in its cradle, shaking her

head. She'd tell Elise the next time she phoned that he'd called. Then, frowning, she decided it was best to write it down. She'd been forgetful lately. Damned menopause. She grabbed a pen and began searching for a notepad.

"What do we have here?"

Ed waltzed into the kitchen, a smile as wide as the sun on his face. He swaggered over to Marie and pinched her backside.

Startled, she wondered if Sally wasn't the only one stealing Harry's Viagra next door, then saw her blouse crumpled on the kitchen table. She looked down at her breasts bulging out of the white lace bra and weighed her options. Tell him she'd had a hot flash, which made her as attractive as a zoo animal, or let him go on thinking she'd decided to get frisky in the kitchen.

She smiled. "Come and get it, Ed."

He took her in his arms as the pen in her hand fell to the floor.

Professor Marston rounded out the lecture with a diatribe on the effects of the French Revolution on literature, then mercifully ended class. Elise shoved her notebook into her backpack and felt a tap on her shoulder.

"You've got some time before your next class, right?" Parker asked. He pulled a windbreaker over his black t-shirt and dark green cargo pants.

"Yeah, why? Want to get some coffee at the Café?"

"No, let's just sit on a bench outside. It won't take long."

He seemed rushed, as if this was something he needed to get over with, like a breakup or a dentist appointment. Necessary, but painful. He led her out of the classroom, and she followed him outside, her eyes adjusting to the bright light.

The sky was pastel blue with sparse white puffs of clouds. Leaves had started to turn gold and red, but still clung to their branches. Students streamed around them, lost in their own busy lives. Elise heard snippets of several conversations as they walked around the corner of the building to a place where they could be alone. The metal bench felt cool beneath her jeans as she settled next to him. He got right down to business.

"My dad got the information you wanted about the adoption agency. They were shut down five years after you were born."

"Shut down," she repeated. "Why?"

"They weren't legitimate."

She knew he was holding back the final punch. He didn't want to hurt her. She pushed him forward. "What does that mean? Why weren't they legitimate?"

"They were buying babies."

All the oxygen left her lungs, leaving her hollow inside. She drew her legs up and rested her chin on her knees. "I was a black market baby?"

His hands fluttered to her face, then retreated. "Your parents didn't do anything wrong. They thought the agency was legit. More expensive than other agencies, but they told people like your parents that it was because they worked faster, cut through the red tape. From your parents' perspective there was no difference between them and any other agency."

"But they were different," she said.

"Yes. Your mother got paid for you."

She leaned back against the cold metal bench. "How much?"

"You don't need to know specifics like that."

"How do you know what I need?"

"I don't want you to get hurt, that's all. Focusing on this is only going to hurt you."

She raked her fingers through her hair as the knowledge pounded in her head. Her mother sold her.

"All I want is to protect you, Elise." He coughed into his hand and lowered his voice. "That's also why I wasn't happy to see you alone with Gavin Shaw last night."

"What?" His sudden change of course surprised her.

"I don't want you to be alone with him. I understand that you want to ask him questions, but do it with me."

"You can't tell me what to do. You're not my boyfriend."

"I know that. But I don't trust the guy."

"I can look out for myself." How dare he? Was he jealous? He hadn't shown the least bit of romantic interest in her lately. It made no sense. She felt the need to profess her independence and maybe slightly hurt him. "I'm having dinner with him Thursday night."

His eyes widened. "How could you do that? He could be the one."

"The one?"

"The one who killed your sister! Remember? Hannah? The woman you were convinced was murdered? The one you were so intent on finding the answers about? Now your only concern is how fast you can get in the pants of her ex!"

Her fingers curled and it took all her strength not to slap him. Instead, she rose silently and walked back into the classroom building. She hurt, inside and out, from the knowledge that she had been sold by her own mother and from Parker's words. Not only were they sudden and biting, but they struck harder because he said what part of her had been thinking all along. She had talked herself into dinner with Gavin by reasoning that she would get answers about Hannah. But she couldn't deny that she was also attracted to him. And it made her sick.

By the time Elise's classes were done it was rush hour, so the drive to Dorchester took two hours. Road rage mixed with fury over what she had learned from Parker in the afternoon. She did a half-assed job of parallel parking her Civic, the tail sticking into the street, and barged up to the door. She rang the doorbell insistently four times in a row, then began beating the black door with her fists.

A tall, broad man answered the door. He was probably handsome in his day, but sloppy now, his large gut bulging underneath his stained t-shirt.

"Who are you?" she asked.

He chuckled. "I guess I'm your step-daddy."

She swallowed the vomit that rose in her throat. "Is she home?"

He opened the door wide and motioned for her to go in. He paused at the bottom of the stairs, but she insisted he go first. She didn't want him ogling her ass the whole way up.

Beth sat on the couch, one-inch ash dangling on the end of her cigarette, watching a talk show with a lot of screaming. Elise had always hated those shows, looked down her nose at the type of trash the people were. But she gazed around the filthy living room and looked at her mother and realized she belonged on one of those shows now. Her life was that messed up.

Beth sat glassy-eyed, wearing a gray sweater and jeans so tight they'd have to be removed by the Jaws of Life. Her eyes left the screen for a moment and, seeing Elise, she jumped up, dropping the cigarette on the couch.

"Damn! Roger, why didn't you tell me? Oh, shit." She tossed the cigarette in the dice-shaped tray and tried to dust the ash off the couch, but instead smeared the stain, making it worse.

Elise stepped fully into the room. "How much did you get for me?"

"What . . . what are you talking about?" Beth stuttered.

"How much was a pretty blond-haired, green-eyed baby girl worth? Probably good dough, huh?"

"I don't know what you're talking about."

Elise closed the distance between them and screamed, only inches from Beth's face. "How much?!"

"Twenty," she answered, her whole body shaking.

"Twenty thousand dollars?" Elise pulled back. Parker was right. Knowing this hurt even more.

"I did it for your sister. I wanted to keep at least one of you, but I didn't have any money. Your father abandoned me. I blew everything I had on drugs and booze. I didn't want to turn tricks. I was a mother now. So, yeah, I sold one of you, but they promised me you would go to a nice, rich family. And I used that money to move into this place and to raise Hannah."

"You think that makes it okay?"

"What do you want? Should I have aborted you both? I could have done that, you know. All my friends told me to do that." Her lips curled. "Your father told me to do that."

"You are twisted."

"I never said I wasn't. And I never said I didn't regret it. I changed my mind. I tried to take it back. I begged the adoption agency. I said I'd even give the money back, but they wouldn't because you were already gone. I tried to get the address or the name of the couple, but they wouldn't give it out."

Elise knew she was lying. If anything, she probably went back to the agency to try to sell Hannah. She wanted to turn around and walk out. That would be the best thing to do. But her masochistic side wanted to know it all.

"How did you choose which one to keep?"

Beth shrugged. "I flipped a coin. Hannah was heads. You, Holly, were tails. It came up heads. So I let the lady from the agency take you."

Her nonchalance infuriated Elise. "You know what? You should have done Hannah a favor and taken forty grand. Maybe she wouldn't have been a drunk or a druggie or a slut or anything else I've learned about her. Why didn't you give both of us away? Hannah would have been better off with me. My parents would have adopted both of us. They would have taken better care of her. She'd probably be alive right now."

Beth's face paled. Elise brimmed with satisfaction because, no matter how much Beth had hurt her, with those words, she just hurt her worse.

CHAPTER 15

Wickman desperately wanted to be an old New England college with ivy clinging to the walls of its two-hundred-year-old buildings. But the truth Wickman couldn't escape was that it was formed in 1960, and no matter how hard the gardeners tried, the salt air always stunted the growth of the ivy. Despite its youth, Wickman tried to maintain the look of the Ivy League, knowing the reputation would always elude it. The Wickman Library was built in 1962, but looking at it, you'd never know. The style was Victorian Gothic, complete with towering spires and turrets, detailed arches, and colorful stained-glass windows. Elise and Kat had taken over a table deep in a corner of the library. Their notes, books, and laptops were strewn across the dark wood. Kat leaned over Elise's shoulder.

"What are you working on, anyway?" Kat's whisper was husky and sexy, like the lovechild of Demi Moore and Kathleen Turner.

"A paper on Mary Shelley for Marston's class."

"*Frankenstein,* a romantic novel? Wouldn't it be horror or gothic?"

"Yes, but it has romantic themes. Romanticism wasn't about sex. It was the power of nature, emotional behavior, remote and exotic settings, and the trend toward irrationality and the supernatural. These themes run all through Frankenstein."

"Huh." Kat returned her attention to her own laptop and tapped at the keys.

"What are you working on?"

"Some World War I shit."

"Nice."

Elise couldn't wait to finish her paper, so she could slink home and crawl under her covers and sleep. Hopefully she wouldn't dream. She just wanted her mind to be blank. She had been thinking so much lately, her brain throbbed. Planning her next steps. Questions to ask Gavin. More questions for Faith. Maybe another visit to the police station. After yesterday's visit to her mother, the need for answers plagued her, stronger than ever.

The tapping beside her stopped, and she looked to find Kat staring at her.

"Can I ask you a personal question?"

"Shoot," Elise said.

"How come you never tried to find your biological parents? I would have been so curious, you know? To know why. And to meet them. To see if I had siblings, cousins, grandparents. Why didn't you?"

"I guess I just wasn't interested."

Kat crossed her arms over her tight peach sweater. "For someone who is so incredibly smart and for whom everything seems to come so easily, sometimes you're frustratingly lazy."

"It's not laziness."

"What is it then?"

Elise saved her work and leaned back in the chair. "Honestly, it's fear. My whole life, I've taken the easy route. I've never taken risks."

"Out of fear?"

"I got into Harvard, you know. I told my parents I was rejected."

"Why?"

"Because of the money and because if I went to Harvard, I

wouldn't be one of the smartest students there. I'd have to really try and after I did my best, I might still fail. So I decided to come here. Not only would it be free, but I'm guaranteed success. I'll graduate in the top five percent with minimal effort."

"And Nick?" Kat prodded.

"Same thing. He didn't cheat on me. He didn't slap me around. He wasn't cheap. He wasn't ugly or stupid. There was nothing wrong with him other than he moved too fast for slow, timid me. I didn't have to completely break it off with him. I could have asked him to postpone our wedding or break off the engagement, but still stay together. But I didn't. Why? Because I didn't want to have the conversation. And sometimes now I think I miss him, but I don't want to call him because I'll have to face up to what I did, and I don't want to have that conversation either."

Elise had come to admire Kat for her impulsiveness, her wild streak. As much as she wished no one else's opinion mattered, it did. She wanted Kat to like her. And the disappointment in Kat's eyes now sank Elise's heart.

"Why are you telling me all this?"

She wished she had a mouth-sized cork she could shove in, but the words tumbled out. "Because you asked why I never tried to find my biological family. It's not because I wasn't interested. It's because I'm a coward. I was scared of what I might find. And look now. I was proven right. My mother sold me. I was better off before I ever came here and found out any of this shit."

Elise turned away, pouting like a child.

"I'm going to head home," Kat said, filling her laptop bag.

"Okay, I'll be there shortly."

Elise kept her head down until Kat was gone. Why did she have to go on blabbering like an idiot? Her fingers returned to the keyboard, but *Frankenstein* was the farthest from her mind now. She stood quickly, nearly knocking her chair backward, and trudged down the main aisle until she found the water fountain.

Though the taste left something to be desired, the coolness of the water soothed her dry throat. She wiped her chin and turned back, keeping her head down the entire way, not wanting eye contact or conversation with any living thing. She settled back into her chair and took a deep breath, ready to reimmerse herself into Mary Shelley's world.

But something was wrong.

Her last sentence was there as she left it, but two more sentences typed in all caps had been added below.

I TOLD YOU TO STOP.

YOU WON'T LIKE WHAT I DO NEXT.

Like many places, Cape Cod had a caste system. Cape natives were the highest rank. Next came the transplants, people who have lived on the Cape for years but weren't lucky enough to be born there. College students took the next rank, and tourists filled out the bottom position, blissfully unaware that they were looked down upon as, at best, a necessary evil.

The men sipping beers at the L-shaped bar at Murphy's Shiphouse nodded at Gavin Shaw as he passed by with Elise at his side. Not only was he a native, but now that he had promised to protect and serve, he was among the highest in the social order. The men smiled approvingly at Elise's brown suede skirt, pink blouse, and long blond hair swept up into a French twist. She would have felt pride, but instead felt guilt at being her sister's boyfriend's dinner date.

"I know it doesn't look nice," he whispered in her ear. "But the food is the best on the Cape."

The hostess showed them to their table, a candlelit corner

table for two, and Gavin pulled out the chair for Elise. Murphy's Shiphouse was best known for its seafood. Cape's Best Chowder! screamed across the front of the menu. The design of the restaurant was a nautical theme, with black-and-white photographs of boats and oil-painted seascapes on the walls and empty lobster traps hanging from the ceiling. Even the napkin holders were sailors' rope knots.

Elise read the menu with trepidation. She'd rather eat rabbit droppings than seafood. Something that would have been helpful to mention to Gavin before he chose the restaurant. Every menu item claimed to be a Cape Cod specialty: Cape Cod Chowder, Cape Cod Scrod, Cape Cod Haddock, even Cape Cod Chicken. She ordered the Cape Cod Chicken—specially glazed with cranberries from a Cape Cod bog—and a glass of chardonnay.

The waitress was a young brunette, probably a high school student. Her eager blue eyes stared at Gavin as she took his order like he was this month's cover of *Teen Dreamboat Magazine*. Elise wondered if Hannah ever got jealous of the female attention Gavin attracted. He had played football at Wickman. That, along with his good looks, must have made him a magnet for young co-eds. He looked especially handsome tonight out of his uniform, wearing khaki Dockers and a baby blue dress shirt. Their eyes met, and hers retreated down to the crimson tablecloth.

"I'm sorry if I'm staring," he said. "It's just going to take some time for me to get used to how you look . . . you know."

She smiled to put him at ease. "I'm getting a lot of looks like that lately."

Uncomfortable silence blanketed them as Elise sipped her wine and let her eyes bounce around the room while her mind searched for something to say.

"I loved her." His words tumbled out quick and loud.

She placed her wineglass gently on the table. "What was she like?" she asked softly.

His face beamed like a child's when handed a colorfully wrapped present. "She was fun. You couldn't be bored with her. She was crazy, wild at times. Spontaneous. Painfully honest. You wouldn't ask her something unless you really wanted to know the truth, because she did not pull any punches."

He fiddled with his silverware as he spoke. "She held people at arm's length. She didn't trust easily. But once she let you in, your reward was her complete loyalty."

"Why did you break up?"

His eyes lifted to the ceiling as if searching for rehearsed words and his mouth opened, but then the waitress slash Gavin groupie came with their salads and a litany of questions—would you like more drinks, is this enough dressing, is there anything else I can get for you—and the moment was gone.

"It feels strange to have a Thursday night off," he said between bites.

The wine slipped down her throat, warming her belly and soothing her nerves. "You were supposed to work tonight?"

"Yeah, I asked another officer to switch nights with me. Unfortunately, I now have to work Friday, Saturday, and Sunday night." He paused as if considering how honest to be. "But it's worth it to be here with you."

"Why didn't you just ask me to pick a different night?"

"I wanted to make it easy on you. I guess I was anxious that any change would scare you off and you'd cancel completely."

His intense interest unnerved her. He couldn't be interested in her in that way, could he? His ex's twin sister? It seemed almost incestuous.

Their meals eventually came, and Elise had to admit he was right about the restaurant. The food was delicious.

"Are you having a good time?" he asked, flashing his perfectly spaced white teeth.

"Oh, yes. The food is great. And it's nice to talk with you under more comfortable circumstances."

"Maybe we can do it again sometime, then." He smiled hopefully.

"Dinner, you mean?"

"Sure. Or a movie. I know of a great dinner theater a few towns down."

Elise gulped the last of her wine. He was interested. Yes, in that way. The wooden chair morphed into a torture seat made of a thousand metal spikes. She wriggled uncomfortably and shifted her gaze away from him.

"Can we talk about Hannah some more?"

Disappointment shadowed his face. "Sure. What else do you want to know?"

"Was she suicidal?"

"I don't know. She never said anything to me about wanting to kill herself, even after we broke up. But this was a girl who had done her share of drinking and drugs. Those types of people tend to be the ones who have the capacity to kill themselves. Self-destructive, I think they call it."

"Did anyone have any reason to want Hannah dead?"

His fork paused in midair. "Not that I know of."

He didn't like these questions; she knew that. So she cut to the important one. "What do you think happened that night on the bridge?"

Confidence returned to his face. "I think she fell into old habits after our breakup. She got drunk, decided she wanted to see the ocean, and fell off the bridge on her way there. A plain and simple tragedy."

Dessert came. They shared a slice of Cape Cod Cheesecake. On her third bite, another thought occurred to her. "Do you still see Faith?"

He choked a bit, then took a long sip of his beer. "Sorry. Went down the wrong way. What did you ask?"

"Do you still see Faith, Hannah's roommate? The three of you were good friends."

"I run into her here and there, but I don't go out of my way to stay in touch."

"That's too bad," Elise said, remembering the picture of the three of them on the beach.

He shrugged. "Eh. Toward the end, she was really getting on Hannah's nerves, anyway, with her hero worship."

"What do you mean? Faith seemed like she genuinely liked Hannah."

"Oh, she did. Maybe too much." He dabbed at his full lips with a napkin. "At first it was the little things: reading the same books Hannah had read, liking the same music. Then came borrowing her clothes, using the same phrases, mimicking her hand gestures. Faith's hair used to be really long, below her waist. Then she cut it short like Hannah's, a real drastic change. I tried to convince Hannah it wasn't a big deal, it was all innocent, flattering even. But she thought it was creepy after a while. In retrospect, I agree with her."

Elise leaned forward, resting her elbows on the table. "Why?"

"Because with what I know now, it wasn't just that Faith wanted to be *like* Hannah. She wanted to *be* Hannah."

CHAPTER 16

The Riverwalk was Elise's favorite place in downtown Providence. Following the Providence River, it sliced through the center of the city. Outdoor concerts and art festivals often lined the waterfront attraction, but even when nothing was going on, there was plenty to see: sculptures, people watching, tourists gliding down the river on hokey gondolas. The Venetian-style footbridges and cobblestone walkways made the Riverwalk a romantic place, a place where your heart floated and your mind wandered. A place where anything could happen. It was on her regular Sunday afternoon Riverwalk stroll during her senior year at Providence that she met Nick Carrano.

"Did you know that it used to be hidden?"

Elise was lost in her thoughts, her eyes traveling with the slow current, as she leaned against the bricks of the footbridge above the river. She turned and squinted at the man beside her, the bright November sun behind him forming a halo around his head.

"What?"

"The Providence River," he repeated, pointing at the water. "It used to be hidden. It was paved over, polluted with sewage." He shook his head. "Disgusting what they did to it. But then they redirected the road, removed the concrete, and let the people see the river again. They built this Riverwalk and Waterplace Park and now look at it. It's like a brand new city." His chest puffed out as he took a deep breath. "I just love it."

Nick's looks weren't immediately disarming. He was short, only an inch taller than Elise. And his features could best be described as common: brown hair, brown eyes, medium build. But he had a smile that made her little heart pump faster and the more he spoke, the more attractive he became. Every conversation was passionate, every word intense.

For their first date, little more than five minutes after they met, he took her to the historic eighteenth-century landmark home of Sarah Helen Whitman, a poet in her own right, but best known for being engaged yet never married to Edgar Allen Poe. Nick held Elise's hand and recited a poem Poe had written to Sarah. As the words effortlessly slipped out of his mouth, Elise felt herself sinking and held tighter to his hand. She feared, more than anything else at that moment, that he would not kiss her. She tilted her face up, closed her eyes, and prayed for the touch of the lips of this mysterious stranger.

Now, as she stood outside Bourne Hall, she prayed for the opposite. She shuffled her feet and inched back from Gavin as he reached toward her. She thrust her hand out.

"Thanks again for dinner, Gavin."

Disappointed, he gently shook her hand and retreated to the warmth of his idling black sedan.

She cast a look up at the windows on her way to the front door and saw that Parker had been watching. Her shoulders sagged as she mounted the stairs. She wasn't in the mood for an argument.

As she reached the third floor, Parker's head popped over the banister. "Can you come up here for a minute?"

She didn't want to hash it out in the stairwell with raised voices, so she complied and hefted herself up the extra flight of stairs to the fourth floor. Parker stood in his apartment doorway, the door half-closed.

He waved her toward him. "I have something to show you."

"Listen. I'm not in the mood to talk to you about anything right now."

"I'm sorry about our fight and what I said." He seemed sincere. "This isn't about Gavin. I promise."

"What is it then?"

He peeked down the hallway and returned his eyes to her.

"Would you like to see your father?"

"My biological father? Where is he?"

"Right here."

Gavin drove aimlessly around Oceanside, not ready to go back to his empty one-bedroom apartment. Dinner with Elise could have gone better, but it could have gone worse. She didn't accept his offer to go out again, but she would soon. They all did what he wanted eventually.

His car was cleaner than usual. He had picked up the empty Styrofoam coffee cups and vacuumed the rugs. It even smelled fresher as he took a deep breath. He fiddled with his radio tuner until moody jazz seeped from the speakers, then he turned it up. He hated jazz, but Hannah had loved it. Slow jazz with a smooth saxophone always turned her on. He remembered the way she swayed to Coltrane in her dorm room, slipping off items of clothing one by one with her eyes closed and her lips parted.

Suddenly aroused, he shifted uncomfortably in his seat. Elise looked so much like her. He knew they were two different women, but he felt as if he already knew Elise. How her lips would taste, how fiery she'd be in bed.

At first, he didn't know what to think about the sudden existence of a twin, but now he realized it was a dream come true. He'd get to start from scratch. Except, he'd do it right this time.

Make no mistake this time.

Parker opened the door all the way and held up an old issue of *Rolling Stone* magazine, its cover faded and yellow beneath the protective plastic.

Elise draped her coat on the back of the low, forest green couch in Parker's living room and plopped down. The layout was identical to Elise's apartment, but the furniture was older and the rug worn down. A masculine scent permeated the air, a mixture of male sweat and cologne.

She carefully slid the magazine out of the plastic. "Is this what I think it is?"

Parker sat beside her. "My father did a little research on Jesse McPhee of Dorchester. He found out the band's name, and I got this for thirty bucks off eBay. They called themselves Harborfly."

"He was famous? He made it big?"

"Unfortunately, no. The article in *Rolling Stone* is more of a cautionary tale. What might have been."

She sighed, torn between needing to know about her father, but not wanting any more bad news. "I don't want to read it right now. Will you just tell me about it?"

He leaned back, resting his arm over the back of the couch. "The band formed in Boston. Your father, Jesse McPhee, was the lead singer and quite a talent. He was the big draw at all the local shows. They drove a van out to California and started playing small venues there. Bigger gigs and a strong following came next. Then they scraped together enough money to make a demo."

He paused. "Can I get you a drink?"

She shook her head. "I just want to know. Keep going."

"Several record companies heard the demo and were interested. The band narrowed it down to one, and it was going to be big money. The contract was nearly signed when one night Jesse passed out on stage, wasted from booze and drugs. He was a junkie. The band had hidden it well from the record company, but now they considered the band a risk they didn't want to take. So they backed off."

"What about all the other interested companies?"

"Word got around. No one wanted them anymore. They kept trying, kept playing, but eventually the fans disappeared and even the smallest clubs weren't interested and their fame faded."

"So, where's my dad?"

Parker lowered his eyes to the floor. "He died of a drug overdose in a Vegas hotel room. You would have been about five at the time."

She rested her chin in her hands. What a motley crew her family was. Everything she found out made her happier Beth gave her away.

Beth.

She straightened as fury calcified her bones.

"What is it?" he asked.

"The one thing I couldn't figure out was why Beth kept Hannah at all. I didn't buy that sob story about how she wanted to keep us both, but could only afford one. That didn't jive."

"But now you know?"

She glanced down at the discolored magazine that had given her the answer, in all its disgusting glory. "Why does Beth do anything? One reason: money."

Parker looked confused, so she spelled it out. "Beth thought Jesse was going to make it big with his band. He dumped her though, so she wouldn't see a dime of those millions. But if she kept one of his children, she could take him to court and squeeze huge monthly payments from him. She didn't need both of us for that, only one."

She tossed the magazine on the coffee table, not wanting

anything associated with her biological family touching her. "Money is all that matters to her. She sold me for it and kept Hannah for it."

CHAPTER 17

The Wickman College mailroom was a square box lined with numbered metal mailboxes from floor to ceiling. Elise slid the silver key into box 177 and opened the small rectangular door.

"I thought you said you got the mail a couple days ago," she said, pulling bundles of mail from the box.

"I meant to, but I guess I forgot," Kat said, her voice echoing.

The overflowing pile of envelopes and catalogs slid from Elise's hands to the floor.

"I'll get it." Kat crouched down, picking up the envelopes one by one. "How was your date last night?"

Elise rolled her eyes. How many times had she insisted to Kat that her dinner with Gavin was not a date? "It was about as much fun as a vaginal exam."

Kat laughed, loud and wicked, like she was auditioning for the witch in the *Wizard of Oz*. "Yeah, if your gyno was Dr. Delicious."

"He's attractive, but he's my dead sister's ex-boyfriend. That's just wrong. Besides you and I both know that wasn't the point of the dinner."

Kat raised an eyebrow. "Do you think he's the one who pushed her?"

"I have no idea. At this point, it could be anyone. But he had a few interesting things to say about Faith. Her friendship with Hannah was not as simple as it first seemed."

Kat rose, frowning at a nine-by-twelve brown envelope in her hand. "I recognize this block writing. I think it's the same as that note someone shoved under the door before. It's addressed to you."

Elise grabbed the envelope. It felt thick beneath her fingers. "No postage, so it's intercampus mail."

"That doesn't mean anything. Anyone can come in here off the street and toss mail in the intercampus slot."

"Sure it doesn't mean the person is a student here, but it does mean the person stood in this room." She ripped open the seal and peeked in, not wanting to shove her hand in without looking first.

"What is it?"

Elise squinted. "Looks like photographs."

She slid out two black and white photos and held one in each hand. In her left, her mother knelt in the garden at the side of her house. Her back was to the camera, and Elise knew exactly what she was doing: planting her tulip bulbs. She always planted in early October before the ground froze, and the tulips bloomed in early spring all along the perimeter of the garden.

In Elise's right hand, the torso of her father lay in the driveway, his head concealed by the bulk of his old Buick. Despite how easy it was with the drive-thru lube shops that littered the suburbs nowadays, he still performed his own oil changes just like always. A heavy wrench lay on the concrete like an implicit threat. Her eyes shifted back to her kneeling mother and the garden shovel on the ground beside her. They both seemed so vulnerable, without any clue that a murderer snapped pictures while they were lost in their chores.

Elise's hands trembled and her breathing came in ragged spurts. She tried to speak, but her throat felt full of sand. She wanted to give the photos to Kat, but her fingers wouldn't move, as if the pictures were glued to her hand. They were already burned into her memory.

The door slammed against the wall as Elise burst into the apartment. Her backpack slid off her shoulder as she punched the numbers. Her finger slipped and pressed the wrong key.

"Shit, shit!" she shouted, hanging up the phone and picking it up again, impatiently waiting for the dial tone.

Kat fell into the room, bundles of mail in her arms. "You're fast." She dumped the mail on the table and hunched over to get her breath.

"Listen," she said, gasping. "You need to calm down. Your parents are fine. It was just a threat, that's all. They're fine for now. If you call them screaming, you'll give them both heart attacks."

Elise laid the phone down. "You're right."

She took a deep breath and let it slowly whoosh out of her lungs. She wiped her clammy hands on her jeans. Leaning on the end table, she took a few more deep breaths, then lifted the phone again. Her fingers slowly selected each number, then she calmly put the phone to her ear. After a few rings, her mother's sweet voice came through the line.

"Hi, Mom!" She tried to control her tone and stay casual.

"Elise, I was just going to call you."

"Why? Is everything okay?"

"Of course it is. It's just been a few days and I miss my little girl."

Relief eased the vise off her heart. Elise wished she could transport herself home, pull her mother into her arms, feel her warmth, bury her face in her hair. "I miss you, too, Mom."

"Maybe you and Kat could visit again soon. And bring your laundry, of course."

"That would be nice. Anything new?"

"Nick called last week. I meant to tell you before, but forgot."

She paused and added, "I didn't tell him where you were."

"Thanks, Mom."

"Honey . . ." That one word was filled with so much: advice, disappointment, reminder.

"I know, Mom. I took the easy way out and I hurt him. I know."

Nonconfrontational as always, Marie changed the subject. "This morning someone else called for you. A young man who said he worked for some lawyer and wanted to know where you lived. I assumed Nick got one of his friends to call, so I told him no such person lived here. It wasn't a lie; you don't live here right now."

"That's good, Mom. Thanks again." She gritted her teeth, angry with herself. "I hate to put you in this position with Nick."

"I may not agree with your decision, but I'll always do what you want, sweetie."

Elise filled her in on the paper she was currently working on. A teacher herself, Marie had always been interested in Elise's work. Neither of them mentioned Hannah, and Elise preferred it that way. She didn't want her parents to know how deeply she'd gone into her research. After sufficiently catching up, they exchanged pleasantries and hung up the phone.

Elise sank into the couch beside Kat, who had stretched out languidly, her bare feet on the coffee table.

"Everything's okay?" Kat asked.

"Yeah. For now."

The phone rang, loud in the silent apartment.

"My mom must have forgotten to tell me something," Elise mumbled as she pulled herself back to the phone.

"Hello?"

A muffled male voice said, "It would have been so easy."

Fear gripped her senses as she pressed the phone harder to her ear.

"I could have snuck up behind her and picked up the garden shovel. She would never have known what hit her. Unless the first strike didn't do the job. But I would have just kept hitting until it was done. Wouldn't want to get too messy, though. Wouldn't want dear old dad to see the blood on my boots as I approached his car, pulled him out from underneath it, and killed him with the wrench he carelessly left in the driveway. Or I could have just put the car in neutral and pushed it over him. Either way. The point is, that's just how easy it would be."

"What do you want?" she asked, each word strained with panic.

"This is very simple, but you don't seem to get it so I'm going to speak precisely and slowly. I want you to leave it alone. Stop digging in the past. Forget her."

The line went dead. Elise dropped the receiver and ran to the bathroom. The phone dangled on its cord like a hanged man while she vomited, her stomach contents mixing in the water with her tears.

The tea reminded her of the muddy water of the Drowning River. It didn't taste much better, so she set it on the coffee table. Kat meant well, and Elise appreciated that she wanted to take care of her. She cuddled the yellow afghan in the corner of the couch, her legs drawn underneath her, shivering despite the warmth in the apartment. She hadn't been able to shake the cold feeling that overtook her during the phone call.

Her stomach grumbled, but she doubted she'd be able to eat the Chinese food Kat went out to pick up. A knock on the door came, hard and fast. At first she assumed it was Kat returning, her arms too full to unlock the door, but it wasn't Kat's upbeat three-knock special. It was someone else.

She rose, dragging the blanket with her, and squinted through the peephole. A distorted, circus-mirror Parker waved at her from the hallway. She unlocked the door and pulled it open, then sloughed back to the couch.

Parker sat on the edge of the recliner and clasped his hands in front of him. "Are you sick?" he asked, taking in her green face, teacup, and blanket.

"No, just had a bad day."

"I'll make it better, then. I was able to persuade my mom to use her administrative resources to get me a copy of Hannah's schedule from last year. All her classes. So you could visit the professors she had at the time. Talk to them under the pretense of wanting to know what Hannah was like, of course. Feel them out."

"Why? Do you think she was sleeping with one of them? Probably, huh? Probably all of them."

Parker blushed. "What's gotten into you? I thought you'd be happy with this. It's a lead. More people to talk to." He reached across the space between them and laid a warm hand on her knee. "I know it's frustrating, but we'll get to the bottom of this. All we need is time."

"My parents' lives were threatened today." She pulled the photographs from under the couch and tossed them at him. "I got these in the mail."

He looked at both of them, frowning. "I don't get it."

"Then I got a phone call, from a man reminding me how easy it would be to kill them." She stared at his gray-blue eyes. "He'll do that if I keep looking into Hannah's death. He'll kill my parents."

"You don't know that."

"You don't know he won't," she snapped back.

"Whoever pushed Hannah did it because he or she wanted Hannah dead. For a reason. This person isn't a serial killer."

"So you think he won't kill to save himself? If I get too close?"

He settled back in the chair and drummed his fingers on his

forehead. "There's a risk involved, yes, but—"

"But what, Parker? Risk my parents anyway? For someone who's already dead? It's not going to bring her back, but it just might get more people killed."

"It's all the more reason to catch this person. We're dealing with a murderer. Someone who needs to pay. If he or she is capable of killing once, isn't it our duty to catch them so this never happens to someone else?"

She ripped off the blanket and leaned forward. "My parents are good people. The best I've ever known. Hannah was a slut and a drunk and a druggie and who knows what else. She obviously did something very bad to piss off someone enough to get killed. I'm not going to put my parents' lives in jeopardy for someone like that."

Anger flared in Parker's eyes, and his face contorted until he was unfamiliar to her. It was as if she had called his mother a whore.

"There are two sides to every person," he said through tight lips. "We're not all good or all bad."

"Yeah, what's so bad about me?"

He stood and leaned his face close enough to hers that she thought she could smell the fury on his breath. "You're a coward."

Her face couldn't have been redder if he had slapped her. He slammed the door as he left, leaving her alone with his insult and her own shame hanging in the air.

CHAPTER 18

The week skittered by like a leaf caught in the wind. Elise threw herself into work, spending long hours at the library, giving in to sleep when it overcame her, and eating when Kat forced her. She saw Parker in class and he smiled at her in that cute boyish "please forgive me" way, and she ignored him.

No more threats arrived via mail or phone. But every time she closed her eyes, she saw Hannah's face just underneath the water, her golden hair splayed out like a flower around her face, her dead eyes staring up at nothing, her mouth open in a plea for help.

She lay on her stomach on her bed, the Sunday paper spread around her, when Kat shuffled into her room, yawning.

"Good party?" Elise asked. She had stayed home under the guise of needing to study, when in reality she had spent the night staring at the wall. Her thoughts skipped like a stone across a lake—from her parents, to Hannah, to Parker—until she fell asleep with the sound of party music booming from down the hall.

"You missed a good one," Kat said, stretching in her tank top and boxer shorts. Her long legs still carried a summer tan. "Drama Geek was there."

"What about Math Boy?"

"I still like Math Boy, but Drama Geek has this thing he can do. Pick a play, any play, and he'll recite lines from it. *Uber*-sexy. I made him recite *Romeo and Juliet* as we made love last night.

Unfortunately, we never got past Act One. What did you do?"

Elise lowered her eyes to the newspaper and pretended to skim the headlines. "Studied. Got a lot done."

"Parker was there. He asked about you."

She snorted. "I care about that as much as I care about the molecular content of salt."

"Liar," Kat taunted, jumping on the bed. She reached down and tossed the newspaper to the floor.

"What are you doing? I was reading that!"

"You need to get dressed. We're going out."

"Where?" she said, like a child being dragged to her bath.

"I'll give you a hint. It's wet and fun to watch and involves people stripping their clothes off."

Curiosity won, and Elise allowed Kat to drag her out of bed. They dressed and piled into Elise's black Civic, lazily driving the mile to the beach parking lot, which was strangely full of cars.

"What are all these people doing at the beach in October?"

"You'll see," Kat said in a singsong voice, pulling Elise past the river and over the bridge.

Elise kept her eyes forward, on the dunes, and refused to look down into the river, sure that Hannah's face would be there. She followed Kat down the path between the dunes and entered the beach, sand creeping into her sneakers.

A group of twenty people, most older than herself, peeled off layers of clothing while a crowd cheered and clapped. Once stripped to their bathing suits, the group roared and charged into the water, the foam waves crashing over them.

Elise laughed in shock. "They're crazy," she said, raising her voice above the cheers of the crowd.

"Oh, this?" Kat waved her off. "This is nothing. It's just practice."

"For what?"

"The Polar Bear Plunge on New Year's Day."

"They do this on New Year's Day? They're nuts."

"Maybe so, but they're having a good time." Kat jabbed her playfully in the ribs, then ran off and joined the cheering crowd.

Elise watched the Polar Bear Club, young and old, splashing and laughing. She couldn't remember the last time she'd had that much fun. A cracking noise came from beside her, and she looked down at a seagull pecking at the remains of a crab. She couldn't remember the last time she'd eaten, either.

She didn't know what was bothering her more, Parker's words or the truth behind them. Was she doing it again? Taking the easy way out? What kind of person didn't care who killed her sister? Didn't try to find out the identity of the murderer? A coward, that's who.

She strolled farther down the beach, away from the frolicking pack, until she came to a breakwater. A father sat with his fishing rod as his young son toddled along the rocks of the jetty. The little boy wore a Disney World t-shirt, and his pale face was shielded from the sun by a miniature version of his father's green fishing hat. They were a cute pair, and she managed to smile as she passed them.

She jumped across deep crevices from rock to rock until she reached the end of the breakwater, then looked down. The green water turned navy here, too deep for her to see the bottom. The ocean stretched out to infinity, melting into the blue of the horizon miles away. She felt as if she were standing at the end of the world. One more step and she'd fall off the edge.

Water splashed beside her, and she dismissed it as a wave hitting the rocks until she heard a panicked scream.

The father stood jumping in place, screaming. "I can't swim! I can't swim! My wife can swim, but she's down there!" He motioned to the crowd in the distance. Elise didn't understand why he was screaming at her, until she glanced around and realized they were the only two there.

The boy had fallen in.

His face broke the surface, enough for him to gasp, then another wave crashed over him and all that remained was a tiny pale hand flailing at the surface. She tore her coat off and dove into the water, the shock of the cold like a thousand needles. She swam toward him and got close, but the current pulled him away. She ducked under and kicked and pulled at the water with her hands, using all her strength, until with the next stroke her arm brushed against something solid and she grabbed hold and pulled it to the surface.

She floated the boy on his back, his face to the air, but he didn't seem to be breathing. Water pounded in her ears, and behind that she heard the muffled screams of the father. She held the boy at the surface while she kicked toward shore. A large wave gave her the boost she needed, and soon she felt gravel under her feet.

She stood and ran with the boy in her arms. He seemed even smaller now, his face pale, as she laid him on the rough sand. He immediately turned to his side and expelled more water than she thought he could hold in his tiny frame, followed by the contents of his stomach. His father picked him up off the sand and cradled him like a baby, tears of joy reflecting off his cheeks.

The cheering of the Polar Bear Club raised to a crescendo and she looked up, realizing for the first time that she and the boy's father were no longer alone. The father's anguished cries must have caught the crowd's attention, and a stream of people came running down the beach. The ones who were already there formed a circle around her, clapping and slapping her on the back.

"Good job!"

"Thank God you were here!"

"So brave!"

A woman, the boy's mother, she assumed, kissed her on the cheek. "I don't know how I can ever repay you."

Elise had never been a hero before, never felt the puffed-chest pride of changing or saving someone's life. As Kat came to her side, her eyes lit in awe of what her roommate had done, Elise knew.

She was no coward.

Elise banged her fist on the door with renewed energy.

"Come in!" yelled a hoarse voice from inside.

Parker and Robbie's apartment smelled like the world's largest gym sock. An empty pizza box lay on the kitchen floor, too big for the wastebasket. Empty beer cans littered the coffee table. The cleaning lady had obviously taken the weekend off.

Parker aggressively shut the TV off. "I can't even watch the news with you anymore."

Robbie stood, fists balled at his side. "Just keep your head in the sand, ostrich."

"You're saying I'm naive? Just because I'm not a conspiracy nut job?"

"Turn on your laptop and Google Operation Northwoods. Then we'll talk about what they are and aren't capable of doing." Robbie turned to Elise. "Will you two make up already? Ever since your argument, he's been acting like a little bitch."

Parker glared at him. "I'm just sick of your constant—" Elise threw him a look, and the anger drained from his face. "I'm sorry, Robbie. Let's just forget it. Elise, please help me change the subject."

She tossed herself into a haggard gray armchair and crossed her legs. "I want to break the law."

"Oh, great, just what I need," Parker said, scooping a book off the chair beside Elise and sitting down. "Another crackpot on my hands. Why would you want to do that?"

"First of all, you were wrong. I'm no coward."

Parker's cheeks flushed, and he lowered his eyes.

"Secondly, I'm ready to solve this thing. I want to know who killed my sister. But I want to know now, so I can move on with my life. So let's kick this thing into high gear, shall we?"

A smile spread across Parker's face, and Robbie whooped.

She continued, "First lead. I've been thinking about Abby Frost and something she said at that party."

"What did she say?" Robbie asked.

"We were having a back and forth, and I went a little over the line, and she said I was just like my sister. But the way she said it, with venom in her voice, got to me. There's something between those two. I'm sure of it."

Parker waved his hand. "Don't even ask me to talk to her because I just can't. It ended badly."

"Why did you break up?"

He sighed and his shoulders sagged forward. "She got drunk one night and cheated on me. I ended our relationship, and she lost it. We're not capable of having a civil conversation."

"That's okay, because I don't want you to talk to her."

"Then what do you want to do?"

"I want to snoop around her apartment."

Parker's mouth dropped open. "You're kidding, right?"

"I want to have a little look around and see if there's anything there that can explain her hostility toward my sister and me. Worst case, there's nothing there."

"Um, no. Worst case we get arrested for breaking and entering."

"She might be onto something," Robbie said in nearly a whisper.

"What?" Parker asked.

"You know I was at Dolan's the night Hannah died. I saw

her there. She got pretty drunk. I didn't see her leave or who she left with, but I did see one thing." He rubbed his temples with his fingers, drawing out the memory.

"What, Robbie?" Elise begged.

"She talked to a lot of people that night and Abby was one of them."

"Abby was there the night Hannah died? They spoke?"

Robbie took his glasses off and looked into Elise's eyes. "Yes, and they weren't happy with each other."

CHAPTER 19

Thursday came and Gavin needed duct tape to keep his eyes open. He had worked six nights in a row, had Monday night off, and instead of resting, chose to drink at Dolan's with the guys. Two more nights of work without enough rest in the day to recharge. Then came this morning, and he should have climbed under the comforter, but instead went deep sea fishing with his buddies. Dumb move when he had to work tonight, but he had trouble saying no when it came to a few hours of fun.

Now he leaned back in his patrol car and allowed his eyes to close. The car was hidden behind a billboard advertising a lobster house. The locals knew this speed trap and automatically slowed as they passed the billboard, but tourists speeding down Route 6A were often picked off and ticketed.

The night shift was miserable, but he had to pay his dues like any rookie. His dad had offered him day hours, but he refused, not wanting special treatment for being the chief's son. He appreciated his dad always looking out for him, but sometimes both his mother and father could be overbearing. The best day of his life was the day he moved out of his parents' beachfront home. They couldn't understand why he'd leave that prime real estate for a claustrophobic one-bedroom apartment in the center of town. Though small, that place was heaven to him. No parents, no college roommates, just him for the first time in his life.

A red Mustang raced by, easily twenty miles over the speed limit if Gavin had been using the radar gun. But he was too tired to care. He rolled down both windows, hoping the cool air would keep him awake, but the smell of the pine trees in the woods behind him hypnotized him more. He'd just close his eyes for five minutes. A little catnap was all he needed, then he'd get back to work. No one would even know. He leaned his head back and his mouth opened slightly as sleep drifted in.

"Snoozing on the job?" a female voice teased.

Gavin straightened and his eyes snapped open. No one was in the car with him. Did he dream the voice?

"Boo!" A small face thrust itself in the open passenger window.

"Damn it, Faith. You scared the shit out of me."

She opened the car door and slid inside, her short skirt exposing her thin thighs. "Serves you right for falling asleep while you're supposed to be protecting the town."

Her voice grated on his nerves. It was high and squeaky and reminded him of Smurfette. What a whiny blue bitch she had been.

"What do you want?" he said, rubbing his eyes.

She moved closer. He noticed her hair was getting long again, just past her shoulders. She had stopped forcing her natural curls to stay straight, too. "I was driving by and saw your car hiding back here, so I thought I'd say hi." She ran her hand down his arm. "Is that against the law, Officer?"

He turned his head to look into her large brown eyes. They reminded him of a deer he shot with his dad once. "What are you doing, Faith?"

Her hand slid across the front of his uniform, her fingers splayed out across his chest. He grabbed her wrist and pushed her hand back into her lap.

"I know you're used to getting what you want, but there are

some things Daddy's money can't buy you."

She giggled. "I didn't think I'd have to pay you, honey."

He inched away from her. "I don't want to hurt you, but you don't seem to get it, so I'll spell it out. I am not interested in you."

She retreated and crossed her arms. "You seemed to be quite interested last year. As a matter of fact, I can still remember what it felt like to lie underneath you and feel you move inside me."

"Stop it. Just stop it! Why are you talking like that?" He looked out the window, peering into the woods behind them.

"Are you scared someone will hear? Are you embarrassed of what you've done?"

"You know that's not what it is."

"Then what is it? Is there someone else you'd rather be with?"

He kept silent and anger flashed in her eyes. "It's her, isn't it?"

"Who?"

"Elise. Your little replacement Hannah." She pushed open the door and slid out, slamming it behind her.

She stormed over to the driver's side open window and lowered her face to meet his. "I've just got one question for you, Gavin. How many of these carbon copy bimbo blond bitches am I going to have to wait through until you figure out it's me you really want?"

Thursday was the busiest night at Dolan's Pub. Friday and Saturday nights, students traveled to Hyannis for the bigger bars. But Thursdays belonged to Dolan's because, smart as owner Jimmy Dolan was, he marketed Thursday nights as Wickman nights. A student ID got you dollar drafts and half-off appetizers. Of course, the only draft for a dollar was a homebrew Jimmy Dolan made in the basement and after one, you'd hap-

143

pily pay five bucks for a Bud Light, but the students streamed in, packing the booths and the rectangular bar centered in the middle of the pub.

Elise, Parker, and Robbie huddled in a booth in the back, their eyes on the crowd. An empty mega-sampler plate lay on the table, the nachos, mozzarella sticks, and boneless buffalo wings already devoured.

"She's here every Thursday night with her roommate," Robbie said. "She'll come."

Parker nodded. He'd run into Abby here before on a Thursday. "Does she still live with Sasha?"

"Yeah," Robbie said, rolling his eyes.

Parker grunted. Sasha was a loud, obnoxious woman who didn't think before she spoke. She could offend a cockroach with minimal effort. She had always been a point of contention in his relationship with Abby. He never understood why Abby was best friends with her. Perhaps they enjoyed treating each other like shit.

"There she is," Elise said.

Parker's eyes turned to the door. Abby Frost was pretty, but in a fake way: red dyed hair, expensive makeup, artificial nails. She wasn't a natural beauty like . . . well, like Elise. The only makeup on Elise's face was a subtle lip gloss. Her hair looked soft and natural, her clothes—cargo pants and black sweater—seemed effortless, yet looked so good on her petite frame. He pushed away that thought and focused on Abby. Overdressed as usual, she wore slim-fitting black pants, a pink blouse, and heels. Why they lasted a year was a mystery to him now.

The mega-sampler mass in his stomach churned as he became nervous at the prospect of breaking into his ex's apartment. Best just to get it over with. He nudged Elise with his elbow and she nodded and stood up.

"You know what to do," he said to Robbie, patting the cell

phone in his pocket.

"I'm sure she's here for at least a couple of hours," Robbie said. "But I'll stay here until you're done and call you if she leaves."

Moments later, Parker started the engine of his Jeep as Elise slid in beside him. They drove five minutes to Beachview Condominiums, where Abby's dad had bought her a place that she now shared with Sasha. Parker knocked first to be safe, then, with no answer, slid the tension wrench into the keyhole, turned it, and inserted the pick.

"Where did you get that?" Elise whispered.

"Internet." The lock clicked, and the door swung open.

The condo's floor plan was identical to Faith's and offered the same ocean view from the bay window. Parker and Elise crept down the hallway past a bathroom. He ducked his head into the bedroom on the left, saw the poster of Toby Keith, and knew it wasn't Abby's room. The bedroom on the right showcased M.C. Escher prints on its walls, hypnotic geometrical labyrinths that Parker had lost himself in on mornings when he lay in bed, waiting for Abby to wake.

"This is her room," he whispered.

Elise followed him into the bedroom, her fingers grazing the bedspread, her eyes taking stock.

"So what are we looking for?" he asked.

"I don't know. Anything to do with Hannah."

A large oak desk rested in the corner of the room, papers and books piled on its shelves. "I'll start with that," he said, motioning to it. "You can have the honor of the underwear drawer."

He opened all the books on her shelves and flipped through them, but nothing fell out or seemed out of place. The middle desk drawer contained only office supplies. On the lower left of the desk were three drawers. If he didn't find anything in those, he'd tell Elise this was a dead end. What more could they do?

She wandered over. "Other than designer underwear that cost more than the entire contents of my closet, there's nothing there. Shall I take the first desk drawer?"

"Sure. I'll take the second."

The drawer slid smoothly and his fingers found a glossy item on top. He pulled it out and quickly regretted his find. His own face smiled up at him from the photograph, his arms around Abby's bikinied waist. He remembered that day at the beach, at the beginning of their relationship, when everything was new and exciting. Their smiles were sincere.

"Looks like she's not over you," Elise said, spying over his shoulder.

He stuffed the photo back in the drawer and continued searching. A pink notebook glared up at him and his blood surged through his veins. A journal? This could be what they needed. He flipped through the pages, but it was only a notebook of to-do lists, schedules, and assignments. Abby was organized to the point of being obsessive.

A shrill ring echoed through the condo, startling him. The phone rang four more times, then the answering machine picked up. Moments later, Abby's pissed-off voice filled the room.

"Sasha, where the hell are you? I've been waiting here at Dolan's for ten minutes. I'll wait five more minutes and then I'm leaving."

The answering machine clicked off. Elise sat on the bed, sifting through a pile of bills and mail from the drawer.

"Damn," he said. "We only have about ten minutes then, counting her drive time."

She didn't even look up. "Then work faster."

He pulled his cell phone out of his pocket and placed it on the desk. Robbie would call the minute Abby left. That would give them plenty of time to get out.

A small gasp came from Elise, her hand covering her mouth.

"Parker, I found something."

He walked toward her, the world in slow motion now, seeing Abby's check register in her hand, wondering what she found, what it meant. How well had he really known Abby?

The front door slammed shut.

Panic streaked across Elise's face, and he held a finger to his lips, hoping she'd stay quiet. He pointed to the closet, then silently picked up the drawer and the pile of envelopes and shoved it under the bed.

He padded to the closet and slipped in, closing the door behind them with a soft click. With barely enough room for the both of them in the dark space, he took her into his arms. She trembled slightly and buried her face in his chest.

"Don't be scared," he whispered, resting his chin on her head and breathing in the sweet smell of her hair.

He held her like a captured dove, strong enough to hold, yet light enough not to hurt. He felt the rise and fall of her body with each breath she took. She looked up at him, her face blurry in the darkness, but her green eyes glowing, pleading. In that moment, the danger, the closet, the reason they were there, everything melted into the background and there was only her face, her lips. His overwhelming desire to kiss her shocked him. It crept up from deep inside and took over, making his whole body tingle. His parted his lips and leaned toward her face.

Then Abby's voice careened down the hallway, scaring him rigid. The answering machine replayed the message while a loud voice mocked it.

"Where the hell are you?" A woman sneered. "I'm late you idiot, that's where I am. Try some common sense."

He lowered his lips to Elise's ear and whispered. "It's only Sasha. She won't even come in here. We're safe."

She nodded but didn't let go of him.

The phone rang again, closer this time, and with a familiar

singsong ring. A cell phone.

His cell phone.

He peered through the slats of the closet door. His cell phone lay on the desk, ringing insistently. Robbie calling to tell them Abby had left. Sasha's loud footsteps trudged down the hall and into the room. He felt Elise tense beneath his arms.

"Moron," Sasha said. "She'd forget her own tits if they weren't surgically installed."

She swooped out of the room and as the front door slammed a moment later, they simultaneously released all the air held in their lungs.

Elise pushed open the closet door. "We're okay!"

"No, we're not," he said, staying behind in the darkness.

"What's wrong?"

"She took my cell phone."

Elise looked at the desk, back at Parker, and understanding hit her.

"She thought it was Abby's and that she had forgotten it. We bought those phones together last year at the mall. We have the same one." His shoulders sagged as dread churned in his stomach. "Abby will find out whose phone it is two minutes after Sasha gives it to her. My mother is on memory dial. My call logs. She'll know it's mine. She'll know I was here."

CHAPTER 20

Elise pushed open her apartment door with a grunt as Parker followed her into the living room. They sank onto the couch next to Kat, who was stretched out, her legs bare under a short denim skirt. From the recliner, Robbie stared at her like a dog watching its owner eat a steak, living with the hope that a piece will drop to the floor.

"What happened?" Kat asked. "You two look awful."

"Yeah, why didn't you answer your phone?" Robbie asked.

"I don't have it."

Silence followed as Elise waited for Parker to finish. He rubbed his temples with his fingers and groaned. She realized she'd have to do the talking. "His phone was on Abby's desk. We were looking through the drawers. Sasha came home unexpectedly, and we had to hide in a closet." Kat's eyebrows rose, and Elise threw her a look that said, "Shut your mouth," and continued. "Then Robbie called and Sasha came into the room and took the phone, assuming it was Abby's."

"Oh, shit," Robbie said, his eyes widening. "Sasha's going to give it to Abby and Abby will know you broke into her place."

"Ding ding!" Parker said, his finger in the air. "Give this man a beer. And give me twenty."

Kat went to the kitchen and returned, cradling four beers in her arms. Elise gratefully took one, twisted off the top, and took a long swig. The cold gliding down her throat soothed her nerves.

"There's more," Elise said, after everyone was comfortable.

"That's right," Parker said with new life in his eyes. "Before Sasha busted in, you said you found something."

"I was flipping through Abby's checkbook register. It dated back two years."

She paused and looked up at the eager faces. This information about his ex would hurt Parker. Robbie would be hurt, too, since he seemed to have liked Hannah so much. What she was about to say didn't bode well for her reputation, either.

"Out with it!" Kat said, her legs bouncing in the chair.

"I saw three checks for one thousand dollars each, written on the fifteenth of each month."

"Who were they made out to?" Parker asked, leaning forward.

"The check register said H.M. My sister's initials."

"When did it stop?" Robbie asked.

"The next check was due two days after she died."

"What would she have been paying Hannah for once a month?" Kat asked.

Elise took a deep breath. "Her silence. It all makes sense now. Abby's immediate contempt for me, her hatred of Hannah. At the party, I threatened to tell the gossip pages about her drinking." She looked at Parker. "I wouldn't do that, though. I was pissed off and wanted to be mean. But that's when she said I was exactly like my sister."

"Hannah was blackmailing her," Parker said.

"The question is," Kat said, "what did Hannah have on her?"

Elise sank deeper into the chair and added, "And was it worth killing for?"

Elise plodded through the next day like a prisoner on death row waiting for his ultimate appointment. She didn't know if Abby had any Friday classes, but kept her eyes on the floor through the hallways all the same. She ate her lunch with her face buried behind a textbook. Rather than heading to the library in the afternoon to study, she sprinted back to the apartment.

She closed the bedroom door behind her, feeling safe at last but knowing it was just a stay of execution. The inevitable confrontation with Abby would come. She just didn't want to be caught off guard. The conversation was necessary, but Elise wanted it to be on her terms. She had quite the list of questions for Abby Frost.

Tossing herself on the bed, she sank into her Laura Ashley comforter like a baby into its mother's arms. As she closed her eyes for a few moments of relaxation, Parker's face materialized beneath her eyelids. There was a moment in the closet yesterday when she thought he was going to kiss her. His lips parted, his face moved down slowly, and she lifted hers up. Then the damned cell phone rang and the moment vanished.

What a pair of mixed signals they were. A month ago, she'd assumed he had romantic intentions, and that was something she wasn't ready for. Now she found herself feeling something for a man for the first time since Nick, and he only wanted to be her friend and help her. She always looked down her nose at those women who only wanted what they couldn't have. Was she one of them now? No. If Parker knocked on her bedroom door right now, pledging his love to her, she'd throw him on the bed like a rag doll and not let him leave for two days except for food, water, and bathroom privileges. She blushed at her private fantasy.

A knock shook the door. Her eyes snapped open, and for a moment she wondered if she was dreaming. She lifted herself from the bed and gingerly stepped to the door.

Kat peeked her head in. "Heading to the Café for some eats. Wanna come?"

Elise exhaled. "No, thanks. I'm not hungry."

"Suit yourself, Shorty."

The front door closed, and she heard the click of Kat setting the lock. With the apartment to herself, Elise didn't know what to do. A pile of books on her desk sat as a constant reminder of the work she needed to do, but she wasn't in the mood to start anything yet. A tattered forest green notebook lay on the bottom of the pile and she immediately knew that was what she wanted. She pulled it out and settled back into the bed with the notebook on her lap.

The cover was worn and faded, the pages tattered. She reminded herself that someday soon she should transcribe this all into her laptop. For the past ten years, she'd kept this notebook of favorite quotations. Some were from famous people, others anonymous. Some were lines from novels or poems. But all of them had stopped her when she heard or read them and moved her enough to include them in her notebook. They read of love, loss, inspiration, and sorrow.

Her favorite had always been a quote from Scottish poet Alexander Smith: "Love is but the discovery of ourselves in others, and the delight in the recognition." She'd always assumed that the quote would one day make her think of a particular man. Maybe she'd even use it on her wedding invitations. She never thought it would make her think of a woman and most certainly not a twin she never knew she had.

But it did. Her fingers traced the swoops and curves of her handwriting. Did she love Hannah? Yes, of course she did. It was strange to love someone she had never met. One would assume that she loved her because it was like loving herself, but that wasn't it. Her sister hadn't been perfect. They were quite different from each other. But Hannah didn't have to prove anything to Elise. She didn't have to earn her love. Elise loved her merely because she had existed.

She sat up in bed and closed the notebook. She wasn't going

to hide from Abby like Parker. She was going to confront her. Now.

The setting sun melted orange across the horizon as Elise pulled into the parking lot. As she scanned the cars, her bravado shriveled, and she found herself hoping Abby wasn't home. But the silver BMW convertible she'd seen Abby zipping through campus in sat parked in front of the condo, dashing any hope that the meeting would be forcibly delayed.

Parker wanted to wait until Abby came to him. She had to know by now that the phone was his. But Elise couldn't wait. Now that she was committed to investigating Hannah's death, she didn't want anyone to slow her down, not even him. She marched to Abby's condo and banged her fist on the door. A shuffling came from inside and a moment later the door opened.

Abby grinned, her red hair tied back tightly in a ponytail. "Wow, I thought he'd have the balls to come himself. But to send his little minion? Cowardly, don't you think?"

Elise shrugged. "He didn't want to confront you. I did."

Abby tilted her head like a confused dog. "You must be pretty whipped to do his dirty work for him. Hmm, let's see." She tapped her finger on her lips in mock thought. "If a man is pussy-whipped, what does that make you? Cock-whipped?"

She took a moment to laugh at her own joke, then a grave look possessed her face. "Wait a minute." She pointed her finger accusingly. "You were here, too. That's why you came. Both of you were here."

Elise just smiled.

"I should have known. I thought I smelled skank when I came home last night."

Elise groaned, feigning impatience. "Are you going to let me in or what?"

"To give you back Parker's phone? Hell, no. I could have you arrested and thrown out of Wickman."

"Looks like we both have something to hide then." She paused for effect. "What were you paying my sister for once a month?"

Abby's mouth formed a giant "O" and she opened the door wide, casting a glance at the parking lot for eavesdroppers as she allowed Elise to enter.

Her confidence returned, Elise sauntered into the living room and made herself comfortable on a white high-back chair. "Where's Sasha?" she asked.

"She's out on a date." Abby stood a few feet away from her, refusing to sit. "Now, what's this bullshit about your dead sister?"

"I want to know why you were paying her once a month."

"I don't know what you're talking about. Have you been smoking some Miami hashish from your slut roommate?"

"I saw it in your check register." She took a chance. "I know she was blackmailing you. A grand once a month until she died—conveniently for you, I might add."

Abby threw herself into a chair. "What do you want? Have you come for your share, too? I'm not a freaking bank machine, you know."

"I don't need your money. I just want the truth."

Abby crossed her arms and looked up at the ceiling, obviously deciding how much to tell her. Elise took it up a notch. "I know you were at Dolan's the night she died."

Abby grimaced. "Robbie told you that, huh? Did he tell you that he fought with Hannah that night at Dolan's? No, he skipped that little tidbit, didn't he? He was obsessed with her. He got a little piece and wanted more, and she wasn't having any of it."

Elise ignored her and pushed on. "I have a theory. Want to hear it? You two fought at Dolan's that night, probably about the payments. You told her to come with you and you'd give her the money. You led her halfway across the bridge, then pushed her into the Drowning River."

Fear tightened Abby's features. "You think I killed her?"

"You didn't?"

"No! I hated her, but I would never kill anyone. You've got this all wrong." Her hands flew about in the air like frightened birds.

"What did she have on you?"

She pinched the bridge of her nose for a moment, then leaned back. "She found out somehow that I had purchased a midterm paper on the Internet. I'm not a cheater. I only did it that one time. She threatened to tell the administration. I would have been expelled, my family would have been humiliated. It would have hurt my father's career. So, I paid her off."

"Whose idea was it? The money?"

"Mine. She had no intention of blackmailing me; she wanted to hurt me. We never got along. She had something on me, something that would get me expelled, and before she went to the Dean, she wanted to see the pain on my face. I brought up the idea of payment and talked her into that."

"And fortunately for you, she died after only three payments."

"Yes, it was advantageous for me that she died, but I never wanted that. I just wanted her to leave me alone. I understand that you have this gut feeling that she was pushed. I'll admit the thought crossed my mind as well. But you're looking in the wrong places, girl." Abby cackled.

"That's interesting, considering that you're the only person I've found so far with a motive. Where do you think I should be looking?"

"Closer than you have been."

"What's that supposed to mean?"

"I wanted the payments to stop, but I wasn't willing to resort

155

to violence. I figured maybe I could get incriminating information on her and we could trade and call it even. I'd keep quiet about her if she'd keep quiet about me."

"Go on."

"She was a little whore, so I figured she was probably cheating on Gavin with someone, and all I had to do was follow her for a week and I'd find something to hold over her head."

"Did you?"

"She died the next week, so what little information I got ended up useless to me, but you might find it interesting now."

"Tell me."

Abby grinned, taking delight in winning control of the conversation. "One day that I followed her, I lost her in the student center. She just disappeared. Then, an hour later, I saw her in the hallway of the center talking with a guy. Intimately."

"Who?"

Her smile widened to reveal tiny polished teeth. "Parker Reilly."

Abby stood and smoothed her white blouse. "This calls for some wine. Would you like some?"

Elise shot her a look but stayed mute. Ghastly thoughts slithered through her mind. Abby returned after a minute, her wine glass filled to the brim.

"Maybe they were in a class together or something," Elise said.

Abby sipped slowly. "I checked that. They weren't."

"Did they kiss or embrace?"

"No."

"Did you hear what they were saying?"

Abby took a long swallow. "No."

"Then she may have been asking for directions, for all you know!"

"She was crying. This was not a run-of-the-mill conversation.

It was emotional."

"This is bullshit, you're just trying to take the spotlight off yourself."

"Has Parker told you what his relationship was with your sister?"

She swallowed hard. "He told me he didn't know her."

Abby downed the rest of her wine in salute to her victory. "Obviously he lied. If I were you, I'd look into why."

CHAPTER 21

Downtown Oceanside had old Colonial village charm. Small shops and restaurants lined both sides of the street. They were open year-round, except for the old-fashioned ice cream shop. Mama Rosie's was a casual Italian restaurant with checkerboard tablecloths and a menu with everything from pizza to fettuccini carbonara. After the meeting with Abby, Elise was starving and decided to head to Mama Rosie's alone, to clear her head and drown her sorrows in a never-ending bowl of pasta for $7.99.

She searched the street for a spot, but none were available, so she pulled her Civic into the lot behind the block. She'd have to walk around. She zipped up her red nylon jacket against the cool October air and strode down the narrow alley between two shops.

She didn't believe Abby. She was just trying to get the attention off herself with that bullshit about Parker. *Abby's the only one with a motive.* Elise repeated that silently like a mantra. The alley opened onto the sidewalk, and Elise was about to take a left to head to Mama Rosie's when she spied a police cruiser parked in front of her. She dropped back into the darkness of the alley and spied.

Gavin was in the driver's seat. A woman was in the passenger seat, but her head was turned away from Elise. She made fast and jerky hand movements. The rolled-up windows muffled the raised voices. The passenger door abruptly opened and the woman got out.

Faith. She wore jeans and a tight pink sweater that matched the hue of her face. Gavin slammed his door and came around to the other side.

Elise pushed back farther, the brick wall cool against the back of her neck. The streetlight illuminated the arguing couple in the dusk, and she felt sure that she couldn't be seen in the shadows of the alley.

Faith reached up and put her hands on his cheeks, pulling him down, trying to kiss him. He grabbed her arms and pushed her away.

"Give it up!" he yelled.

"I was good enough for you then, but not now, huh?" Faith's high voice screeched, on the verge of sobbing.

Gavin stormed into his cruiser and drove off. Faith's face crashed down into her hands as she walked away.

Elise stood glued to her spot, her appetite gone. Gavin and Faith had more than Hannah in common. They had a history. More likely than not, they'd had an affair.

Locals never visited the Sea Mist Lounge, the bar of the Sea Mist Hotel, the only hotel in Oceanside to stay open year-round. Only tourists and traveling businessmen sat in the round leather chairs, sipping overpriced drinks. A chandelier hung in the center of the room, and the bar and tables were trimmed in fake gold. The decor was supposed to look elegant, but instead reminded Elise of a cruise ship lounge: dated and tacky. She glanced around the room. Two men in loosened ties stared down their drinks at the bar, a couple of tables were full, but the place was mostly empty. Good. She needed to bend the ear of the bartender.

Kat had started working behind the bar of the Sea Mist three nights a week a couple of weeks ago. Tourists were scarce in the off-season, but the hotel was popular with traveling businessmen, and Kat was popular with them. The lower the v-neck, the higher the tips, she'd told Elise.

Elise sidled up to the bar and collapsed into a chair.

Kat placed a napkin in front of her. "What can I get you?"

"Nuts."

"Excuse me?"

"You know, those little wooden bowls filled with nuts that you give the customers? I want one of those. I'm starving."

"You have to order a drink to get one of those."

Elise groaned. "Fine. Corona with a lime."

"You haven't eaten dinner yet? It's eight o'clock. You're wasting away, girl. Do you have an eating disorder or something?"

"I tried to go eat, Mom, but I was interrupted."

Kat stuffed the lime into the beer bottle with her thumb. "By whom?"

"Gavin and Faith fighting. I think they had an affair."

Kat whistled. "The plot soup thickens."

Elise filled her in on the evening's events. First, her confrontation with Abby, then the fight witnessed between Faith and Gavin. Kat interrupted her twice to serve tired-looking men who smiled eagerly as she leaned over the bar to push drinks toward them. By the time Kat was done, so was Elise's beer, so Kat popped her open a second.

"Who do you believe, Parker or Abby?" Kat asked. "Sounds to me like she's trying to redirect you."

She nodded. "He has no reason to lie. She has every reason."

"Are you going to ask him about it?"

"Not yet. I just want to keep this to myself for a while."

Laughter erupted from a table of four older women. She raised an eyebrow.

Kat leaned close and whispered, "Some sort of quilters' convention this weekend. Those quilting ladies look like innocent old ninnies, but they toss 'em back better than the men in here. Not beer, either. They're drinking high balls, whiskey on the rocks, brandy straight up. Hard core."

"You know what I think is strange? I haven't heard from my stalker since the photo incident."

"Maybe he or she thinks you've stopped investigating."

"But I haven't stopped, and I haven't been hiding it. I've been out in the open, asking questions. It's like the person just disappeared or stopped watching me."

"That is strange."

"Maybe he's gearing up for something big. A harsh punishment for not listening." She shivered and knew it wasn't because she was positioned under an air vent.

"Don't think like that." Kat scooped up some tips left on the end of the bar, then returned to Elise. "What about Faith and Gavin? You have to get more information on that. That's a solid lead."

"Yeah. I think Faith's the one to go to on that. She obviously had some *Single White Female* thing going on with Hannah, and I think she seduced Gavin because she wanted everything Hannah had."

"Twisted," Kat said, drying a glass with a towel. Her eyes lit up. "You should let me question her."

"Why?"

"First off, I feel useless. Everyone else is helping you: Parker, Robbie, even Parker's dad in D.C. I haven't done anything. I'd like to help. Secondly, if she had some obsession with Hannah, she's not going to open up to her mirror image. I have my ways. I think I could get her to be honest with me."

Elise was flattered that Kat wanted to get involved. "Couldn't hurt to try. Go for it."

"Why did Hannah and Gavin break up?"

"I haven't found that out."

"Would Gavin have dumped her for Faith?"

Elise shook her head. "No way. That's what Faith wanted but never got."

"More likely that Hannah broke up with Gavin, then."

Elise nodded as she swigged the last of her beer.

Kat drummed the bar with her fingers, a sly, knowing smile spreading across her face. "And I wonder why she would have done that."

Kat steered Elise's car past the valet and into a parking spot. After making a call to Robbie in the morning, she had found out where Faith worked. He seemed to know everything about everyone. Armed with information, she put on her highest—and hence most intimidating—heels, borrowed the car, and headed out on her own. She was going to get some answers from this psycho-chick.

The Half Moon Yacht Club had a seasonal boating program and a year-round social program. Meaning that its members could stop by any time for a twelve-dollar salad and to circle-jerk each other with stock tips and tales of expensive purchases. Kat tossed a smile at the parking attendant who stood open-mouthed by the door, no doubt in approval of her snug crimson mini-dress.

A glossy mahogany plaque hung above the door with the club's motto: "To promote yachting and maintain a suitable clubhouse." She snorted at "suitable," knowing they didn't mean clean silverware. She wondered if she was the only Latina who had ever pushed these doors open without carrying a mop with her.

A large deck fronted the clubhouse, overlooking the harbor. Inside, fans circled on the vaulted ceilings, and the elegant tables were flanked by floor to ceiling windows on three sides. Eleven o'clock was an off-time to arrive, a little too early for lunch, and she had planned it that way. Only two tables had customers. She waited a minute at the hostess desk until a familiar face emerged from a small room marked OFFICE.

"Hi, Faith," Kat said with an exaggerated wave.

Faith paused and quickly regained her composure. She smiled politely, smoothing her white blouse and gray wool skirt. "Kat Herrera, right? What are you doing here?"

"Thought I'd buy you a drink during your break."

"Excuse me?"

"Can you take a break or do they work you to the bone here?" Kat knew Faith didn't need this job, didn't need money. She had her parents for that. She assumed Mommy and Daddy had forced her to take the job anyway. Perhaps they were members, or maybe they thought this would be an easy way for her to meet a proper young man. Either way, it would be insulting to someone like Faith to insinuate that she was working hard rather than lazily socializing in her upscale position as hostess of the club.

"Of course," Faith snapped. "I can take a break whenever I want."

So easy. "Let's have a seat, then. I'd like to chat."

Kat motioned to the table closest to the hostess desk and Faith followed, uneasiness spreading across her face as she sat.

During the drive to the club, Kat had pondered an opening to her interrogation. Should she start slow and turn aggressive? Play dumb? But as she looked at Faith's darting eyes, she knew the best way was the direct hit.

"So tell me, did Hannah break up with Gavin because she found out you were screwing him?"

Faith's gaze dropped to the table, and she busied her hands lining up the already straightened silverware. Bull's eye. Kat's instinct had been correct.

"How did she find out?" Kat asked.

"She found a note from me at his place," Faith replied in a

small voice.

"Convenient, huh?"

"I don't know what you mean," Faith said, fingering the strand of pearls around her neck.

Kat tossed her hair off her shoulders. "Come on, we're a lot alike, you and I. I've done those tricks before. Accidentally leave the panties under his bed where she'll find them. Call when you know she'll be there so you can hang up and arouse suspicion. Been there, girl." She winked conspiratorially.

Faith smiled weakly. "Yeah, I left the note where she'd find it. I didn't want to hurt her, but she had a right to know. I didn't want to tell her myself. So, I figured—"

"You'd take the coward's way out."

"Yeah." Her shoulders sagged. "I'm a horrible friend. The worst. I wish I could go back and change everything."

Kat upped the ante. "Gavin's been saying a lot of shit about you to Elise."

Faith's eyes widened. "Like what?"

"That you wanted to be just like Hannah, you copied her, you were obsessed with her, that's why you seduced him."

Faith banged her small fist on the table. "That asshole. He was always bitching at me to make sure I never told anyone. He never wanted this to get out. And now he's blabbing his trap to her."

"Is it true?"

She thought for a moment, and the anger faded from her eyes. "It's not as lurid as it sounds. I really loved him."

"You still do."

She nodded sadly, her hair a curtain of trembling curls.

"But he never loved you."

"Not yet. He may someday."

Kat inched closer to her. "Did you kill Hannah? To get her

out of the way? Thinking that maybe if she was gone, he'd love you?"

Faith's thin lips tightened. "That's ridiculous. I loved her. I was jealous of her, but I never wanted her dead. Her death wrecked me. I had to take a month off from school."

"What about Gavin? Could he have killed her?"

"I don't know. He was possessive of her." She rolled her eyes. "Obviously a double-standard since he cheated on her with me, but he was. And she's the only girl who ever dumped him." She spoke in a faraway voice, as if she were talking to herself and not Kat. "For a guy who always breaks the hearts, it must have cut to have his broken for the first time."

"Could he have done it?" Kat repeated.

She tilted her head, considering. "Maybe in a moment of passion." She waved her hand, shooing the nasty idea away. "No, he just couldn't. He didn't. She fell. She fell."

Faith's eyes teared up, and she used a royal blue cloth napkin to dab at the corners.

"No one's ever fallen from that bridge, Faith. Hannah would have been the first to fall. What are the chances of that?"

"Then she jumped. It's the only logical answer." She sniffled and refused to look Kat in the eye. "Could you leave now?"

Kat stood and bent over, her hair in Faith's face as she whispered in her ear. "You never for one moment believed that she jumped."

"Are you okay? Faith? Can I get you anything?"

Faith lifted her face from her hands and glanced up at Rosie, the only waitress on the clock this afternoon. Her dark skin and the sexy Hispanic lilt to her voice immediately reminded her of Kat.

"I'm fine, Rosie," she snapped. "Get back to work."

She couldn't have the help thinking that they were on the

same level. They weren't. She didn't need this job. The contents of her closet cost more than Rosie made in a year.

Rosie straightened and muttered something under her breath as she dashed away.

Faith craned her neck to look out the window and watched Kat drive away in Elise's car. Who did she think she was? Coming in here, not a member, and dressed like that. Then making all sorts of accusations. Gavin should have kept his mouth shut. She wondered what Elise was doing to him to draw all his secrets out.

Secrets. Faith was sick of them. The burden of them all sometimes made it hard to breathe. Everyone in this town had an agenda.

The door to the office opened, and he peeked his head out, furtively looking both ways, like he was some sort of gangster. Faith sighed and waved him out. She appreciated his heads up that Kat was coming, but never expected the interrogation she had been given. She didn't think Kat would know as much as she did.

The chair screeched as he pulled it out and dumped himself into it. "What did she want?"

"What do you think, Robbie? She knows."

His black glasses slipped down his nose, and he roughly pushed them up. "How much does she know?"

"Not everything."

"What did you tell her? You'd better not have said anything about—"

"Don't worry, I didn't say a word about you. You're safe for now. She doesn't know what we did. And neither does he. And for our sake, hopefully it will stay that way."

CHAPTER 22

Elise reclined on the bed and gazed around Kat's bedroom. Her white walls were covered with shirtless male Calvin Klein models pouting for the camera. A red and black South American tapestry hung loosely from the ceiling. A pile of the past week's outfits lay in a heap at the foot of the bed, including the red number she wore to the yacht club that day when she ambushed Faith.

Elise had been right. Faith and Gavin did sleep together. From what Kat found out, Faith was still hopelessly in love with him. Faith had hoped that when Gavin and Hannah broke up, he'd come rushing into her open arms. But that didn't happen. She must have been crushed. Was Faith crazy enough to take it to the next step and eliminate the competition? Elise closed her eyes and pictured Faith standing on the dark bridge, eyes like a lunatic's, pushing the unsuspecting Hannah to her death. She had trouble imagining it realistically. It couldn't have been Faith. Mentally, she was as balanced as the Atkins Diet, but that didn't mean she was a killer.

Elise fingered a French maid costume laid out on the bed, her fingernail catching in the lace trim. "You're really going to wear this to work?"

Kat stared in the mirror, her mouth a large "O" as she applied mascara to her already lush lashes. "Hell, yeah. It's Halloween, you prude. I'll garner a lottery winner's amount of tips tonight, babe. We're still going to the party after I get home, right?"

"Yeah, sure." Elise's track record at parties wasn't good, but she had to admit she was looking forward to tonight's Halloween bash.

Kat reached for the blush and put a heavy amount on her already well-defined cheekbones. "We could skip it if you wanted. We can wear masks, pretend we're tall twelve-year-olds, and trick-or-treat around town."

"That's okay. I can handle a party."

Kat caught her eyes in the mirror. "But can you handle Parker and Gavin? Word on the street is they're both going to be there."

"I'm just going to have a good time. I have no interest in either of them."

Kat turned to face her, her hands lost in her hair, manipulating the strands into a twist. "Are you still upset about what happened the last time you kissed Parker?"

Elise rolled her eyes to the ceiling, not wanting to relive that scene at the moment.

At her silence, Kat returned to the mirror, slid a shade of hooker red lipstick across her full lips, and smacked them together. "You know what would be the best way to get back at him? Kiss Gavin. Right in front of him. Sometimes guys need to be reminded that you aren't twiddling your thumbs waiting for them to come to their senses. Sometimes they need a little poke in the ego."

Gavin idled in his cruiser a block away from the man he was staking out. It was a personal mission, but he had an eye out for speeders at the same time to justify his position. He bent back the white plastic top on a coffee cup and took a sip. Still too hot, it burned the roof of his mouth, and Gavin winced at the pain.

Normally he kept away from college parties. He didn't go to Wickman anymore and felt above it all—the nasty keg beer, the crowded apartments, the drunken masses. But he had a good reason to attend tonight's shindig: Elise Moloney. Tonight, they would take the next step. He'd been patient, called her a couple of times, but she always brushed him off. That was harder to do in person. He knew from experience. Women melted under his touch. Charisma alone usually worked for him, but tonight he had another trick up his sleeve.

He tipped his cup and took a slow sip, the coffee now pleasantly warm. He straightened in his seat as the door he was watching opened. Parker Reilly stumbled out clutching a large bag and strutted to his Jeep, a goofy smile on his face. Cocky bastard, Gavin thought. He thinks Elise has it for him. Not after tonight, pal.

The Jeep pulled out of the parking lot, and Gavin guided his cruiser in. He swaggered up to the glass door and entered the store. Charisma on.

"What are you anyway? A weimaraner?"

"What? I'm a cat."

"Oh, I get it," Kat said. "You wanted to be me for a night. Flattering."

Elise groaned and nudged her into the party. They arrived fashionably late. They couldn't blame the commute since the party was in Bourne Hall, but their lack of punctuality was truly Kat's fault. She insisted on going to the store first to buy a feather duster to bring as a prop. Before Elise could take a deep breath, Kat was gone, off feather-tickling men on her way to the keg.

The hosts had gone all out—cobwebs strung from the light

fixtures, orange food coloring in the beer, a jack-o-lantern in every window. An alien ambled up, handing Elise a cup full of orange beer in his outstretched three-fingered hand.

"What are you supposed to be, a mouse?" the alien asked in Robbie's familiar nasal tone.

"Cat."

"She's in the kitchen."

"No, I'm a cat."

"No, your whiskers are too short, you're a mouse."

"I know what I'm supposed to be, Robbie!"

The alien shrugged and moved on.

Elise was thankful that it was a costume party because this was Brittany's apartment. The last time they'd crossed paths, she'd been doing her best green-eyed monster impersonation, and elbowed the poor girl away from Parker. She may have even used her nails; she couldn't remember. Hopefully Brittany wouldn't recognize her in her cat/mouse/weimaraner costume and kick her ass out of the apartment.

Brittany was already loaded and dancing on the coffee table, fully immersing herself in the persona of her costume, a hooker. No doubt she had high hopes for some role-playing with Parker.

Elise backed up to the closest wall and nonchalantly slipped one hand behind her so she could pick her wedgie in private. If her gray leotard was going to creep up her ass every five minutes, this was going to be a long night.

After several minutes of people-watching, the French maid dusted her way back to Elise. "I'm heading to the keg. Want a refill?"

"No, I've got to pace myself. I have a self-imposed two-beer maximum tonight."

Kat rolled her eyes. She'd been doing so much eye-rolling lately, Elise worried she'd give herself a seizure. But all the eye-rolling, chicken-clucking, and forced yawning in the world wouldn't make Elise break her two-beer rule tonight. Not after her last party performance. Forcing her tongue down Parker's throat and then being rejected by him was as close to a kick in the balls as she'd ever feel, being testically challenged. Her heart couldn't take that again. So, in addition to the two-beer rule, she had another: no kissing anyone. Whatsoever.

"Okay, Hillary," Kat said with a teasing smile.

She desperately didn't want to take the bait, but couldn't resist. "What's with the Hillary?"

"Parker's here as Bill Clinton. Mask and all." She tickled Elise's whiskers. "I know that turns you on. I saw you reading Bill's book. That baby was a thousand pages, there's no way you'd read it if you weren't hot for him."

"Oh, for God's sake, Kat!"

"What? There's nothing wrong with it. I'd do him. Embrace your crush."

Elise pointed to a crowded corner of the living room. "Isn't that Biology Boy?"

"Where?" Kat turned, and Elise grabbed her opportunity to escape, mixing with witches and hobbits in the kitchen.

She wanted to find Parker, but in a crowded party the short girls are the first to get lost. She stood on her tiptoes and peeked over shoulders. She glimpsed Bill Clinton heading from the bathroom to the living room and followed him down the hall. Squeezing herself between a six-foot condom and a doctor with fake guts glued to his scrubs, she got stuck. She wiggled and writhed until someone caught her arm and pulled her out from behind.

Relieved, she threw her arms around her savior's neck, then pulled back, pleasantly surprised at who it was. "Good evening, Mr. President. I thought I saw you in the living room."

President Clinton shrugged and titled his head, motioning

toward one of the bedrooms. He took her by the elbow and guided her down the hall, then took a quick left into a darkened bedroom, closing the door behind him.

Before she knew what was happening, he pressed her up against the wall. Her fingers curled over his suit jacket. His fingertip swept along her jaw line and down her neck, making goose bumps rise on her flesh. She tried to lift the mask up, but he grabbed her wrist hard and held her arms down at her sides. All she could see were two full lips in the mouth opening of the mask and the darkness of the eyeholes. He leaned harder against her body and kissed her. His mouth was hungry, insistent. More aggressive than she imagined Parker would kiss her, but she lost herself in the moment anyway. His hands were tight on her waist, then slid down her hips. The kiss grew deeper and hotter until someone coughed behind them, shattering the moment. She hadn't even heard the door open. She turned around, ready to perform several organ extractions on whoever it was.

Parker stood glaring at her, his Bill Clinton mask in his hand.

She turned back to her Bill as he lifted his identical mask off his face. Gavin smiled, both in delight and victory. She did her best not to crumple to the floor, her knees buckling only momentarily. Pride straightened her back, not allowing her to show disappointment. She didn't want Parker to know she had thought and hoped her make-out session was with him.

Caught in a moment she didn't want to face, she did what she did best. Ran.

"I need a drink," she said, heading to the keg for her second and last beer of the night.

CHAPTER 23

Fog slithered in from the sea and smothered East Street, as thick clouds obscured the Sunday midday sun. The threatening gray sky kept most people home, but Elise had to run. It had been three days since the last time, and the unused energy built up inside her, and her muscles ached for release. Her sneakers pounded the pavement, giving her body what it wanted.

Another party, another fool of herself made. She stuck to her two-beer rule, but the no-kissing statute was shattered by her lusty kiss with Gavin. Part of her was pissed that Parker saw it, but another part—that had developed as a by-product of too much Kat time—was delighted because of the flash of jealousy on his face.

She spent the rest of the party in hiding, from Brittany and both Bill Clintons. She breathed a sigh of relief when Kat said she wanted to go home. The next time a party came around, Elise might go with a mouthguard on.

She had her rhythm now, her legs pumping almost effort-lessly as she ran past homes and storefronts, most of them still displaying Halloween decorations in their windows and pumpkins on their stoops. The buildings ended, but the road stretched on, and she followed it through the mist to the beach parking lot. Five cars were parked, probably fishermen or beach joggers. Other than that, she was alone.

Since the night she'd followed the strange person—she had named him the "lanky man" in her mind—to the marsh, she had only jogged during the day. Just in case.

She'd always felt safe, until now.

She stopped at the base of the bridge, feeling watched. Hunted. The Drowning River was hidden in fog, the sounds of rushing water the only hint that it was there at all. Her usual run took her across the bridge, through the dunes, and down the beach. She wanted to keep going, not let jittery nerves get the best of her, but her heart wouldn't let her. It pumped wildly, a primitive reaction to danger. She closed her eyes, willing herself to remain calm.

Fine, she thought, *I'll follow my instinct and go home.* She spun around.

A man stood one hundred feet away, unmoving, openly staring at her. He was in his late forties, short but wide, with a shaved head. His gut hung over his belt, pushing his pants unnaturally low.

The hairs on the back of her neck stiffened to attention, and she shivered as if ice water had trickled down her spine. The man strode purposefully toward her, eyes focused on her face. He held no weapon in his hands, but one fist was clenched.

She wanted to run, but her feet were rooted to the asphalt. She reasoned with herself. He wasn't going to hurt her. Not out in the open, in daylight. Anyone could see. Her eyes glanced around the parking lot. No one was around.

He picked up speed as he neared, and in a swift movement grabbed her forearm. She yelped as he squeezed her wrist.

"I warned you," he said, his face close to hers, his breath rancid. "This is your fault."

He pried open her hand and shoved something hard into it. "Close your eyes," he said.

She complied, fear's grip a vice on her body. She heard his footsteps retreating on the sandy pavement, and kept her eyes closed until she couldn't hear him anymore. Then she opened them and twirled in a 360, searching for anyone to help her.

She was alone. The man was gone.

She looked down at her arm, still outstretched, her fingers clasped over the object he had given her. She opened her hand and gasped.

No, it's a copy. It's someone else's. This doesn't mean what I think it means.

She turned the watch over and read the engraving.

To Mom: Love Always, Elise

Elise bolted back down East Street, toward campus, searching both sides of the street for the man with the shaved head. People passed her, slipping in and out of stores, and paid no attention to her panicked face and ragged breathing. She collapsed onto a rock wall lining the front yard of an old Cape-style home and ripped into her fanny pack, her fingers searching for the cylindrical shape her lungs needed.

She puffed on the inhaler and breathed deeply for thirty seconds, then ran again. She burst into Bourne Hall, her calf muscles throbbing as she bounded up the stairs and into her apartment.

"Kat! Kat!"

Silence greeted her. Dropping to the floor with the cordless phone in her hand, she pounded the numbers on the dial. After an interminable silence, it rang. Her mother had to be home. They would have come home from church hours ago, maybe run a couple errands. Dad would be at the Bowl-a-Drome. Mom would be puttering around the house, watching TV, reading, doing laundry. She saw this in her mind's eye, the Sunday ritual her parents had kept her entire life.

It rang again. And again. Until the answering machine picked up, and helpless tears streamed from Elise's eyes.

★ ★ ★ ★ ★

He steered the car around a tight bend past a breathtaking view of the ocean, then pulled onto Route 6A. He glanced at the clock on his car radio. He had two hours to get to Logan Airport. No problem. His morning appointment had been in Quincy, an hour away, but this little sojourn was worth the effort of driving down here. And swinging by Hingham was not an issue since it was right on the way.

That look on her face was priceless. If he wasn't busy driving, he'd reach around and pat himself on the back. Nothing's more important than protecting family. He'd do whatever it took.

Pulling onto Route 3 North, he flipped open his cell phone and hit the memory dial. A voice quickly picked up the other end.

He recalled his morning adventure to the voice, expecting praise. He didn't get it.

"Why are you breaking my balls?" he whined. "I thought this would make you happy. The little threats didn't stop her, so I had to step it up."

He listened for a moment, pulling the phone away from his ear when the voice got loud.

"Yeah, she saw my face, but who cares? She'll never see me again. I don't live here, remember? Stop being a paranoid jackass."

He slammed the cell phone shut and tossed it on the seat.

"Damn it!"

Someone asks for your help, you give it, and this is what you get. Next time, he'd leave the dirty work to others.

Dread formed a heavy knot in Elise's stomach. Her vision blurry, she wiped tears from her face with the palm of her hand. The line of cars on the exit ramp advanced too fast, and she slammed on the brakes, filling the air with the smell of burnt rubber.

The man's words resounded in her head. *This is your fault. I warned you.* Her mother's watch felt heavy in her pocket, weighing her down with its implied guilt. She pictured her mother's trusting smile as the man approached her. Her eyes widening, not understanding. The man grinning, raising an arm above his head . . .

She forced the train of thought away, not wanting to imagine the possibilities, and focused on the road. Narrow and winding, it had double lines and a thirty mph speed limit, but now that she was minutes from home, she drove even faster. She passed an elderly couple in a Buick and swung a right onto Bluebird, her parents' yellow colonial looming with uncertainty at the end of the road.

The driveway was empty.

Ed had a Sunday bowling league, so his car wasn't expected. But Marie was always home on Sunday afternoons. She ran errands after church in the morning and spent the afternoon doing housework or relaxing.

Elise's muscles turned to stone, her neck stiff and aching with tension. She closed her car door quietly and approached the house. The front door was unlocked. Her mother would never have left it unlocked if she wasn't home, but her car wasn't here.

The living room was decorated in Americana. The colonial flag framed on one wall, its thirteen stars faded. The new flag on the opposite wall, bright red and white. Boyd's Bears—her mother's obsession—littered corners and tabletops.

"Mom?" Her voice came out small and unsure, like a punished child. She cleared her throat as she crossed into the kitchen and tried again, louder. "Mom!"

Movement pulled her eyes to the right, and she stared at the sliding glass doors that led to the backyard. The late afternoon sun reflected off the glass, blinding her, but what she had seen wasn't a trick of light. It was the absence of light.

Someone had walked past the door. Someone was in the backyard.

A cool gust of wind hissed at her face as she gingerly stepped outside and slid the door closed behind her. A noise came from the west of the yard, around the side of the house. She looked for a weapon, found nothing but a brittle stick, then remembered her car keys. She angled the largest key between her index and middle finger, poised to remove an eye if necessary.

The smell of new mulch in the bushes nearly suffocated her as she crept down the yard, hugging the side of the house. She reached the corner, stopped and listened. Something or someone was definitely there, a few feet away. The sound was familiar, but she couldn't place it at first. Then it hit her.

Digging.

Someone was digging.

It was an animal, she told herself. A dog burying a bone.

The sound stopped. It was suddenly quiet, too quiet. She clutched the key tightly, took a deep breath, and jumped around the corner.

A scream shattered the silence and Elise shrieked back in turn.

"You scared the shit out of me!" Marie yelled, her hand on her heart.

Elise didn't know what shocked her more: that it was her mother creeping around the yard, obviously safe and unharmed, or that her mother had said the word "shit."

"I'm sorry, Mom. I didn't mean to scare you."

The color returning to her face, Marie pushed herself off the ground where she had been kneeling, surrounded by gardening tools. "What in the daisies were you doing jumping out at me like that?"

"I didn't know it was you. Your car isn't in the driveway, and I saw someone creeping around the backyard and figured it was a prowler."

"I'm fifty-five, sweetheart. What you see as creeping is me, speed-walking." She sighed, dusting off her jeans. "You've been watching too much TV. No more karate jumps at your old mother, okay?"

Elise pulled her in and hugged her tightly. She smelled of dirt and perfume.

Marie pulled back. "Are you okay? What are you doing here?"

"I missed you, that's all. I thought I'd surprise you, come home for Sunday dinner. I didn't mean to scare you."

Marie patted her face. "I'm glad you're home. You're too skinny. A home-cooked meal will do you good. I'm sorry I yelled like that before, but I think you took a year off my life."

Inside, Elise sank into an overstuffed flowered couch and focused on stilling her trembling hands while Marie changed her clothes upstairs. She returned with fresh clothes and two cups of tea. Marie had never really accepted the fact that her daughter hated her tea, but today Elise decided to humor her and drink it.

"Where is your car, anyway?" she asked with forced nonchalance.

"I've had the worst day," Marie said, settling beside her. "I came out of the nursery with a new bush I wanted to plant, and my car battery was dead. Daddy was already at the bowling alley, and we don't have a cell phone yet. He still insists they should only be for doctors and important people." She rolled her eyes. "But anyhow, luckily a man parked beside me helped me out."

"How did he help?"

"First he tried to jump the battery. I have no idea what to do with all those cords, but he knew. It wouldn't work though. Dead as roadkill, it was. He gave me a ride down the road to a station, and they towed the car and drove me home. I'll get the car back with a brand new battery tomorrow."

Guilt passed over her face. "Unfortunately, I think I lost my watch along the way. I'm so sad because you bought me that years ago, and I loved it. I never had it serviced, and I should have because now look. The clasp probably broke. Maybe in that man's car, but I didn't get his name."

The watch felt like a lava rock in Elise's pocket, heavy and burning. She considered giving it to her, letting the truth spill out of her like water over the falls. She would someday, but not now.

She wanted to chastise her mother for getting in a car with a strange man. Wanted to ask her what he looked like. But Marie was a smart woman, and she'd get suspicious. Plus, Elise already knew exactly what had happened, knew what the man looked like, what his breath smelled like. The only thing she didn't know was his name.

CHAPTER 24

The dispatcher had big blond hair, black at the roots, and held up a finger in the air as she spoke into her headpiece. The nail polish was brown with an intricately painted pumpkin on each tip.

"Have you tried talking to your neighbor yourself, Mrs. Cutler?"

She nodded, as if Mrs. Cutler could see through the phone line. "The noise ordinance starts at ten P.M. If the music is still too loud in thirty minutes, call back, and we'll send an officer over there."

She blew a bubble with her gum while listening, then sucked it back in. "Uh-huh. You're welcome, Mrs. Cutler."

She slid open the glass divider. "Thanks for waiting. How can I help you?"

"I'd like to speak with Gavin Shaw, please," Elise said, her voice calm after the hour drive back to Oceanside.

The dispatcher snapped her gum. "Officer Shaw is out on patrol."

"Can you radio him in? I really need to speak with him."

A door behind her opened, and a low, hard voice said, "I'll take care of this, Bonnie."

"Thanks, Chief," Bonnie said, sliding the glass divider closed.

Elise turned around and faced the Chief of Police. If she hadn't known he was Gavin's father, she never would have guessed. They shared the same build—tall, muscular, broad-shouldered, but Gavin's heart-stirring good looks must have come from his mother. Chief Shaw's skin was pockmarked, and his large, gray, plastic-framed eyeglasses had been in fashion when she wore legwarmers, color coordinated with her Jordache pocketbook, of course.

"Miss Moloney, is it?" The tenor of his voice demanded respect.

"Yes, sir. I'd like to speak with your son."

"Want to cause more trouble, is that it?"

"No, sir."

He narrowed his indignant eyes. "You made quite the scene the last time you were here. Outrageous accusations."

"I don't want to cause trouble. I need help."

His face didn't soften, but his voice did. "Come to my office."

She followed him through a door, past the rows of desks where she had incited fury in Officer Lisa Federico, and into a corner office. The blinds in the two tall windows were raised, and light from a streetlight cast an orange glow across his face as he sat behind his desk, reminding her of a carved pumpkin lit from a candle within.

He motioned for her to sit. "What do you need help with?"

"A man has been following me, harassing me, threatening my parents' lives."

He pulled a notepad and pen from his drawer. "What's his name?"

"I don't know."

"Shouldn't this be handled by the Wickman campus police?"

"He's not a student. He's older, late forties."

"Wickman accepts students of all ages, no? Graduate students especially could be in their forties."

"True, but I don't think he's a student."

"Do you know anything about him at all?"

"No, just that he wants me to stop investigating my sister's death."

He capped the pen and laid it down on the blank notepad. "I have the solution to your problem."

She leaned forward, delighted that she was finally getting somewhere. Chief Shaw could put a tail on her, and they could track down the guy, catch him in the act of watching her, charge him with . . . what? Stalking, maybe.

"All you need to do," he said, "is tell him the case is closed and has been for quite some time. There is no investigation."

She blushed at her foolishness, thinking he was going to help her. "Chief, with all due respect, this could be the guy who killed her."

"Didn't your mother ever read you the story about the boy who cried wolf?"

"You think I'm making this up?"

"I think you're mentally unbalanced. I think something inside you snapped when you found out you had a twin who died. I think you want her to be more than she was, and a stupid, drunken accident is beneath this facade of a person you created in your mind. She was a real person. She had faults, many of them, and she got drunk and fell, maybe even jumped. End of story."

"You're not going to look into this at all?"

He groaned and looked up at the ceiling. "Has this man ever talked to you or do you just think he's stalking you?"

"He talked to me on East Street this morning."

"Okay, then, bring me a witness."

"No one saw."

"On East Street on a Sunday?" He threw his head back in laughter.

"It was in the parking lot, past the shops!"

"Miss Moloney—"

183

"What about my mother? She saw him. He took her watch."

"Where did this happen?"

"Hingham."

"Did she file a report with the Hingham P.D.?"

"No, but—"

"Miss Moloney, I'm afraid you're through wasting my time for the evening." He pointed to the door. "I assume you can show yourself out without causing a ruckus?"

Her mouth gaped open. She was furious, yearning for a biting retort, but the words wouldn't come. She rose and tore open the door, letting it bang against the wall.

Footsteps shuffled away as she stepped into the corridor. She recognized the officer even as she hurried in the other direction, her back to Elise. She wondered how long Officer Federico had been standing at the door, how much she had heard, and why she had bothered to listen at all.

The week passed in a shuffle of classes and books. Midterms were next week, and Elise felt the pressure on her chest like high altitude. She told Kat and Parker everything that happened on Sunday. Kat told her she should back off, stop investigating. Parker stayed silent. She had expected him to pressure her, to show up at her door with some lead he wanted her to follow, but he was unusually quiet. They studied together a couple of times in the week, and he remained focused on his work, stealing glances at her and quickly looking away when caught. She felt like he had a sudden secret, something he was keeping from her, yet always tempted to tell.

Elise hadn't said Hannah's name in days, but she was never far from her thoughts, always in the background, hovering like a ghost over her shoulder. She was there now, as Elise hunched over a book from her Nineteenth Century Irish Novel course. She didn't trust herself to study in her bedroom; she was too tired. So she spread her work across the coffee table and read on the couch, a two-liter of liquid caffeine within arm's reach on the floor.

The door to Kat's bedroom opened, and Elise glanced up. Kat was bent over, lacing up a black leather boot, her face hidden by a veil of black hair. She straightened, tossing her hair back, a tan flash of thigh visible where her black mini-skirt met her thigh-high boots.

"You look like a dominatrix," Elise muttered, reaching down for a swig of her soda.

Kat's face lightened. "Thanks! Just the look I was going for."

Elise swallowed the fizzy soda, begging the caffeine to work quickly. She glanced at her watch. "It's eleven o'clock. Where are you going?"

"Grand opening of a new club in Hyannis. A few of us are going to blow off some midterm steam. Wanna join? It's Friday night. Come on."

She shook her head. "No, too much to do."

Kat crossed the room and peered out the window. "Plus, I can't study anymore tonight. The wind is wigging me out."

"The wind?"

She flicked the window with her fingernail. "Yeah, these old windowpanes rattle every time the wind gusts, and it freaks me out."

Elise snorted. "And you think I'm a wimp?"

"It's not my fault. I blame Stephen King. I read *Salem's Lot* when I was twelve and never fully recovered. Anytime a windowpane makes the slightest sound, my first assumption is that Ralphie Glick is there, scratching at the glass, begging me to let him in." She checked her reflection in the glass, pulling her hair to the side. "Stupid Stephen King. I should sue his ass. How can you quantify lost sleep into a dollar amount?"

A car horn beeped twice.

"Please tell me that's your ride," Elise said, her hands together in prayer.

Kat peeked out the window. "Yep, it's for me. You're free to return to geekdom now." She patted Elise on the head and locked the door on her way out.

The apartment was silent before, but knowing Kat was studying in the bedroom gave Elise a safe feeling. Now that Kat was gone, the silence moved in like fog off the water. She shivered and pulled the afghan off the back of the sofa, covering her legs. She opened her book again and reread the same passage three times before the words melted and the room went to black.

Elise woke with a start, a sound in the apartment ripping her from the confusing images of a dream. Hannah floating down the Drowning River, her lifeless green eyes open to the sky. Then her mind cut to the shack where she thought she had trapped the lanky man that night when she met Gavin for the first time. Then she floated over the shack and into the marsh. Seagulls circled her, crying, louder and louder. One swooped at her with a screech, and that's when she bolted awake.

She pulled the blanket off her legs and squinted in the dim light. Did she really hear something or was it just the cry of the seagull in her dream? She had been jumpier than normal this week, since the shaved-headed man approached her with her mother's watch clasped in his sweaty, pudgy hand. She held her breath and listened to the air, wondering if the noise would come again. The fridge growled to life, startling her in the silence.

The wind picked up, and it rattled the windowpane as if an unseen hand tap-tapped from outside, suspended in midair. Annoying Kat and her Ralphie Glick bullshit. Because of her, she was sitting here thinking about little boy vampires. She had something real to be frightened of.

She rose from the sofa and double-checked that the door was locked. Darkness reached out toward her from both bedrooms, and she rushed through the job, turning on lights, checking both rooms and the bath.

Nothing. It was that crazy dream with the Hitchcock birds, that's all.

Returning to the couch, she gazed down at her pile of books and felt lonely. Maybe she should have gone with Kat. The clock on the cable box read 11:45. She wondered if Parker was home. She suddenly needed the presence of another person like she needed oxygen in her blood.

She combed her hair, tossed some books in her backpack, and headed upstairs. She knocked lightly, in case he was asleep, but within seconds the door opened, revealing a room filled with the blue light of the television.

"What's going on?" she asked, feeling foolish for showing up at nearly midnight.

Parker yawned and scratched at the blond stubble on his chin. His hair was cutely mussed. "Robbie went out. I wasn't in the mood."

She nodded. "Me, too. Can I hang out here for a while?" She held up her backpack. "I have my books. If you're busy, I can sit and do my work. I was a little nervous alone downstairs."

He opened the door wide. "Yeah, come on in. I was just lounging and watching TV."

She followed him inside, letting her backpack slip off her shoulder to the rug. Some mindless reality show was on the television. Parker flounced back on the couch, but instead of joining him, she went to the window.

Leaning one hip on the sill, she gazed out at the night. After a few moments a car went by, then the sound of high-pitched laughter rose from the sidewalk. A couple walked hand-in-hand under the glow of the streetlight, heading back to the dorms after a night of drinking and flirting. A dull ache throbbed in her chest, and Nick floated into her mind. She wondered if she missed him or just missed being part of a couple. Two girls screeched on the reality show, their voices getting higher and more urgent.

"I don't know how you can watch this crap," she said and chuckled.

Male voices joined in on the argument. Something about dishes left in the sink and someone bringing home a whore.

She turned from the window and caught Parker staring at her. She expected his eyes to dart back to the screen, but they didn't. They remained on hers like a dare. For a moment, all her senses dulled. The light dimmed. The screams on the television were muffled as if from an apartment down the hall. The ground shifted beneath her trembling legs. She mentally begged him to look away, to sever the moment, because she didn't have the will to do it.

Mechanical music broke the spell.

She blinked quickly, wondering where the muted sounds were coming from, taking a few moments to realize it was her own cell phone, the eighties' song she had programmed as its ring.

Parker's eyes drifted to the floor as she answered.

"Hey, it's Gavin."

"Oh, hi." She felt a mixture of annoyance and relief.

"I just called your place and you weren't there so I figured I'd take a chance on your cell."

He paused as if waiting for her to tell him where she was.

"What's up?" she asked instead.

"I know that you've repeatedly turned me down for dates, and I just want to make clear that this is not a date I'm asking for. It's a favor."

"Go on." She cast a sideways glance at Parker who had turned the volume down on the television. Out of respect for her conversation or to listen in on it?

"My cousin is unexpectedly getting married next weekend. They've been engaged for a while, and the wedding was supposed to be this summer, but she's pregnant—unplanned—so the wedding has been moved up to next weekend instead. A quick job. It's a big family drama, but anyway, I'm stuck for a date and I have to bring someone or my family will think I'm gay. Please? I'm begging here."

She sincerely laughed at his predicament, but knew there were scores of other women he could ask. She didn't want to lead him on by going, but this was a good opportunity to ask him more questions, even check out his family. You never know what secrets you can unearth at a wedding after everyone's tossed back a few. And she had to admit that knowing the chief would be pissed to see her there with his son gave her a little tingle of joy.

He filled in the silence. "Please come with me, Elise. I'll owe you big time. You'll never pay a parking ticket in this town, I swear."

Please, Elise. The words drifted from her past, surfacing another memory where she wanted to say no but said yes. She could never refuse a begging man.

"Okay, I'll go with you."

He whooped in the background, and she pictured him dancing a little jig in his uniform. She held back a laugh. "I've got to go now. Talk to you later."

She flipped the phone closed and caught Parker's look. His arms were crossed and he frowned at her, his pale face flashing vibrant colors as a soda commercial reflected off his skin.

"Was that Gavin? Are you going on another date with him?"

She waved him off. "No, I've already turned him down a couple times for that. This is a favor. He has a last-minute wedding next weekend for his pregnant cousin and needs to bring someone."

"You agreed to go?" His words were controlled, smooth, but she felt the anger vibrate beneath them.

She nodded.

"How is that not a date?"

"It's just a favor." She turned back to the window. "Plus, who knows who else might be there. More people to question about Hannah, you know?"

She turned back to him, but his eyes stayed on the screen, refusing to look at her. He was obviously upset, but why? Was he concerned for her safety? Jealous? Both?

"I'm getting a drink," she said.

She dashed into the kitchen and helped herself to a glass of water. She wasn't in a confrontational mood, so rather than return to the living room, she hefted herself up onto the counter. The ice cubes clinked as she sipped from the glass, her legs dangling, her feet kicking like a toddler in a high chair.

Parker padded across the threadbare rug and onto the yellow linoleum of the kitchen floor. He leaned against the wall, in bare feet and faded jeans, his black t-shirt haphazardly tucked in on only one side, his eyes burning into her.

The uncomfortable moment from before the phone call returned.

Hoping to change the subject, she said, "I was thinking about the possibility that Faith had—"

"I don't want to talk about all that stuff."

Her instinct was to snap at him for rudely interrupting her, but something in his stare made her hold back. He wouldn't look away. She swallowed hard; her throat felt dry despite the water she just drank.

"What do you want to talk about then?" she said, her voice small.

He pushed himself off the wall and sauntered over to her. "You."

He placed his hands on the counter on each side of her, parted her legs with his hips, and leaned into her, their eyes at the same height. She was so used to looking up at him all the time that being at the same level made her feel confident and powerful. Her fingers lightly stroked the blond hairs on his arms, causing goose bumps to rise on his flesh.

He gently pulled her hair back, exposing her neck and kissed the arch where her shoulder rose to meet her throat, then moved his lips slowly up to her ear, across her jaw line, then pulled back. He gazed at her lips as if they were a delicacy and parted them with his thumb. Their lips and tongues met in a warm, wet, deep kiss. His hands moved to her hips, and he pulled her to meet him at the edge of the counter, where she felt his arousal and moaned.

In one swift motion, he lifted her off the counter. She wrapped her legs around his hips. He carried her to the bedroom like that, their mouths breaking apart only for gasping breaths. They fell to the bed in a tangle of arms and legs and pulled each other's clothes off, with no regard for buttons or seams. She lay bare and exposed on the bed, but felt no need to cover herself as she'd had in the past with others. He looked at her as one would stare at a priceless artifact or a famous painting seen in person for the first time.

She raked her fingernails down his chest, her nails tickling his stomach, and he moaned as she explored further. Then he lowered himself onto her, and the night was theirs.

Elise woke frightened that it was all a dream. Scared that she would open her eyes and find herself tangled in the afghan on the couch, surrounded by her books. She squeezed her eyes shut, unwilling to let the beautiful dream go, the memories of

Parker. The taste of his skin, the smell of his hair, the pressure of his hands on her body.

She desperately listened for the gentle rhythm of sleep breathing beside her, and when it wasn't there, she steeled herself for disappointment as her eyelids drifted open. Morning sun filtered through a two-inch space at the bottom of the shade, lighting up a room that wasn't hers. She recognized the disheveled desk and the plaid comforter immediately. It was real. She was in Parker's bed.

Grinning, she rolled to her left side, but she was alone in the bed. A note curled on Parker's pillow. She picked it up and squinted at it.

DON'T YOU DARE LEAVE. WE'LL HAVE BREAKFAST.

She smiled and clutched the note to her chest. Pipes groaned as the shower started. She flirted with the idea of joining him, but instead decided to get them a treat. She slid on her jeans and grabbed one of his t-shirts. She'd head to Dunkin' Donuts and grab them some fresh coffee and tasty treats. Something gooey and dipped in honey.

She was about to leave the room when she realized she'd better leave him a note. She rifled across his desktop looking for a pen, but found none, so she opened the top drawer.

Something caught her attention. At first it didn't register, but she knew something familiar was out of place, like running into someone from high school at college. Then her eyes focused on what it was. Her handwriting.

She pulled the object out of the drawer. It was a wallet-sized photo, her handwriting on the back, though she was sure she never gave Parker anything like this. She read the inscription:

I wanted to give you this picture and write something totally moving on the back. But I've sat here for an hour and can't put all my thoughts down. A million words could not express what you've done for me, so I'll choose one. Thanks.

Hannah.

With a trembling hand, she turned it over and looked into her sister's face. Coldness spread through her chest, squeezing her heart.

He lied. He did know her, and well.

Betrayal singed like a third-degree burn. Tears welled in Elise's eyes as she slid her apartment door closed with a quiet click. She didn't want to wake Kat, but at the same time she desperately needed to talk to her. Needed to tell her how alone she felt. She had been tricked, used. For what, she didn't understand. All she knew was that Parker had lied, and the weight of that lie felt like a rock on her chest.

Kat's door stood slightly open, a couple of inches, enough for Elise to peek and see if she was sleeping. She crept to the door and peered through the crack. The mirror on the wall opposite the bed showed Kat's reflection. She was sitting up, whispering furiously to someone. The form sat up beside her, the blanket falling from his shoulders. Elise held back a gasp.

Robbie.

His chest was bare, and she assumed he was completely naked beneath the blanket around his waist. Kat's exposed breasts swayed as she leaned in toward him, her finger pointing in his face.

She couldn't make out any of their muffled words, but the intensity of the conversation rose until Kat, in nearly a yell, clearly said one word louder than the rest.

"Hannah."

Elise reeled back from the door as if an unseen fist had punched her in the gut. She had never been a paranoid person, but now she felt the world closing in on her, whispers surrounding her. Everyone here had an agenda, secrets, lies to hide.

Tears flowed freely down her cheeks as she realized she had no one left to trust.

Steadying herself against a wall, she wished she could go back in time. To last year, to Providence, a happy place where she didn't know Hannah existed, didn't know Parker, Gavin, Kat, Robbie, Faith, Abby, or anyone else in this damned town. She was safe then. Comfortable and safe.

She slithered into her bedroom like a prowler, quietly slipping on fresh clothes and pulling her hair back into a ponytail. She slid her car keys off the desk and into her pocket, not knowing if this was the right thing to do, but feeling that she had no choice. Right now, there was only one person she wanted to see, and the urge filled her until she felt nothing else.

CHAPTER 25

Nick Carrano had proposed on Elise's twenty-second birthday, Valentine's Day. He had been quiet and introspective the entire week prior. She found him gazing at her when he thought she wasn't looking and anytime he wasn't doing that, he was staring at blank walls, floors, his hands. He was strangely nervous, and it made her anxious. She even wondered if he was seeing someone else.

The day before her birthday, he was gone all day and night. He didn't even call. His behavior was so strange that when he showed up at her apartment the next day, she assumed he was there to break up with her. On her birthday, like a bastard. But then he dropped down on one knee, and with a heartfelt speech she couldn't remember a word of now, he asked her to marry him. The ring was small but beautiful, and his eyes seemed so vulnerable. She was shocked, but relieved that his actions of the previous week all made sense now.

"Please, Elise," he begged. "Please make me the happiest man alive. Please be my wife."

She remembered feeling dizzy, shaking all over, looking into his eyes and knowing she didn't want to hurt him.

She said yes.

Now, in the parking lot of his old apartment building in Providence, she sat in her Civic feeling dizzy and shaken all over again, but this time she would be doing the begging. What she had done to him was awful. She left him a letter and the engagement ring and took off to Europe, never speaking to him again. Sure, she explained in the letter that she wasn't ready, she didn't feel like they were making the right decision, she needed space, she wasn't sure if she loved him. But she should have done it face-to-face. She closed her car door and stared up at the gray cement block that was his building. How could she think for a moment that he'd forgive her?

Approaching the door to apartment 202, her veins filled with fear. What if he hated her? Screamed at her? She stopped, ready to turn away, then forced herself to knock. She'd come all this way; it would be cowardly to turn back now. He might not even live here anymore anyway.

A shuffle of footsteps came from the apartment, and the door swung open. Nick stood, slack-jawed, color draining from his face. He was unshaven and his bushy brown hair needed a cut. His Patriots sweatshirt was stained and his jeans wrinkled.

In the shocked silence, the thought occurred to her that he might hit her. Instead, relief flooded his face.

"Is it really you?" he asked, his voice raspy.

She nodded, still feeling unsure.

"You're back," he breathed and pulled her into a tight embrace.

After a moment, she pulled back. "You don't hate me?"

He traced her face with his fingers. "How could I ever hate you? I love you. I've never loved anyone, but I love you. You can't just shut that off."

Tears of shame stung her eyes. "I was horrible to end it that way. Slime! Spineless, gelatinous slime. I came here because I wanted to ask if you could ever forgive me."

He smiled. "Already done."

They spent the day on the couch, talking, crying, hugging. She told him about Europe and Wickman, eventually explaining Hannah and everything she had been through the last two months. He seemed stunned by it all and dutifully rubbed her shoulders while she poured it all out, never interrupting her with questions. He seemed to instinctively know what she needed.

By the end of the day, she got exactly what she wanted. It felt like last year, comfortable and safe. They laughed at old stories and inside jokes, cuddled and stared at each other. He didn't excite her like Parker did, but she could trust Nick, and that made up for all the rest.

"Come back to Oceanside with me," she said.

His mouth opened in surprise. "I don't think that's a good idea."

"Why not? You could get an apartment there. We could start over."

He scratched at his disheveled mop of hair. "And my job?"

"You could get a new one. I'll be your sugar-momma until you find one." She tickled his side. "Come on."

He moved back from her, slightly. "Moving too fast is what caused all of this to happen, Elise. I'm not going to make that mistake again."

"But that was just me being frightened and stupid. I've changed. I'm not like that anymore. I want you there with me. You're the only one I trust, the only one who matters."

"I can't do it. I'm sorry. I want to start over with you, be a couple again, but we have to go slow for now. I'm not going to Oceanside with you."

She dropped her eyes to the hardwood floor. Of course he couldn't. She'd hurt him deeply; no wonder he was reluctant to give his heart to her completely. She trusted him, but he no longer trusted her. She needed to earn that again.

With one finger, he lifted her face up by her chin. "I have an idea, though. Spend the night with me."

She thought of all the work she didn't get done last night,

midterms coming up this week, but his eyes pleaded with her. It's the least she could do. Tomorrow was Sunday. She could lock herself away in the library and catch up then.

"Deal." They smiled at each other for a moment. Then she rose. "I'm heading to the kitchen for a drink, want anything?"

"No thanks."

The setting sun cast a red glow through the window and across the white and black tiles on the kitchen floor. The day had been so draining, she couldn't wait to crack open a cold beer and relax. She opened the fridge and remembered. Nick didn't drink. His father was an alcoholic, and Nick was always careful not to follow in his path. She always had the feeling that his father might have abused him, but Nick never spoke of it. It was just an undercurrent she felt whenever he spoke minimally of his family.

She settled for a soda, and as the carbonation tickled her throat, her eyes fell on the kitchen wall phone. She was wary of Kat after eavesdropping on her and Robbie this morning, but didn't want her to worry about her too much, or even call the police and report her as missing. She had no idea what Kat would think about her spontaneous trip to Providence and reunion with Nick. But as she picked up the green phone, she knew she was about to find out.

Parker locked the door behind him and descended the stairs, trying to hide the goofy grin he'd had all day. When school first started, all he could think about was Hannah and his plan. But now things were different. All he thought about was Elise. At first, she was just a vessel, something to get him what he wanted. Now, she was her own person to him.

He thought about the way she smiled, not suddenly like most people, but slowly, starting with her eyes, then spreading like a blaze as her cheeks lifted and the sides of her mouth turned up.

He thought of her voice and how sometimes she spoke so softly it was as if she were only talking to herself. About how timid she was at first, a little mouse, scared of everything, and now, she had this boundless courage, which shocked and impressed him.

He wondered why she disappeared in the morning without leaving a note. He assumed she'd come back, and he waited all day for her, not wanting to call or push her. The last thing he wanted now that he had her was to scare her away. But maybe this was some sort of test. He had to come to her or something. He'd play. He'd do anything she wanted.

He knocked on her door and Kat yelled out, "Who is it?"

"Parker!"

"Come on in, surfer boy!"

He found her in the kitchen cooking a stir-fry dinner, the smells making his stomach growl. She shook her hips as she stirred the food, hip-hop booming from the radio.

"Elise isn't here," she said, bobbing her head to the bass line.

"Where is she?" he yelled over the volume.

She kept her eyes on the wok, stirring the meat and vegetables with a wooden spoon. "Shouldn't you be studying?" she called over her shoulder. "Midterms start in two days, pal."

A chill came over him. Kat wasn't one to ignore questions. Something was going on. He put his hand on her shoulder and turned her around to face him.

"What are you hiding from me?"

Her mouth turned down like a doctor delivering bad news. "She went to Providence."

He shrugged. "So. For what?"

"To see Nick."

"Her ex? What, does she want to get back with him?"

"I have no idea. She acted very strange on the phone, like she

199

was mad at me. She's spending the night there. She'll be back tomorrow."

The room spun, and he didn't know if it was from the smoke of burning chicken or the pain throbbing in his head.

Kat turned away from him again, to salvage her meal. "Maybe she got sick of you leading her on." She threw one last glance at him. "You're too late, Parker."

Elise sat on a bench outside the graduate classroom building, feverishly reading through her notes, cramming every last fact she could fit in her brain for her first midterm, which started in ten minutes. She was terribly nervous, but not about the test. She had studied as hard as she could and felt that she had a handle on all the topics that would be covered. The reason her leg bounced with anxiety was not for the test, but for seeing Parker. She couldn't avoid him now; he was in the same class.

Worse, she realized as she glanced up from her notes. He was headed right for her.

He threw himself down on the bench beside her, anger distorting his features. "Where have you been?"

She kept her eyes on her notes. "Busy. Midterms, you know."

He yanked the notebook out of her hands, forcing her to look at him.

"The other night," she said, "was a mistake."

"Are you back together with Nick?"

She gazed at the stream of students filing past, the wind whipping their hair. "We're talking about it."

"Did you sleep with him?" He looked at her as if her answer could stop his heart from beating.

"No, I didn't," she said, and it was true. Nick wanted to, but she wasn't ready, didn't feel right about it so soon after sleeping with Parker. They literally slept together, side by side, but that was it.

She looked at Parker, his lips, his outstretched hands. She wanted him, wanted to fall into his arms and make love to him again. But he'd lied to her. She couldn't trust him.

"Did I do something wrong? Did we move too fast?"

She turned from him, gazing across the quad at dozens of other students cramming for the first day of midterms, biting their nails, bouncing their feet, tapping their pens in a strange orchestra of nerves. He put his hand on her shoulder, his touch sending warmth down her spine.

"We don't have to do that again," he continued. "We can take a step back, move slower."

"It's not that."

"You suddenly want to get back with him, then?"

"No, that's not it, either."

His cheeks flushed, and he threw up his hands in frustration. "Then what is it?"

"Don't yell at me!" she screamed back, rising from the bench and snatching her notebook from his fingers.

"I'm sorry. Just talk to me."

She shook her head and marched toward the classroom building. She closed herself off, like an animal retreating into its shell.

CHAPTER 26

Midterms were the perfect week to avoid people. It wasn't considered strange to lock yourself in your room for hours, disappear into the stacks of the library not to be seen until the next day, eat dinner at midnight, sleep in the afternoons after a test. Elise lost herself in her work all week, avoiding everyone, even Kat.

What she couldn't avoid was Hannah's ghost. The more she retreated into herself, the less she saw of other people, the more Hannah dominated her thoughts. Everywhere she went on campus, she glimpsed Hannah there last year. She imagined her in animated conversation at a booth in the Café, with her head bent over a book in the library, flirting with guys on the quad. Hannah had walked these same paths, opened these doors, sat at these tiny wooden desks staring at a chalkboard, just like her.

For the first time, the power of the coincidence stunned her. She wondered, for a moment, if it was a coincidence at all that she came to Wickman. What if, instead, Hannah had drawn her here? To find out about her, to solve her mystery? Elise shook her head at the silly thought.

"You disagree, Miss Moloney?" Professor Reed's voice boomed.

"Um, no, sorry, just"—she tapped at her forehead. "Inner thoughts. Forget it."

A few classmates giggled, and she sank down into the chair, wishing she could disappear. This had been the longest week of her life and now that it was Friday, she just wanted it to be over. Thankfully this, her last class, had no midterm exam. They turned in research papers instead. So she was done. The pressure was lifted, and now she wished Professor Reed would put them out of their misery and end the week.

Parker was in this class, too, the second class they shared, and she tried her best to ignore the feeling of eyes on the back of her head during the entire lecture.

"I'm passing out a new assignment. This is a group project." He handed stapled papers out to each student while his voiced rumbled on in monotone. "Read these pages and if you have any questions on the topic, see me after class or during office hours. I'm not going to pick your partners for you like you're children. Pick them yourselves."

Elise reached her hand out and touched the arm of the woman next to her, a quiet student about her age who always attended class and answered correctly when called upon.

"Want to be partners?" Elise whispered.

She nodded rapidly, and Elise got the feeling that she was delighted and relieved to be asked rather than put upon to do the asking herself. Elise glanced back at Parker. Hurt stained his face as he turned to talk to the guy next to him.

After class, her partner sidled up to her outside.

"Elise, right?"

"Yeah. Kimmy?"

"Cammy."

"Oh, sorry."

Cammy shrugged as if she'd heard it a thousand times. Her red curls were frizzy and out of control. When the wind picked up, it lifted her hair, reminding Elise of Medusa and her mane of snakes.

"This may sound completely dorky of me," Cammy said, "but do you want to go to the library now and get started on the project? Not too much, just go over it together, make sure we both understand it, and then maybe delegate some work for the weekend?"

Elise held back a groan. All she wanted was a break from schoolwork after this week of hell, but Cammy seemed so eager, and if she hid in the library for an hour, that was one less hour she had to face anyone else.

"Sure."

Minutes later they had a table in a private study room, and Cammy's eyes shot back and forth as she speed-read the assignment. She held a Walt Disney World pen in her hand. It was filled with water, and when she held it up Mickey Mouse floated down in his boat only to float the other way when tipped upside down.

"How did you get this room? I thought you had to reserve these."

"I already had it reserved," Cammy said, still reading. "I knew I'd want to get some work done this afternoon and I like studying alone, so I reserved it for myself." She looked up. "Handy, eh?"

"Yeah," Elise said, wishing they were at Dolan's instead.

Cammy laid the assignment down on the dark wood table. "I'll be honest with you." She wrapped a curl tightly around her index finger. "I'm just stressed because, not to brag, but I'm here on full scholarship. It's the only way I could afford a place like Wickman. But I have to keep a three-point-five GPA to keep the scholarship. So I get kind of stressed about classwork sometimes."

"Do you have the Harvey Wickman Memorial Scholarship?"

"Yeah," Cammy said, surprise widening her eyes.

"I do, too."

A smile lit up Cammy's face, and Elise guessed it was relief that Elise was a good student and she wouldn't be doing all the work on this project alone.

"They give out five each year to incoming graduate students, based on prior academic accomplishments. We must be two of the five for our year. I feel so lucky."

Elise smiled politely, wishing they could get on with the project. "Me, too. I knew I wanted to go to grad school, but the prospect of paying for it overwhelmed me. When I got the application in the mail, I figured I'd give it a try."

Confusion knit Cammy's red eyebrows. "What application?"

"The application for the Memorial Scholarship."

"You mean, after you requested it."

"No, it was just sent to me with the college brochure. You know how your name gets on all these mailing lists and every college from here to Timbuktu starts sending you junk."

Cammy studied her with suspicion. "Yeah, but they don't send out scholarship applications to everyone they send a brochure to. You have to request one, and you only bother doing that if you have the grades and the scores."

"That's strange. Maybe my test scores were sent to them or something."

Cammy frowned, and Mickey Mouse sank to the depths of her pen. "Yeah, maybe."

Elise bent over her knee, deftly painting the nail of her big toe with a pale pink hue as she cradled the cordless phone between her cheek and shoulder. Her baby blue terrycloth robe parted across her bare legs.

"It's not a date. I'm just doing the guy a favor by going to this wedding with him."

Nick sighed across a hundred miles of fiber-optic cable. "Sorry if I'm being an ass."

She smiled, and the phone nearly fell as her cheeks rose. "Nah, you're cute when you're jealous."

"I miss you. I could accept not seeing you all week because of midterms, but I really wanted to see you this weekend."

"Me too, but I can't cancel on Gavin, and tomorrow I have to meet with this girl from one of my classes to work on a group project. Next week, I'll head down to Providence. I promise."

"Okay, I'll let you finish getting ready. Don't make yourself look too beautiful. I love you."

"Love you, too." The words rolled easily off her tongue, even if she wasn't sure she meant them.

She hung up the phone and tossed it on her bed. Her toes twinkled up at her, sparkly and feminine. She dabbed the brush at her last toe, then replaced it in the bottle. She loved an excuse to dress up and waddled on the heels of her feet to her closet to choose one of her three formal dresses to wear. The black one was boring and conservative, more for a funeral than a wedding. The purple one was matronly and a couple years out of style. The red one was sexy, form-fitting, with a low scoop that revealed all of her back. She tugged it off the hanger and draped it across the bed.

"I don't think Nick would approve of you wearing that dress out with Gavin."

The voice startled her, and she clutched at her robe as she twirled around. Parker leaned against her desk with his arms crossed, his eyes taking her in from head to newly painted toes.

"What are you doing here?" she snapped.

He lifted himself up onto her desk and sat, his legs barely touching the ground. The position reminded her of sitting on his kitchen counter, her legs wrapped around his waist, her tongue lost in his mouth.

"Kat let me in. Am I not allowed to visit you anymore? We're not even friends?"

"I'm busy. I have to get ready for—"

"Your big date with Gavin. I remember."

She was about to remind him for the hundredth time that it wasn't a date, but decided not to waste the oxygen.

He jumped off the desk and in one swift move picked up a chair and maneuvered it under the doorknob. "No one's going in or out of this room until you tell me what happened. Why you suddenly changed your mind about me."

She rolled her eyes and glanced at the alarm clock on her nightstand.

"Yep, you're going to be late for the wedding unless you start talking. I deserve answers, Elise! Why did you sleep with me, then, with no explanation, leave me for Nick?"

A groan escaped her lips as she sat down on her bed. Her robe slipped off her shoulder, revealing the swell of her chest. She groped at it, roughly pulling it back up. "I'm not even decent. Can't we do this another time?"

"It's nothing I haven't already seen, remember?"

Embarrassment and anger flushed her cheeks, and she rocketed out of bed. "Fine, you want this? We'll do it now. You're a liar, that's why!"

He took a step back, stunned. "What?"

"I found the picture of Hannah in your desk drawer, read the inscription on the back." She rushed at him, pointing her finger at his chest. "You lied, asshole. You knew her."

Realization settled over his face, and she knew he hadn't expected this. He looked down at the floor, his face twisted in anguish.

"Yes, I knew her," he said, his eyes slowly lifting to meet hers. "Better than anyone else did."

Gavin turned the wheel for the sharp right onto August Road, a twisting wooded street that was mostly vacant and only served as a shortcut to avoid Route 6 on the way to his cousin Pete's house. Pete was the best man in the wedding and had all the tuxes corralled in his home. He was known in the family as a control freak, but Gavin never minded him. Out of his seventeen cousins, Pete was probably his favorite.

It was hard for Gavin to imagine being part of a small family. He had three siblings, one brother, two sisters. He was the baby of the family, and they all treated him like one, constantly trying to protect him and steer him in the direction they wanted. He could roll with it when he was younger, but now he was a man with his own life, and he resented the monologues of advice that dribbled off their tongues every time he saw them. He momentarily wished he had been an only child like Elise or Hannah. Then he stopped and nearly laughed out loud at his mistake. They were raised as only children, but unbeknownst to them, they were not. Even his huge, dysfunctional family was less complicated than that mess.

August Road ended in a stop sign, and he took a left onto Harvest and a quick right onto Glen Drive, slowing to a stop in front of Pete's house, a quaint cape style with clapboard siding and two dormers on the roof.

"Shit," he muttered, spying his father's truck in the driveway.

He was hoping to get there early and avoid him. The last thing he wanted right now was to listen to another diatribe from his dad about how Elise was more trouble than she was worth, blah, blah, blah. Gavin had spent his whole life trying to satisfy his father. First football, then Wickman, then joining the force. His father had made all his choices for him. This was where he drew the line, though. He wanted Elise Moloney, and no one was going to talk him out of it.

He grabbed his wallet off the passenger seat, but before he slid it into his pocket, he opened it and felt for the hard circle underneath the leather. He knew it was wishful thinking. Just getting Elise to agree to go to the wedding had been a feat of grand proportions; she wasn't going to put out tonight. But he was prepared if she changed her mind after a few drinks and slow dances.

He killed the engine and closed his eyes, savoring one last moment of quiet. He pictured Elise, her stunning beauty, her keen intelligence. She was stubborn, and in that way different from Hannah. The more he got to know her, the more he realized how separate the two of them were. His charm had worked quickly with Hannah. It was at the end when he couldn't hold onto her. He wished he could go back and change what happened. But there was no use in dwelling on that. Elise was like a second chance from God, an angel placed in his path. He wouldn't let this one float away.

Elise reached out one hand on her desk to steady herself from the shock of Parker's words. He knew her sister. Better than anyone else did.

Concerned, he pulled the chair from under the doorknob and gently eased her into it, kneeling beside her.

"Are you going to tell me the truth now?" she asked. "All of it?"

He nodded and took a deep breath before he began. "You know I was a psychology major here as an undergrad. Part of that degree requirement was to work a few hours a week at the counseling center. Answer the anonymous helpline, do paperwork, filing. Each year, two seniors are chosen to be peer counselors and take regular appointments from students. It's an honor, really, to be thought of that highly. That the department advisor thinks you can really help someone."

His eyes seemed far away, as if he were looking through the wall of her bedroom and into the past.

"I was chosen and I got a few, I guess you would call them clients, who would come to see me once a week for counseling. Hannah McPhee was one of my clients. She had been arrested for possession, and I think she felt bottomed out and wanted to turn her life around. So she started coming to see me once a week."

"What did you do?"

"Me? Not much. Listened, asked open-ended questions. She did all the work: introspection, talking it out, thinking, challenging herself. And she really did it. She turned her life around. It was an amazing metamorphosis to watch. To see a person at her lowest and watch her over time come to be the best she could be."

"So Gavin wasn't the reason her grades got better and she stopped the drinking, drugging, and promiscuity?"

"No, Gavin came shortly after she had already turned that corner. I think she thought of Gavin as her reward, because she felt that he was the type of guy she would never have been able to get before. But now her self-esteem was up, her confidence high, and she had a wholesome, successful boyfriend. She was truly happy."

She chewed on her lower lip to stop it from trembling. "Why didn't you tell me this from the beginning?"

"It's all confidential. I'm not allowed to mention anything about my clients. No names, no information at all. No one knows that I counseled Hannah. Not even Robbie. What I just did by telling you this broke the confidentiality agreement I signed with the counseling center. I broke an agreement with Hannah to tell you this."

He raked his fingers through his hair. "Besides, you never really needed to know. How does knowing this help you? It doesn't. It's not like it gives you any answers to what happened that night."

She closed her eyes, not wanting to ask the next question, scared of the answer. "Did you develop feelings for her?"

"Not romantic feelings, no. I was dating Abby the whole time

I counseled Hannah. I just wanted to help her. I felt a responsibility toward her."

The pieces began to fall into place. Snippets of conversation. Things about him she had pondered while trying to fall asleep at night. "Her death is the reason you quit psychology."

He nodded. "I failed her. My first patient was dead. That told me that I wasn't fit for that line of work."

"Did she see you right up until the end?"

"Yes. She was very vague at our last meeting. She said she and Gavin were over, but didn't want to talk about why. She had always spoken so openly to me, but was shut off that day, only touching upon the subjects she wanted to and ignoring the others."

"Was she depressed?"

"No, and that's why I couldn't easily accept suicide as the answer. Something was troubling her, and she had been through a breakup, but she seemed strangely optimistic at the same time. She told me she had something new to live for, something she never expected."

His eyes met Elise's, and she felt his heart reaching out to her. "I prodded her, and she told me that she found out she had a twin sister. All she needed now was to find her. Then she died."

Elise straightened in her seat, understanding now. "And you couldn't accept that."

His hands waved in the air as his face reddened with conviction. "The authorities were useless. Everyone here forgot about her after two weeks. But it made no sense. Yeah, she was drunk, but after everything she'd been through and so much to look forward to, she wouldn't have just thrown it all away by falling or jumping off the bridge."

Elise swallowed hard. "Mighty coincidence, me happening to come to Wickman, huh, Parker?"

He rose and sulked to the other side of the room, facing the wall.

"I met this girl Cammy," she continued. "She's here on scholarship, too, but they never sent her the application with her brochure. She had to request it. I got the scholarship application randomly in the mail. Wasn't so random, was it?"

He stood in a penance of silence.

"Your mom's a secretary here. I knew that, but never questioned anything until my talk with Cammy. After that, I looked up your mom to see what department she's in. I wasn't surprised when I found out it was Admissions."

He returned to her side, and spoke without facing her, the bedroom his confession box. "You earned the scholarship yourself. I couldn't have fixed that. You had the grades for it already."

"But you lured me here."

"All I did was have my mom insert the scholarship information and application into the regular brochure and send it to you. Then I hoped you'd come."

"How did you know my address?"

"My dad found you for me. He used his contacts."

"Why bother bringing me here? For what?"

"My instinct said Hannah had been murdered, but I had no proof. I wished that she could reach through the space between the dead and the living and just tell me who did it. Then the idea hit me. I couldn't speak to Hannah, but I could get the next best thing."

He faced her, his eyes apologetic. "You share one hundred percent of your DNA with Hannah. Yes, you're not her and you haven't lived her life, but if anyone could get into her head and figure out what happened, it would be you. No one else seemed to care anymore. She was old news. But I knew that if you came here and found out about all this, you would grab onto it with passion like Hannah would have. That you wouldn't quit until someone paid for what he did to her."

She turned away from him, disgusted. "And maybe in the meantime, I'd lure the killer out for a second try. You used me."

"I'm sorry, Elise. Truly, I am. But I don't regret any of it because if I hadn't done it, I wouldn't have met you."

He touched her face lightly, a flutter of butterfly wings. Her heart ached, but she steeled herself against his touch.

"I never expected to fall in love with you, Elise, but I did. It has nothing to do with Hannah. I was never attracted to her in that way. She was broken, wounded, and I'm not like Gavin. I don't choose women who need me to save them. I like women who are strong, confident, smart. Women who can save me. That's why I fell for you. Not because you're Hannah's twin, but because you're you. I didn't plan for this, but it happened."

She rose, pulling the robe tightly around her neck. "Thank you for telling me the truth, but right now I want you to leave."

Resigned, he nodded slowly and backed out of her room, his eyes wistfully leaving hers as his shape disappeared from the doorway.

CHAPTER 27

A dark-planked wooden deck wrapped around The Harvest Country Club's banquet facility, providing views of the manicured greens of the golf course in front and a sprawling cranberry bog in back. Elise pulled her sheer black shawl tight across her chest, as the cool late October wind whispered down her neck. She was alone on the deck and relished the quiet moment away from all the other wedding guests who were busy inside getting as sloshed as they possibly could at the open bar.

The slider hissed open and shut behind her, and she felt eyes on the bare skin of her lower back. She glanced over her shoulder, the wind whipping her blond locks across her face. Gavin stood transfixed, a champagne glass in each hand, his lips parted. She wished she hadn't chosen the red satin dress. She wanted to look nice, but its eye-popping effect on Gavin had been more than she had planned for.

He shook his head, waking himself from his trance and stepped to her, holding out a glass.

She accepted it with a polite smile and returned her gaze to the view, leaning her elbows on the deck railing. The last remnants of the setting sun blazed paths across the sky in red and orange, matching the dead leaves scattered on the grounds below and the scarlet of the bog in the distance. She cursed the encroaching darkness for pushing the sun beneath the horizon.

"Beautiful sight, isn't it?" she said, to fill in the silence.

"The most beautiful I've seen," Gavin said, and she knew he

214

was looking at her and not at the vista before them. "I hope you're having a good time. You've been out here for a while. Are you avoiding me?"

"No." She placed a kind hand on his shoulder. "If I'm avoiding anyone, to be honest, it's your father."

"Well then, that makes two of us. Want to head in and avoid him together?"

He grinned, a lopsided, innocent boy-next-door grin, and she was reminded of how charming he could be. With just one wink or a smile, he could momentarily stop a woman's heart from beating. He offered his arm and she linked hers through it, allowing him to lead her back into the ballroom.

A crystal chandelier hung from the ceiling above a plush red carpet. An ice sculpture of a swan glistened on a long table, surrounded by gifts wrapped in silver and gold paper. The wedding cake was gone, probably being cut in the kitchen, and she realized how much of the wedding she had missed, wandering around the grounds. It wasn't fair to Gavin as his date. Even if her mind was underwater, her body could at least be here.

The band slowed the music to a Sarah McLachlan song she loved and when Gavin pulled her to the dance floor, she didn't resist. The warmth of his hand on the small of her back burned her after the cold outside. He held her close, his breath in her hair. With Nick or Parker, she would have taken delight in this moment, but with Gavin she felt trapped, like an animal in the hunter's crosshairs. Then she realized it didn't have to be that way. She could easily switch the balance of power with the information Kat had gotten from Faith.

In the same soft tone that she used to ask for the time or to speak of the weather, she delivered the bullet. "How long were you having an affair with Faith before Hannah found out?"

His body went rigid, and she dared to look into his eyes, which were not angry, but fearful.

"Faith told you?"

She nodded slowly and gripped his hand tightly, a gesture to let him know that he was the one trapped on the dance floor, with nowhere to flee from her questions.

"It was a one-time thing." He nervously licked his lips. "Hannah went to Dorchester for the night. Some family drama with her mother. So Faith and I stayed in and drank too much. Way too much."

He shook his head. "I've never felt like that before in my life. It felt like it wasn't even me, like I was hovering on the ceiling watching it happen to someone else. But the damage was done. I did it, and things were never the same. Hannah found out and broke up with me."

She wondered if he knew that Faith was the one who made sure Hannah found out. The Sarah McLachlan song ended and segued into an Air Supply number, giving the dance floor the reputation of a toxic waste site. As the dancers fled, Gavin didn't use his chance to escape. He kept his hands on her waist and shuffled along.

"If I could go back and take that night away," he said, "I would do it a million times over. It was a mistake in more ways than one. It made me lose Hannah, and it gave Faith false hope."

"So you never had intentions of a relationship with Faith?"

"No, she's not my type. She's too intense, almost obsessed with me. I always liked her fine and never minded hanging out with her when Hannah wanted to. I could never understand at the time why Faith wanted to be the third wheel so often, but now I know it was because she had a crush on me."

His eyes were glassy, but Elise knew it wasn't the champagne. He continued, "Sometimes in the middle of the night, I can't sleep because I wonder if that kick-started everything."

"What do you mean?"

"If I hadn't slept with Faith, then Hannah and I wouldn't

have broken up, and then I would have been with her that night, and she wouldn't have fallen from the bridge."

A chill drifted down her back, and she stopped dancing, her feet cemented to the hardwood floor. It wasn't his words that had seized her heart and stopped her breathing. The dance floor had thinned out, giving her a view of the bar. Two men clinked shot glasses and tossed them back, then one turned to face the crowd. As she recognized him, Elise's throat felt full of dust, dry and brittle and impossible to swallow.

The man was bulky, the buttons of his gray suit jacket bulging. The twinkling light of the chandelier reflected off the dome of his shaved head.

Beth Wells shuffled through the living room, searching with the desperation of a stranded man in the desert looking for water. Her ankles cracked as she fell to her knees, searching under the coffee table and Roger's battered Barcalounger. She crawled to the couch and pulled herself up, her joints aching. A dry, hacking cough spasmed from her chest as she lifted up the cushions.

"Dickhead," she mumbled, picking up a porno mag from its hiding place.

Stupid Roger. She sent him to the corner store last night with her last five bucks to buy cigarettes, and he probably bought this jerk-off rag with her money instead. Now, she had no ciggies and her yellowed fingers were shaking.

She took a deep breath, forcing herself to calm down. She didn't want to bring on a coughing attack. In and out, count to ten. Reach your calm plateau. Soon enough, she thought, none of this bullshit will matter anymore. All her troubles will be gone, poof, like a puff of smoke.

The shrill ring of the phone woke her from her reverie. She picked up the cordless from the top of the television.

"Hello?"

She listened with interest at first, then tightness crept across her face, her lips drawn into a thin line.

"Absolutely not!" she bellowed into the phone.

She shook her head, angry with the voice on the other end. "I don't think that's a good idea."

Her foot tapped as she listened a moment more, then all restraint escaped her body. "We're giving the guy more time and that's final."

She hung up the phone, fingernails digging into her palm, the calm plateau she had managed to reach before crumbling under her feet.

"What's wrong, Elise?"

She had stopped dancing, but held the pose—one hand in Gavin's, the other on his shoulder—like a Pompeii corpse frozen in ash.

"Who's that guy at the bar with the shaved head?"

Gavin looked over her shoulder. "That's my Uncle Larry, my father's brother. Why?"

She strained to keep her tone casual. "He looks familiar."

"He lives in South Carolina now, but you may have seen him around town. He travels for business a lot and anytime he's seeing a client in Mass, he always stops by to shoot the shit with Dad for a bit. They're close. As a matter of fact, Dad is going to be psyched to see him. He had said he wouldn't be able to make it up for the wedding. He must have rearranged his schedule at the last minute. Dad probably doesn't even know he's here yet."

They resumed dancing, more like Gavin spinning a dead weight. Larry hadn't seen her yet, and she was comforted by the fact that Gavin seemed undisturbed by her questions about him. Someone in the ballroom, however, seemed quite concerned.

His father.

Chief Shaw caught her look from his spot at the table closest to the dance floor, where he had been busy holding several people hostage with one dirty joke after another. He followed her line of sight to the bar, to Larry, and froze mid-guy-walks-into-a-bar. He excused himself, dashing to the bar, and as Larry pulled him into a bear hug, he whispered furiously in his ear.

Larry's eyes turned to the dance floor and met hers.

Elise pulled herself from Gavin's grasp and sprinted toward the bar, positioning herself between it and the doorway.

Larry ran in the opposite direction, darting between tables, and out the sliders to the deck.

She followed, partly aware of the scores of guests who stood staring at the spectacle they had created. Pulling the slider to the side, she burst outside, her eyes taking too long to adjust to the darkening sky. The crunch of dead leaves gave his position away. She slipped out of her heels and sped down the deck stairs to the ground below, watching his large form lumber across the grounds.

The night had deepened to a dark gray. She stood atop a short but steep hill that led down to the cranberry bog, a mass of crimson that stretched to the horizon. He stopped at the bottom of the hill and looked up at her, not expecting a woman in a tight red satin dress to follow.

He was wrong.

She teetered down the steep brown grass, brittle against her feet. One foot slipped forward and she faltered, digging her fingers into a clump of dirt to right herself, then continued down at the same pace. She heard footsteps behind her, probably Gavin, but didn't waste a moment to look.

"Stop," she screamed at Larry. "Just stop and tell me why!"

"Screw you, crazy bitch!" he called over his shoulder, running until his designer shoes hit the edge of the bog.

It was harvesting season, and the bog was flooded, a tide of red berries floating atop the shallow water. She reached the bottom of the hill, her breath fogging in front of her, and continued to follow.

He glanced over his shoulder, eyes widening at her pace, then plodded into the bog, muttering words she couldn't hear. The bog was about a foot deep, the berries tickling her shins as she pushed through them. She had expected her feet to sink in mud, but the peat was firm and supported her as she closed the distance.

The darkness grew the farther they went from the country club's lights, and she lost his shape behind one of the loading bins. He could be hiding behind any of them, ready to jump out and attack her. Could he drown her in a foot of water? Adrenaline pumping in her veins, she was unable to stop and pushed on, reaching the first bin when a spotlight lit up the bog.

"Stop! Oceanside Police!"

Elise froze and held her hands up. Larry, behind the closest bin, straightened, but kept his hands at his sides.

"You too, Larry," the female voice called. "Hands in the air."

Elise turned around, blinded by the spotlight until Officer Lisa Federico moved the light to the side, allowing Elise to see her face. Two more forms tumbled down to the edge of the bog, one after the other: Gavin and his father.

Taking a chance with Officer Federico, Elise lowered her hands and slogged through the bog toward the bank. The sound of splashing behind her told her that Larry was doing the same thing.

She reached Officer Federico, who, with a lowered voice, said, "Your words from that day stayed with me. Especially after you came in wanting to file a harassment charge and the chief blew you off. I knew something was going on, so I've been keeping tabs on you when I can."

"What's going on here?" Chief Shaw barked.

"You know damned well what's going on," Elise said. "I recognized your attack dog, here. The guy you sent to do your dirty work."

"What are you talking about?" Gavin asked, looking from her, to his father, to his uncle.

"Your Uncle Larry has been stalking me."

"Stalking how?"

"Harassing phone calls and notes, telling me to stop investigating Hannah's death. He even stole my mother's watch from her and gave it to me to let me think that he'd killed her. To scare me into keeping my mouth shut."

Gavin glared at his father. "You told him to do all this? How could you do something like that?"

The chief put a hard hand on his son's shoulder and growled, "I didn't want my son to end up in Walpole."

"Prison? Why would you think I'd go to prison?" He stepped back, one hand covering his mouth. "You think I killed Hannah?"

"I knew you wouldn't have done it on purpose, son."

"I wouldn't have done it at all! I loved her!"

"You had just gone through a bad breakup, I knew that."

"So you just assumed that I pushed her off the bridge?"

The chief wiped the sweat off his forehead with his arm. "I just wanted to protect you. This girl is trouble."

Larry sidled up to Elise with his head down like a dog who'd bit his owner. "I never would have harmed you. I just wanted to scare you into letting things go."

She ignored him, thoughts rushing at her. "So you took the pictures of my parents, left the message on my laptop, put the note under my door?"

"Yeah, it was me, all of it. Gavin wasn't involved at all. He didn't even know. I was doing what I could to protect my nephew and help my brother out. Family first." He shrugged. Realization shocked her like an ice water plunge. "So the real killer never threatened me. The real killer might not even know I exist."

"Or maybe, genius," the chief said, "there is no killer. Like I wanted you to believe all along. Your instinct is wrong. She wasn't murdered. She got drunk and fell."

Chapter 28

Morning sunlight poured through the bedroom window, a spotlight on the dust motes dancing in the currents of air. Elise winced and rolled to her side, squeezing her eyes shut. She forgot to pull the shade last night when she got home, lost in the confusion of the night's events. Her chest felt heavy, her heart swollen and bruised in hopelessness.

A light knock on her bedroom door alerted her to Kat's presence. She kept her eyes closed as the door creaked open and Kat's bare feet padded across the rug up to the bed. Kat probably wanted to go to Sunday brunch, to ask her what happened last night. She controlled her breathing, making each breath long and deep as if in the throes of sleep.

After a moment, Kat's footsteps receded and the door clicked shut. Elise opened her eyes and set herself to the task of finding patterns in the swirls of white paint on the ceiling. She had no intention of getting out of bed today. She didn't want to speak to anyone. She just wanted to hide.

She felt her life disintegrating around her. Parker had lied to her. And worse, he'd used her, lured her here for his own purposes. Hannah's supposed killer wasn't stalking her; it had just been Gavin's nutjob uncle thinking he was protecting family. Her only proof that Hannah had been pushed was the stalker insisting that she stop the investigation. With that explained, she had nothing. No proof that Hannah didn't just fall or jump.

She didn't even want to think about Hannah anymore.

The phone rang, and she waited for Kat to answer it. On the third ring, she realized Kat must have left, so she groaned and reached to her nightstand, picking up the ivory receiver.

"Hello," she croaked.

"Elise? Are you okay? You sound horrible."

"I'm fine, Mom. I just woke up."

"Sorry to wake you. We haven't talked in a while, I wanted to catch up."

Guilt nagged at her like a hangnail. There was so much she hadn't told her parents. But now was not the time. "Can I give you a call back later? I'm so tired."

Silence sizzled across the line, full of disappointment. "Sure, dear. Oh, just one thing."

"Yeah?"

"Nick had one of his friends call for you again, trying to find out where you live."

"It's not one of Nick's friends."

"How do you know that?"

"Nick and I are . . . in touch again. He knows where I live now, and he has my number. So it's not him."

"Oh," her mother said, pausing in the hopes that Elise would continue and tell her more. When she didn't, she added, "Then who's trying to find you?"

"It's probably a stubborn telemarketer. I'll talk to you later, Mom."

She gently hung up the phone and rolled over, facing the wall. She closed her eyes and willed herself to sleep a dreamless sleep with no visions of Hannah.

The dream came again: Hannah slicing through the black river like Ophelia floating, arms out at her sides, palms up. Then Elise was soaring above the marsh. Birds of all sizes flew with her, whispering in her ear, chirps that were almost words.

Swooping down and up, flocking around her, leading her. She wanted to speak to them, ask them where they were going, what they wanted to tell her, but her mouth opened and no sound came out.

Just a feather.

Her eyes snapped open. She threw the blankets off and pulled at her t-shirt, stuck to her chest with sweat. The dream wasn't a nightmare, really, but it burrowed into her and wouldn't let go. When faced with a problem, she often figured out the solution in her dreams, her subconscious working overtime while her body slept. This dream was coming more frequently, but she had no idea what it meant. Birds. What the hell was her mind working on?

She glanced at the clock. Noon. Just a few more hours of hiding and then the whole day would pass without seeing Kat or Parker or Robbie or . . .

Robbie.

She nearly fell out of bed.

She tore off her clothes and jumped in the shower. Luckily, Kat was out somewhere, so Elise wasted no time. Tossed on clean jeans and a green cable-knit sweater and pulled her towel-dried hair up into a ponytail.

Two minutes later, she was pounding on the door to Parker's apartment, hoping he wasn't home. The door opened, and she sighed with relief at Robbie's inquisitive stare. He wore black track pants and a retro "Who shot JR?" t-shirt.

He took in the sight of her, out of breath, hair still damp. "Parker's at the library."

"Good," she said. "I was looking for you. Grab a jacket. Let's go."

Elise managed to evade his questions during the five-minute drive to the beach parking lot and even as they mounted the pedestrian bridge. But as they reached the middle of the bridge, the spot where Hannah last stood as a living, breathing woman, Robbie lost it.

"I'm not taking one more step until you tell me what I'm doing out here!"

She stopped, several steps ahead of him and turned around, one hand on her hip. "I need your help."

"With what?"

"Parker said that you believed there was a . . . how did he word it?" She tapped her fingernails on the wooden railing. "A crazy bird man who lived in one of the old shacks out on the marsh who took care of the endangered bird nests."

He nodded. "Yeah, crazy bird man. He lives out there. Some people think it's an urban legend, but I saw him once my sophomore year. I was wasted, standing on the top of one of the dunes, and saw him hiking across the marsh with a bird right on the top of his pointy head. What does that have to do with anything?"

"You're going to help me find him. Right now."

"Why?"

"Because it's something that's been bothering me. A loose end I need to tie up."

The salt marsh extended out to the horizon, sliced by shallow estuaries narrow enough for Elise and Robbie to jump over. They reached a tidal creek spanned by a short wooden catwalk and gingerly tested it before putting their full weight on it. The lush, green grass of the marsh had turned golden in spots, a sign of impending winter. They passed one shack whose tin roof lay on the ground beside it, obviously abandoned for several years.

"How much farther do you want to go?" Robbie asked, lagging behind her.

"If the next shack we find is in the same condition, I'll give up. Deal?"

"Yeah. I still don't get why you want to meet him anyway."

She stopped for a moment to allow him to catch up. "I think I've already met him."

Before he had a chance to ask another question, she pitched one of her own. "There's something I've been meaning to ask you about. You told me you saw Hannah that night at Dolan's."

He kicked at an empty clamshell, shuffling his feet back and forth. "Yeah."

"Abby told me something you left out. You had a blowout with Hannah there."

He shrugged. "We had a tiff, nothing much. No bigger than the fight Abby had with her."

"What was it about?"

His right foot slipped, and he grabbed onto her shoulder to regain his footing. He blushed and smiled apologetically. "I had a crush on her, a big one. We slept together a few times, and then she was done with me. She started dating Gavin, and I guess I never got over her. I had a few too many in me that night. I had heard that she and Gavin broke up, and she came into the bar and, like an asshole, I hit on her. She brushed me off rudely, and I snapped back. That was it."

She stuffed a few orphan strands of hair back into her ponytail and started walking again, faster than before. "Let's keep going."

"You believe me, don't you?"

"Why wouldn't I?"

"I don't know. Just forget it."

She glanced over her shoulder at him, watching him nervously plunge his hands into his pockets, and felt that he was hiding something beneath his thick glasses and innocent clumsiness.

The marsh grass was higher here, nearly touching her knees.

A high-pitched shriek came from the sky, and Elise screamed as she and Robbie ducked, covering their heads. A small but determined bird swooped down low, screeching at them. They ran in a crouched position and as they got a hundred feet away, the bird left them alone.

"You're lucky she didn't peck at you."

Robbie straightened and turned to face the voice.

"You two walked right by a nest of endangered birds. You shouldn't be out here, for their safety and yours. That was the mama bird that wanted to take your eyes out back there."

Elise rose and let her hands fall from her face.

The man gasped.

Tall and skinny, he had a yellowed wool hat on his head, a small brown bird on one shoulder, and the head of another bird peeked out of the pocket of his green camouflage coat. The lanky man.

"You saw me, that night last month from the bridge. You ran from me." She had been unable to identify the strange item perched upon his shoulder that night, but worked it out in her dreams.

Panic gripped his face and his hands fluttered wildly in front of him. "I can't swim! I'm sorry! I didn't know what to do!"

"What are you talking about? I was on the bank. You were on the bridge. You gasped at the sight of me and ran away."

His eyes teared, and the thought occurred to her that the crazy bird man might be aptly named.

"I couldn't help you! I know you must be angry, but I can't swim." He shook his head so violently that the bird on his shoulder left for safer ground.

Robbie stood mute behind her, no help at all. She reached forward and placed a hand on the man's shoulder, hoping to calm him. "When? When was this?"

"Last year. I'm sorry."

Her intake of breath was so sharp that it burned her lungs. She inched closer, forcing him to look at her face. "Are you talking about my sister? I'm a twin. A girl who looked just like me, with short hair?"

He stopped shaking and blinked away wetness from the corners of his eyes.

"What did you see?"

"I saw you get pushed." His lips trembled as he spoke. "Off the bridge. You fell, so far. The water so cold. Too cold. I can't swim. There was nothing I could do."

"Did you go to the police?" Robbie asked, his first words to the man.

"Yes, I asked for the captain."

"The chief?"

"Yes. He told me I was drunk and stupid and didn't see shit." He put on a fake voice like a child imitating an angry parent. "He said, 'If you know what's good for you, you'll forget what you think you saw and let this poor girl's family have some peace. The last thing they need is to think their daughter was murdered because of what some druggie hallucinated.' "

He returned to his own voice. "But I don't do drugs or drink, and I know what I saw." His bended shoulders sagged further. "He threatened to kick me out, not let me live on the marsh anymore. Said it's illegal for me to live out here and he could do it with a snap of his fingers. Who would take care of the birds?"

"Who pushed her?" Elise asked gently.

"I know one thing for sure."

"What?" Robbie asked, moving closer to him.

"It was a man."

Robbie grabbed him roughly by the shoulders, and he winced in pain. "Did you see him?" Robbie said, his voice rising. "Describe him!"

"I can't," he said, fear in his eyes. "It was dark. I couldn't see details like hair color or his face. I just know it was a man."

"Think!" Robbie yelled.

"Calm down," Elise said, surprised by Robbie's outburst.

"Anything you can remember! Think!"

"Take it easy, Robbie!" She seized his arm and pulled him backward, forcing him to let go of the man.

"I'm sorry," Robbie said to her, through gritted teeth. "I want to know who did this as much as you do. I want him to pay."

Released, the bird man ran off, intermittently crying and mumbling about not knowing how to swim.

The student parking lot behind graduate housing held shiny BMWs and misused Land Rovers between its faded yellow lines. Elise sat in her Civic alone. Robbie had gone into Bourne Hall several minutes ago, but she wasn't ready to leave the solitary comfort of her car yet. Thoughts ebbed and flowed through her like tidal currents. But one crashed on the shore, louder than the rest.

Hannah was murdered.

It was certain now. She had a witness. Chief Shaw had covered it up, thinking the murderer was Gavin. Though at this point, she had no evidence that it wasn't Gavin. Maybe Uncle Larry wasn't so off the wall after all.

Her instinct had been correct. Hannah didn't jump or fall. She was killed. Emotions toiled in Elise's heart. Anger for Hannah. Sadness for herself, cheated out of her sister for the second time. Strangely, she also felt a sense of relief, for finally knowing the truth.

But not all of it.

She wouldn't know the whole truth until she uncovered who the man was who stood behind Hannah on the bridge and thrust his hands to her back, pushing her to an icy death. But she was closer to the answers now than ever before. She would find them, and avenge her sister.

With renewed energy, she left her car and crossed the parking lot, dried chunks of mud in the soles of her sneakers scraping across the asphalt. The stairs echoed with her footfalls as she ascended to the third floor and opened the door to her apartment.

Kat lounged on the couch, one mile-long leg draped over the other, her head thrown back in laughter. Elise knew all of Kat's laughs now: sincere, uncontrollable, drunk, fake, and flirty. This one was the latter, meaning a man was in the house.

At the sound of Elise closing the door, Kat cut off her come-hither giggle and pointed. "There she is."

A man rose from the recliner, handsome, in his late thirties, with a white oxford shirt and khaki pants. His hair was prematurely gray, but in a hot way. He looked Elise up and down like she was a shiny new car in a used lot, and sighed with relief.

He held his hand out. "Greg Gilmore."

She shook it, trying to keep her eyes on him instead of Kat panting like a dog in the background. "Elise Moloney."

He smiled, revealing a line of pearly white, perfectly spaced teeth. "You were hard to find."

Chapter 29

The law offices of Attorney Malcolm Burton were located in a short, mirrored building resembling a toy skyscraper in North Quincy, straddling the Dorchester line. To use the word "offices" was a stretch, since the suite contained only one office and an entryway where a receptionist would sit if he had one. Mr. Burton had to run downstairs to use a copier—strangely didn't have one of his own—and promised to be right back. Elise's patience was trickling to the floor like sand through a sifter.

Greg Gilmore hadn't told her anything other than it was imperative that she rush to Attorney Burton's office first thing the next morning. So here she was, her ass sore already from sitting in the hard, burgundy leather chair for ten minutes. She had skipped her Monday morning classes, which pissed her off because she was supposed to get back her midterm grades, and fought morning traffic for two and a half hours. All she knew was that Greg Gilmore was a private investigator hired to find her, and that he would have found her a little sooner if her parents had been more forthcoming over the phone.

The only thing that kept her seated was the knowledge that whatever Mr. Burton had to tell her, it was important enough to hire a PI for.

The office was gloomy, blinds pulled down, casting no light on the dark paneling and mahogany desk. The walls were bare except for a black and white photo of JFK and a framed map of

Florida. A tall, neatly stacked pile of file folders stood on the desk.

Attorney Malcolm Burton reentered the office, a stately looking man in his early seventies. His gray suit matched his well-groomed beard, and his head was bald on top with a trim skirt of hair around the sides and back. He sat straight as a tomato stake in his chair and folded his hands on the desk.

"I apologize for the time that took. I was surprised to hear that Mr. Gilmore had found you and wasn't prepared." He motioned to the map of Florida. "I've been winding down my practice for some time, and next month I'm retiring to Florida. I'm glad that you've been found because after today, I officially have no more clients and no more work to do."

"Congratulations, Mr. Burton," she said, glad for his well-deserved impending retirement, but wanting to get on with it. "Why am I here?"

"Please, call me Malcolm." A sad look overtook his face, a mix of pity and personal grief. "I'm sorry to have to give you this news, but your maternal grandmother, Martha Mary Doyle, has passed away."

"Beth's mother?"

"Yes."

She rubbed her eyes. "Okay. Again, why am I here?"

His tone remained somber. "Because you're in the will."

"She knew about me?"

"Of course. She passed last November. We've been looking for you for nearly a year."

Elise's mouth gaped open in response.

He leaned back, his voice more casual now. "Your grandmother was a good woman. We grew up together in Dorchester, remained friends our whole lives. Her first husband, your grandfather, was a brave man. Top-notch." He shook his head, lost in memories. "He died too young, shot down over the Pacific in

World War II. Poor Martha was left to raise Beth alone, and Bethie didn't do well without a father in her life. She was a wild child and a worse teenager. Out of control.

"Anyway, Beth and Martha had a falling out. Martha never liked airing the family's dirty laundry, but I knew it had to do with Beth giving you up for adoption. Her mother never forgave her for what she did, and she cut her off forever. Beth never cared for anyone but herself, so losing her mother didn't matter much until her mother finally remarried after being a widow for three decades."

"Why would that matter to her?"

"Martha married the owner of a local supermarket chain. He became an overnight multimillionaire when a national chain bought him out. He died of a heart attack about five years back, but Martha did well by herself, made sound investments."

"The rich grandmother," she said. At Malcolm's raised eyebrows, she added, "Hannah's college roommate told me that Hannah's education was paid for by some rich grandmother."

He smiled shyly, then pride filled his face as he continued. "Martha should have gotten herself a big-time lawyer, but insisted on using friends when she could, so she used me. I drew up her will and the instructions were that her twin grand-daughters were to split the inheritance."

"How much is it?"

"Five million each."

Elise felt herself slipping down the chair and struggled to pull herself back up.

"Do you need some water, Elise?"

"No, thank you. I'll be okay." Her hands began to shake.

"After she passed last year, the hard part was tracking you down. Turns out the adoption agency Beth used wasn't as legitimate as we had originally thought."

"So, you told Hannah about her inheritance."

He nodded and smiled, anticipating her next question.

"And you told her about me."

"Yes. Not right away. Your grandmother wanted me to try to find you first, to reunite the twins and then explain the inheritance. When a few months passed and I hadn't found you yet, I decided to tell her. This was in February, only a week before she died. I read her the will, in private, and she learned of your existence. I had cleared the office of all breakables prior to our appointment, assuming that fury at her mother would be her first emotion, but it wasn't."

"What was?"

"Happiness. I'd never noticed her eyes before, but that moment they lit up the brightest shade of green I'd ever seen outside of Ireland. She was so excited and encouraged me to get started on finding you right away. I was particularly delighted at that, because it proved to me that goodness can skip a generation."

"What do you mean?"

"Your mother was a selfish woman, nothing like Martha. Your sister, however, was just like her grandma." He cleared his throat. "There were two stipulations in the will in the event that only one of the twins should inherit. The first: if you weren't found within one year, Hannah would collect all the money. Martha put an end date on the search for you so Hannah wouldn't have to wait forever if you couldn't be found. If Hannah was anything like Beth, she would have wanted me to drag my feet in looking for you so she could inherit ten million, but that wasn't what she wanted. She didn't seem to care about the money at all. All she wanted was you."

Elise's throat tightened, and she found it hard to swallow. "What was the second stipulation?"

Sadness possessed his face once more as he stroked his beard. "In the event of the death of one of the twins, the other would inherit all the money. So you, as of this moment, are inheriting ten million dollars."

She sat dumbfounded, only able to utter a short grunt.

"I'm sorry I didn't find you sooner. I didn't have a lot of resources with which to search for you, and that last idiot was useless. I'm glad I finally gave up on him and hired Greg. I only held on to him for so long because Beth insisted. After a while, I started to think that maybe"—he paused, unsure of whether to be completely honest—"maybe she didn't want you found. So I hired Greg without telling her."

Her stomach dropped. Her mother knew where she was for the last two months and never contacted Malcolm. "What does she care if I inherit the money?" As soon as the words left her mouth, she knew the answer. "Who would have gotten the money if I wasn't found?"

"Hannah, of course. But with her gone, if you weren't found it would have gone to Beth."

"Why would Martha do that?"

"She didn't. According to Massachusetts Intestate Succession law, if neither of you were able to inherit, her next of kin, Beth, automatically would. Your grandmother never expected Hannah to die, and we assumed that you would be easier to find than you were. So we didn't make contingent beneficiaries beyond the two of you."

"Have you told Beth that you found me?"

He shook his head. "She thinks she's days away from inheriting it all." He put his hand on a black multiline phone. "Would you like me to call her now?"

A wicked smirk crept up her face. "If it's all right with you, I'd like to tell her myself. In person."

Elise stood in the shadows under the second-story deck in the back of Beth Wells's triple-decker, her petite frame leaving plenty of room between her head and the wooden boards above it. She arrived several minutes ago with her left pocket full of stones and her right pocket full of one-dollar bills. She quietly made a path from the front door, down the walk, around the side, and to the back of the house. Then she rang the doorbell, hid in the dark, and waited. But she didn't have to wait long.

The crunch of footsteps on brittle leaves announced Beth's presence. Elise was unable to see her mother's face as she bent down for another dollar, her blond and gray hair covering her expression.

Beth straightened and giggled playfully, her fist full of dollars. "Roger, what are you up to?"

Elise stepped out of the shadows, and Beth visibly jumped.

"Like cheese to a mouse."

Beth's eyes narrowed. "You scared me. What are you doing prowling around my house?"

"I thought I'd give you a little taste of the only thing that makes you happy: money. Right, Mommy dearest?"

Beth shoved the ones into the pocket of her jeans. "What are you going on about? Still bitter about me selling you? Please, you should be down on your knees thanking me that I didn't abort you like everyone told me to."

"Did Grandma Martha tell you to abort me? Sounds like she was a wonderful woman. I doubt she would have told you to do that. She probably wanted to raise me herself. That's probably why she never spoke to you again after you sold me."

Her nose twitched like a cornered rat. "I don't know what you're talking about."

"Yeah, sure." Elise forced a casual tone. "Doesn't matter. I don't have time for this anyway. I have to go find myself a financial planner. Thankfully, Malcolm recommended a couple because, honestly, I wouldn't know where to start."

The color drained from Beth's already pallid face, and her

whole body trembled. Elise wanted her to say something, anything. She wanted a fight. Beth stood silently, gazing at her with what looked like remorse and that made Elise even angrier. She rushed at her with both hands thrust out. Before she knew what she was doing, she pushed her down. Beth fell over like a cardboard cutout and rolled to her side, coughing hard into her hand.

Elise started to walk away, disgusted with her mother and her own behavior, but in between coughs, Beth shouted, "Wait!"

Beth regained her breath, but stayed sitting in the brown grass. "I'm sorry, Elise. I'm sorry about everything. I'm sorry I didn't tell you about the inheritance. But I figured your parents take good care of you, and you didn't need the money."

Elise put her hand up, wanting Beth to just shut up. "I don't want to listen to this."

"I know that you have great parents, and I know you must hate me for everything I've done, but I want to start over. I want another chance with you. My Hannah is gone. I never thought you'd come back into my life and now that you're here, I regret so much what I've done. Please, if I can't be a mother to you, let me be a friend."

She shook her head. "You just want to get your hands on the money."

"No, I know the money's lost to me. I don't expect anything from you."

Elise steeled herself, took a deep breath, one last look at the woman who brought her into this world, and spoke. "Good, because that's what you're getting. Nothing. This is the last time you will ever see me."

A stretch of dark clouds hung low in a colorless sunset. There was no wind, as if the sky was holding its breath. Elise stood before Bourne Hall, a different woman from when she left it this morning. She was now a multimillionaire. None of it seemed real, and she didn't want to face it yet. She decided to tell no one. As soon as word got out, she would be treated differently, whispered about, stared at.

She wished she hadn't gotten physical with Beth, but at least the final confrontation was done and she never had to see her again. Before, she was filled with anger. Now, she almost pitied her. How ill must she be to love money more than flesh and blood? For the love of money, Beth gave up one daughter, held onto another, lied to a lawyer, and schemed to keep the truth from both daughters.

A thought, hidden and evil, scurried out from a dark corner of her brain. Did Beth love money enough to kill for it? After a few months passed and it looked like Elise wasn't going to be found, the only thing that stood between Beth and ten million dollars was Hannah. Could she have convinced Roger to push her for the money?

A chill iced her veins as another option occurred to her. With one daughter dead, there were two ways Beth would have ended up with the money: if Elise wasn't found, or if she was dead, too. Would Roger come after her next?

She shooed the thought away like an insect on her skin as she reached the concrete stairs. She glanced up at the windows and felt ashamed for hoping to catch a fleeting look at Parker walking by or looking down at her. His window was empty.

She missed him with a physical ache. Was what he did that bad? Yes, he wasn't honest with her, but didn't everyone deserve a second chance? Surely she didn't after what she did to Nick, but he forgave her.

Nick. She sighed. She needed to stop daydreaming about Parker and focus on Nick.

She ascended the stairs and turned the doorknob to her apartment. It was unlocked, so she called out, "Kat, I'm home," as she shrugged out of her coat.

Two large hands grasped her shoulders and turned her around.

"Nick? What are you doing here?"

He smiled wide. "Surprise! I couldn't take it. I missed you so much, I had to drive up here to see you."

She looked around the empty living room. "Where's Kat?"

A laugh escaped his throat. "She's a funny one, that girl. She had to go to work, left a few minutes ago. I've been watching some TV, waiting for you."

He looked better, clean-shaved, with a neatly pressed button-down shirt and black pants. He dressed up, drove all the way here to surprise her, and all she felt was disappointment. Her mind was reeling in chaos, and all she wanted was to disappear under the covers of her bed. But one look at his eager eyes, and she swallowed those feelings and threw her arms around his neck.

"This was so nice of you," she whispered into his ear.

He kissed her tenderly, then pulled back to see her face. "Let's go out to eat somewhere romantic. Show me around this small town of yours."

Grabbing his hand, she smiled politely and led him outside.

The gaming controller vibrated in Parker's hands as the sports car on the screen bounced off a concrete barrier and burst into flames.

"Shit," he yelled, tossing the controller onto the floor.

His eyes were dry from staring at the screen, and he rubbed them like a tired child. He'd been playing video games for hours when he should have been studying, but studying reminded him of class and who sat in front of him and her long, smooth golden hair, and her playful smile. He pushed his hands against his forehead. He needed to stop thinking about Elise. It was ripping him apart.

"You should have had some of my chicken marsala, man," Robbie said, strutting in from the kitchen. He rubbed his stomach as he leaned against the wall beside the window.

"No, thanks. I had salmonella once when I was fourteen, don't want it again."

"Screw you, it was damned good. I should drop out and become a chef." Something caught Robbie's attention, and he gazed out the window.

"Who's that guy Elise is with?"

Parker stood so fast the room spun and raced to the window. Elise looked gorgeous in a violet blouse and gray slim-fitting pants. A man about their age with dark hair held the car door open for her, his hand on the small of her back. Parker gritted his teeth against the rising plume of jealousy.

"That must be Nick," he said, speaking as much to himself as to Robbie. "Her ex and possibly current boyfriend."

"Really?" Robbie replied, scratching his head.

"Yeah, why?"

"He looks familiar."

"From where?"

Robbie stared out the window until the car was gone. "I don't know, but I've definitely seen him before." He played with the stubble of the goatee he was desperately trying to grow. "Maybe he's just one of those guys who looks like a lot of other guys. If you ask me, he's kind of average looking."

"Yeah, maybe that's it," Parker said, unsure. A lot of what Robbie said was bullshit, but it was worth checking out.

He plodded into his bedroom, shutting the door behind him before he picked up the phone on his desk. He dialed a number from memory and waited for the familiar voice to pick up.

"Dad, it's me. I need a favor. I know I've asked you for a lot lately. I swear this will be the last thing I ever ask you for."

CHAPTER 30

The heat was on the fritz. Even with the thermostat off, scorched air pumped out of the vents. Elise grunted as she pushed up the sill in the living room, sweat tickling her neck. Fresh air rushed in the open window, smelling like rain, although the ground was dry. She bent over, feeling the brittle leaves of her once beautiful potted plant that was now brown. She poured some ice water from her glass into the fertilized dirt. She should have pulled the plug on the gardenia a week ago, but held on, sure in her desperation that she could bring it back to life.

Kat reclined on the couch, flipping through some gossip rag to see who was dating/cheating/newly anorexic this week. "What about her?"

Elise glanced at the actress Kat pointed to. "Real."

"Why?"

Elise shrugged. "They fluctuate with her weight."

Kat nodded in agreement. "This one?"

Elise looked again. "Real."

"Real? You've got to be kidding me. She has one-percent body fat and D-size boobahs."

"So do you!"

"Yeah, but I'm six feet tall. My boobs are proportional. This chick is short like you."

Elise sighed, sick of the real-or-fake-boobs game. "I still say they're real. They sag slightly. They're not hard mounds that stick straight out."

Kat snorted and flipped the page. "You have a class this afternoon, right?"

"Yep."

"After, want to do dinner before I head to work?"

"No, Nick's driving up."

"Again? Doesn't that boy have a job? How was dinner with him last night?"

"Nice. Went to Murphy's Shiphouse."

"What are you two doing today?"

"We're meeting at the beach at four for a romantic stroll, probably the last one of the year with the temps dropping. Then maybe dinner."

Kat glanced up from a page of the worst-dressed celebrities. "You don't sound too happy about it."

Elise exhaled slowly through her nose, the smell of the ocean filling the room. "He's doing it again. Moving too fast, putting too much pressure on me. Last night he asked me to drop out and move back to Providence with him."

"And he asked you to meet him for a romantic beach stroll. Hmm. Think he might propose again?"

"It's a possibility. He's acting the same as he did my birthday week last year, and that ended with a proposal. I'm not ready for that, but I don't want to hurt him again. It's like history repeating itself."

Kat tossed the magazine on the floor and locked eyes with her. "What about Parker? It's obvious you two have deep feelings for each other."

There was so much Kat didn't know, so much Elise was holding inside. She felt like a basement boiler, heating up, ready to burst. She wished she could open the dam and let all the truths spill out, but she still remembered the morning when she heard Kat and Robbie's insistent whispers and her sister's name. She trusted no one enough to talk to right now.

Instead of taking her silence as a hint, Kat pushed forward. "I'm going to say one more thing, and that will be it on the topic. Remember our talk when you admitted to me that you have always taken the easy road in life? Never took risks, avoided hard decisions, and acted like a coward?"

Elise felt like a child being lectured by her mother. She refused to look at Kat, her words like needles of truth pricking her. "Of course, I remember."

"I don't want to tell you what to do. What I love about you most is that you don't judge me, and I'm not going to sit here and do that to you. But I'll just give you one piece of advice then leave it at that."

"Go on."

The couch bounced as Kat crawled to the other side and tossed her arm over Elise's shoulder. "Here you are at another crossroads with another choice to make. On one hand, there is the easy choice. The comfortable one. On the other hand, the risk." Her eyebrows rose wickedly. "But we all know with great risks, come great rewards. Choose wisely."

Class dragged like a six-part PBS series on zoning variances. Back in the apartment, Elise ran a comb through her hair and checked her watch. Ten minutes until she had to leave to meet Nick. The scent of a looming storm was stronger in the air now, and she wondered if they would have to cancel their beach stroll. She hoped so. Kat was working at the Sea Mist—probably gathering a third world country's gross national product worth of tips in her skin-tight, v-cut electric blue shirt—so maybe they could head there for food and drinks and avoid the whole romantic beach thing.

A loud knock rapped on the door, and she breathed a sigh of relief. Nick was canceling the stroll and meeting her here. She opened the door all smiles, then her face fell.

"Hey, Robbie."

Without being invited, he stepped around her and into the living room. "How's it going?"

"Great, thanks. Kat's working, if you're here for her."

He looked nervous, his eyes darting around the apartment. "No, I just thought I'd stop by and chat."

"I'd love to, but I'm on my way out."

He tossed himself on the couch and reached for the remote. "Just a few minutes. Come on, humor me. I'm bored."

His strange behavior affected Elise in a startling way. She was nervous. But why? She had nothing to fear from Robbie, of all people.

"I can't. I have to meet Nick at the beach in five minutes." She moved toward the door, not even bothering to ask him to leave. "I've got to go."

He shot up and placed himself between her and the door, blocking her way out. His face darkened.

"I can't let you do that," he said in a low voice.

He reached a hand out behind him and locked the door, then stepped toward her, closing the distance between them.

"Elise, I have a confession to make."

Parker's Jeep crawled to a stop in the beach parking lot as he spied Nick standing on the bank of the river. His father's search didn't pull up much. He was hoping for something big: a criminal record, bankruptcy, a shady past. Nick was clean, but that didn't mean he deserved to be with Elise. Parker's father proved one thing: Nick was a liar. He didn't go to Brown University.

It was innocent enough, Parker figured. He met Elise, a senior at Providence, and didn't want to admit that he hadn't attended college. So he lied to make himself more appealing. Parker shouldn't judge him, glass houses and all. He'd lied to Elise, too. But she belonged with him, not Nick. She loved him; he knew it. She never loved this guy. She just felt comfortable with him, like a tattered old teddy bear. But you couldn't build a life on that. As he shut the door to the Jeep and approached the man with the puzzled face, he hoped that after this conversation, Nick would see it his way.

"What confession?" Elise asked, backing up. She prayed for a knock on the door again, for Nick to come to her rescue.

Robbie's face twisted with guilt. "I haven't been honest with you regarding my feelings for Hannah. I was in love with her, obsessed with her."

He moved toward her, wringing his hands. "I wanted her and Gavin to break up and so did Faith, so we teamed up. I gave Faith some Ecstasy I bought at a club, and she used it to seduce Gavin. One night while Hannah was away, they got drunk together, real drunk. She gave him the E, telling him it was one of those hangover preventers. Then they had sex, and Faith made sure Hannah found out. Hannah dumped him, just as we hoped, but then everything went wrong. She died."

Elise eased herself onto the sofa, but Robbie remained standing, anxiously shifting his weight from one leg to the other.

"I don't want you to get the wrong idea," he continued. "I'm not going to pull a Gavin and try to replace Hannah with you. I don't even think of you in that way. First, you're not my type. Hannah was. Second, I've moved on. I've found someone else I care deeply about for the first time since her."

"Kat?"

"Yeah. I ruined it, though. We made love once, after a night at a club, and I said Hannah's name. I didn't mean to. It was a stupid mistake, and as soon as the sound was out of my mouth I knew what I had done and wished I could reel it back in. But it was too late."

Elise exhaled in relief. "That's why you were fighting that morning?"

"You heard?"

"Not the whole conversation, just the tone and Hannah's name."

Regret seeped from his eyes. "I don't think she'll give me a second chance."

"I'll talk to her about it. No promises, but I'll give it a shot." The clock on the wall showed she was late. "I really have to go now, though."

"Actually, you can't."

Her eyebrows rose. "Another confession?"

He laughed nervously. "No, that's all I needed to get off my chest. But there is another reason I'm here. To stall you."

"From meeting Nick? Why?"

"Kat mentioned to us that you were meeting him at four at the beach, so Parker went to meet him instead."

"Why?"

"He's in love with you and wants to protect you. He went to confront Nick."

"About what?"

"Something's off with that guy. At the very least, he lied to you. He never went to Brown."

Her brow knitted in confusion. "Of course he did."

Robbie shook his head. "Parker's dad did a full check."

A small laugh escaped her lips. "On Nick? Dear God, what for? Nick's a straight arrow."

"To see if he had any prior arrests, bankruptcies, DUIs—"

"DUIs? Nick doesn't even drink!"

Robbie froze. His face turned a sickly gray as his eyes searched the ceiling.

"What's wrong?"

The words trembled from his throat. "I thought I recognized him from somewhere, and now I remember. Dolan's Pub. That night. He was there."

Her heart pumped faster. "Talking to Hannah?"

"Yeah. It made me jealous. That's why I remember his face. And I thought it was strange that he was at a bar, but wasn't drinking. I wanted to know who he was and what the hell he wanted with her."

"Did you see them leave together?"

"No, but that doesn't mean they didn't. No one saw her leave."

Elise cradled her face in her hands, sorting through the facts. As the pieces fell together, a sickening thought made her stomach surge. She shot up and grabbed the phone, resting it on her shoulder as she pulled a card from her wallet. It couldn't ring fast enough, every moment of silence a year off her life.

"Malcolm Burton," he answered stiffly.

"Malcolm, it's Elise Moloney. I need to know the name of the PI you hired."

"Greg Gilmore?"

"No, the first one who couldn't find me."

"Nick Carrano, but I fired him months ago. Why?"

She hung up, promising herself she'd apologize for her rudeness some other day.

Robbie stood blankly at her side, still in shock from his revelation. She grabbed his hand to get his attention.

"We have to get to the beach. Now."

Storm clouds hung low, mixing the dark gray of the sky with the rising dunes. Robbie drove Elise's car as she called Gavin from her cell in the passenger seat. The car careened around the bend onto East Street and sped on a straight course into the parking lot, where Robbie slammed on the brakes, the tires screeching as they kicked sand into the air.

Parker and Nick stood in a confrontational style, hands cutting through the air, voices raised. Robbie stumbled out of the car, leaving the door open, screaming in a frenzy. Parker stepped away from Nick to approach Robbie, a baffled look on his face.

"You killed Hannah! You pushed her! I saw you that night at Dolan's!"

Rage flaring in his eyes like a struck match, Robbie advanced to Nick until they were face-to-face. Nick reared back and head-butted him square in the nose. Robbie's eyes went wide with shock, blood gushing from his nose like a busted pipe. He stumbled backward and fell to the asphalt, unconscious. Parker dropped to his knees and cradled him. Blood pooled on his khakis, leaking from Robbie's face and the fresh slice the concrete made on the back of his head.

The wind picked up, shrieking through the dunes as Nick fled to the bridge. Elise followed at a safe distance, staying on the base of the bridge as he stopped halfway across.

"I fell in love with you," he shouted. "I never would have hurt you. I wanted that money for us! To start a life together."

"We couldn't have done that with five million? It had to be ten?" Her heart ached with the knowledge that this man she had taken to her bed and promised to marry had murdered her sister. In his twisted mind, he did it for her, for their future.

She took a few steps onto the bridge, still far enough away that she could run if he charged. "How did you do it?"

"I told her the truth. I was a private investigator sent by the lawyer to find her sister." He grinned. "Then, I lied. I told her I had you with me. I said you wanted to meet privately, on the beach, and she came with me quite eagerly. I had already scouted the place and broken the railing to make it easier for me. Then all I had to do was lure her there and push."

Elise bent over as if she'd been kicked in the stomach. Vomit rose in her throat and back down again. She wanted to kill him, strangle him, punch him, tear the skin off his bones.

"I have something for you," he said in a teasing voice. A piece of paper flapped in the wind, held up in his hand. "Hannah wrote a letter to you. Malcolm instructed me to give it to you when I found you. Want it? Come and get it."

She gazed back at Parker, his hands and arms stained red, his face warped in emotion as he crouched over Robbie, taking his pulse. She took a step forward. Stopped.

Nick looked down at the letter, started to read. " 'I don't know what you'll be thinking or feeling when you get the news that you're a twin, but I hope that you decide to meet me.' "

He looked up at Elise. "Oh, how sweet. Come to me or I'll throw it in the river." He held it out over the railing as the clouds opened up and silver rain drizzled down like ash.

"Don't!" She rushed across the bridge, vaguely aware of movement behind her.

Parker rose, shouting, "Elise, don't do it! Stay back!"

She reached Nick and tugged the note out of his hand, stuffing it into the pocket of her jeans. She felt her head snap back as he pulled her hair, then slammed her forward, her head smashing into the railing. Stunned from the blow, she was unprepared for what came next.

Her legs were lifted into the air, and her hands flailed as she was flipped over the railing, fear filling her like a baby's first breath. Her thrashing hands grasped onto a plank, slivers of wood sliding under her skin as she scrambled to hold on. She looked up at Nick, her eyes pleading. But his gritted teeth and black, dead, shark eyes strangled her last ounce of hope. He bent at the waist, ready to pry her hands from the bridge when Parker let out a guttural scream and charged.

Startled, Nick held his hands out, like a shitzu defending itself from a rabid rottweiler. Parker slammed Nick into the railing, which splintered from the weight of the two men, their momentum sending them flying through the air. They looked like one raging beast, a tangle of grappling arms and kicking legs, still clutching each other as they hit the cold water and sank.

Elise watched through a veil of mist and rain, then forced herself to look away from the raging current under her dangling legs and focus on pulling herself up. Her muscles ached and her arms shook as she clawed her way up, kicking with her legs and landing on her side, straining for breath. She felt something warm and sticky in her hair and the slickness of it trailed down her face and dripped a crimson stain onto the wood. Her lungs burned, and her vision was tinged with black at the edges, like a frame. She peered over the edge and counted two heads bobbing in the river, tossed around like stuffed toys.

The bridge vibrated, and she knew this was it; she was losing consciousness, not enough oxygen getting to her brain as her airway constricted. She lay on her back, the hard rain pelting her closed eyelids. The vibration stopped and someone loomed over her.

"Elise! Elise, are you okay?"

Her eyes opened lazily. "Gavin," she breathed. "Inhaler . . . in my car. Parker and Nick in the river."

He peered over the broken railing into the water below, then back at her, and ran across the bridge. The wrong way. He wasn't headed to the parking lot, to her car, to the inhaler to save her life.

My God, she thought. He's going to let us all die. Her breathing became rapid, each exhale a wheeze. She rolled to her side, searching the sand for Gavin. He emerged from the fog, carrying the life preserver from the beach shack.

He looked up at her from the bank, and she leaned on her elbows, sucking in as much air and energy as she could and shouted, "Hurry! I love him!"

"Which one?" he yelled, as her world dissolved and her eyes rolled back.

EPILOGUE

Elise became slowly aware of her senses, smell coming first. The air was stale and sterile, but she didn't mind because it meant she was breathing. Her lungs no longer burned, but a dull throbbing beat in her head. She opened her eyes and immediately closed them, brightness singeing her irises.

"Relax," a soothing older female voice said. "Let your eyes adjust slowly."

She blinked and squinted at the light. A halo circled the head of a woman in her sixties, her black hair curled in a tight perm. She would have thought she was in heaven if it wasn't for the tag on Nurse Weyler's white scrubs.

"Am I okay?"

Nurse Weyler approached the bed. "Three stitches in your scalp and a mild concussion, but you'll be fine. You're lucky Officer Shaw got your inhaler in time."

"I don't even remember that."

"It happens." A conspiratorial smile spread across her face. "There's someone who has refused to leave the hospital until you woke up. Feel like company?"

She nodded, too scared to say yes, too frightened of who might walk through the empty doorway. Her heavy eyelids fell and when she opened them again, Parker sat in the chair beside her, a blue hospital blanket around his shoulders. She floated on her relief and reached a hand out from under the blanket, which he grasped immediately.

"Robbie?" she asked.

"He'll be here a day or two, but he's fine."

"Nick?"

He shook his head. "Gavin saved me first, and after that Nick was already gone."

She nodded, feeling no regret, no sympathy for her sister's killer. At the thought of Hannah, panic gripped her and she pulled down the blanket, staring at her bare legs poking out from the Johnny.

"Where are my jeans? I need my jeans!"

Parker opened the drawer next to the bed, then rose and opened the closet. He lifted a clear plastic bag and pulled her jeans out.

"In my right pocket there's a note."

He reached in and pulled out the white lined paper.

She settled back on the pillow, exhausted from the moment of dread that her sister's words were gone. "Please hand it to me."

He eased himself into the chair, unfolded the note, and passed it to her. She read it silently and slowly, savoring every word.

Hi, I'm your sister. Hell, I never thought I'd be writing that. I don't know what you'll be thinking or feeling when you get the news that you're a twin, but I hope that you decide to meet me. Our family isn't much. Our mother is selfish. Our father is dead. We have some cousins scattered around, but I've never been close with any family member, really. That's why I think that finding out about you is like a gift.

I can't wait to meet you and see what you're like. See how different our lives have been. See if nature vs. nurture makes a difference. Sociologists would love us! I haven't led the cleanest life, and I've made my share of mistakes. I won't blame that on

Mom or anyone else. They're all on me. But I've turned it around.

Elise paused and tears formed in her eyes.

I've been in counseling with this psych student. He's cute. I'll introduce you. Anyway, after several months of counseling with him, I feel the best I've ever felt, and for once in my life I'm optimistic about the future. Then I find out about you and it just gets better. Anyway, I've written a novel here, so I should stop. I just wanted the PI to have something to give you when he finds you. Something to maybe convince you to come meet me.

Love,
Hannah.

The note slipped from Elise's hand and fluttered to the floor like a feather. Tears trailed down her cheeks as she took Parker's hands in hers.

"Anything good in there?" he asked, smiling.

"Yeah," Elise said. "It's all good."

ABOUT THE AUTHOR

Kim Byrne lives in Massachusetts with her husband and son.